Baroness Orczy was born in Hungary in 1865, the daughter of Baron Felix Orczy, a landed aristocrat and well-known composer and conductor. Orczy moved with her parents from Budapest to Brussels and Paris, where she was educated. She studied art in London and exhibited work in the Royal Academy.

Orczy married Montagu Barstow and together they worked as illustrators and jointly published an edition of Hungarian folk tales. Orczy became famous in 1905 with the publication of *The Scarlet Pimpernel* (originally a play co-written with her husband). Its background of the French Revolution and swashbuckling hero, Sir Percy Blakeney, was to prove immensely popular. Sequel books followed and film and TV versions were later made. Orczy also wrote detective stories.

She died in 1947.

BY THE SAME AUTHOR
ALL PUBLISHED BY HOUSE OF STRATUS

By the Gods Beloved
The Case of Miss Elliott
Eldorado
The Elusive Pimpernel
The First Sir Percy
I Will Repay
The Laughing Cavalier
The League of the Scarlet Pimpernel
Leatherface
Lord Tony's Wife
The Old Man in the Corner
The Scarlet Pimpernel
Sir Percy Hits Back
The Triumph of the Scarlet Pimpernel

THE WAY OF THE SCARLET PIMPERNEL

Baroness Orczy

First published in 1933

This edition published in 2002 by House of Stratus, an imprint of House of Stratus Ltd, Thirsk Industrial Park, York Road, Thirsk, North Yorkshire, YO7 3BX, UK.
Also at: House of Stratus Inc., 2 Neptune Road, Poughkeepsie, NY 12601, USA.

www.houseofstratus.com

Typeset, printed and bound by House of Stratus.

A catalogue record for this book is available from the British Library and The Library of Congress.

ISBN 0-7551-1122-2

1

At an angle of the Rue de la Monnaie where it is intersected by the narrow Passage des Fèves there stood at this time a large three-storied house, which exuded an atmosphere of past luxury and grandeur. Money had obviously been lavished on its decoration: the balconies were ornamented with elaborately carved balustrades, and a number of legendary personages and pagan deities reclined in more or less graceful attitudes in the spandrels round the arches of the windows and of the monumental doorway. The house had once been the home of a rich Austrian banker who had shown the country a clean pair of heels as soon as he felt the first gust of the revolutionary storm blowing across the Rue de la Monnaie. That was early in '89.

After that the mansion stood empty for a couple of years. Then, when the housing shortage became acute in Paris, the revolutionary government took possession of the building, erected partition walls in the great reception and ballrooms, turning them into small apartments and offices which it let to poor tenants and people in a small way of business. A *concierge* was put in charge. But during those two years for some reason or other the house had fallen into premature and rapid decay. Within a very few months an air of mustiness began to hang over the once palatial residence of the rich foreign financier. When he departed, bag and baggage, taking with him his family and his servants, his pictures and his furniture, it almost seemed as if he had left behind him an eerie trail of ghosts, who took to wandering in and out of the deserted rooms and up and down the monumental staircase, scattering an odour of dry-rot and mildew in their wake. And although, after a time, the lower floors were all let as offices to business people, and several families elected to drag out their more or less miserable lives in the apartments up above, that air of emptiness and of decay never ceased to hang about the building, and its walls never lost their musty smell of damp mortar and mildew.

A certain amount of life did, of course, go on inside the house. People came and went about their usual avocations: in one compartment a child was born, a wedding feast was held in another, old women gossiped and young men courted: but they did all this in a silent and furtive manner, as if afraid of rousing dormant echoes; voices were never raised above a whisper, laughter never rang along the corridors, nor did light feet run pattering up and down the stairs.

Far be it from any searcher after truth to suggest that this atmosphere of silence and of gloom was peculiar to the house in the Rue de la Monnaie. Times were getting hard all over France – very hard for most people, and hard times whenever they occur give rise to great silences and engender the desire for solitude. In Paris all the necessities of life – soap, sugar, milk – were not only very dear but difficult to get. Luxuries of the past were unobtainable save to those who, by inflammatory speeches, had fanned the passions of the ignorant and the needy, with promises of happiness and equality for all. Three years of this social upheaval and of the rule of the proletariat had brought throughout the country more misery than happiness. True! the rich – a good many of them – had been dragged down to poverty or exile, but the poor were more needy than they had been before. To see the King dispossessed of his throne, and the nobles and bourgeois either fleeing the country or brought to penury might satisfy a desire for retribution, but it did not warm the body in winter, feed the hungry or clothe the naked. The only equality that this glorious Revolution had brought about was that of wretchedness, and an ever-present dread of denunciation and of death. That is what people murmured in the privacy of their homes, but did not dare to speak of openly. No one dared speak openly these days, for there was always the fear that spies might be lurking about, that accusations of treason would follow, with their inevitable consequences of summary trial and the guillotine.

And so the women and the children suffered in silence, and the men suffered because they could do nothing to alleviate the misery of those they cared for. Some there were lucky enough to have got out of this hell upon earth, who had shaken the dust of their unfortunate country from their shoes in the early days of the Revolution, and had sought – if not happiness, at any rate peace and contentment in other lands. But there were countless others who had ties that bound them indissolubly to France – their profession, their business, or family ties – they could not go away: they were forced to remain in their native land and to watch hunger, penury and disease stalk the countryside, whilst the authors of all this misfortune lived a life of ease in their luxurious homes, sat round their well-filled tables, ate and drank their fill and spent their leisure hours in spouting of class-hatred and of their own patriotism and selflessness. The restaurants of the Rue St Honoré were thronged with merry-makers night after night. The members of the proletarian government sat in the most expensive seats at the Opéra and the Comédie Française and drove in their barouches to the Bois, while flaunting their democratic ideals by attending the sittings of the National Assembly stockingless and in ragged shirts and breeches. Danton kept open house at d'Arcy-sur-Aube: St Just and Desmoulins wore jabots of Mechlin lace, and coats of the finest English cloth: Chabot had a sumptuous apartment in the Rue d'Anjou. They saw to it, these men, that privations and anxiety did not come nigh them. Privations were for the rabble, who was used to them, and for aristos and bourgeois, who had never known the meaning of want: but for them, who had hoisted the flag of Equality and Fraternity, who had freed the people of France from the tyranny of Kings and nobles, for them luxury had become a right, especially if it could be got at the expense of those who had enjoyed it in the past.

In this year 1792 Maître Bastien de Croissy rented a small set of offices in the three-storied house in the Rue de la Monnaie. He was at this time verging on middle age, with hair just beginning to turn grey, and still an exceptionally handsome man, despite the lines of care and anxiety round his sensitive mouth and the settled look of melancholy in his deep-set, penetrating eyes. Bastien de Croissy had been at one time one of the most successful and most respected members of the Paris bar. He had reckoned royal personages among his clients. Men and women, distinguished in art, politics or literature, had waited on him at his sumptuous office on the Quai de la Mégisserie. Rich, good-looking, well-born, the young advocate had been fêted and courted wherever he went: the King entrusted him with important financial transactions: the duc d'Ayen was his most intimate friend: the Princesse de Lamballe was godmother to his boy, Charles-Léon. His marriage to Louise de Vandeleur, the only daughter of the distinguished general, had been one of the social events of that season in Paris. He had been a great man, a favourite of fortune until the Revolution deprived him of his patrimony and of his income. The proletarian government laid ruthless hands on the former, by forcing him to farm out his lands to tenants who refused to pay him any rent. His income in a couple of years dwindled down to nothing. Most of his former clients had emigrated, all of them were now too poor to need legal or financial advice.

Maître de Croissy was forced presently to give up his magnificent house and sumptuous offices on the Quai. He installed his wife and child in a cheap apartment in the Rue Picpus, and carried on what legal business came his way in a set of rooms which had once been the private apartments of the Austrian banker's valet. Thither he trudged on foot every morning, whatever the weather, and here he interviewed needy bourgeois, groaning under taxation, or out-at-elbows tradesmen on the verge of bankruptcy. He was no longer Maître de Croissy, only plain Citizen Croissy, thankful that men like Chabot or Bazire reposed confidence in him, or that the great Danton deigned to put some legal business in his way. Where six clerks had scarcely been sufficient to aid him in getting through the work of the day, he had only one now – the faithful Reversac – who had obstinately refused to take his *congé*, when all the others were dismissed.

"You would not throw me out into the street to starve, would you, Maître?" had been the young man's earnest plea.

"But you can find other work, Maurice," de Croissy had argued, not without reason, for Maurice Reversac was a fully qualified lawyer, he was young and active and of a surety he could always have made a living for himself. "And I cannot afford to pay you an adequate salary."

"Give me board and lodging, Maître," Reversac had entreated with obstinacy: "I want nothing else. I have a few louis put by: my clothes will last me three or four years, and by that time..."

"Yes! by that time...!" Maître de Croissy sighed. He had been hopeful once that sanity would return presently to the people of France, that this era of chaos and cruelty, of persecution and oppression, could not possibly last. But of late he had become more and more despondent, more and more hopeless. When Frenchmen, after having deposed their anointed King, began to talk of putting him on his trial like a common criminal, it must mean that they had become possessed of the demon of insanity, a tenacious demon who would not easily be exorcised.

But Maurice Reversac got his way. He had board and lodging in the apartment of the Rue Picpus, and in the mornings, whatever the weather, he trudged over to the Rue de la Monnaie and aired, dusted and swept the dingy office of the great advocate. In the evenings the two men would almost invariably walk back together to the Rue Picpus. The cheap, exiguous apartment meant home for both of them, and in it they found what measure of happiness their own hearts helped them to attain. For Bastien de Croissy happiness meant home-life, his love for his wife and child. For Maurice Reversac it meant living under the same roof with Josette, seeing her every day, walking with her in the evenings under the chestnut trees of Cour de la Reine.

A little higher up the narrow Passage des Fèves there stood at this same time a small eating-house, frequented chiefly by the mechanics of the Government workshops close by. It bore the sign: "Aux Trois Singes." Two steps down from the street level gave access to it through a narrow doorway. Food and drink were as cheap here as anywhere, and the landlord, a man named Furet, had the great merit of being rather deaf, and having an impediment in his speech. Added to this there was the fact that he had never learned to read or write. These three attributes made of Furet an ideal landlord in a place where men with empty bellies and empty pockets were wont to let themselves go in the matter of grumbling at the present state of affairs, and to go sometimes to the length of pointing a finger of scorn at the device "Liberté, Fraternité, Egalité" which by order of the revolutionary government was emblazoned outside and in every building to which the public had access.

Furet being deaf could not spy: being mute he could not denounce. Figuratively speaking men loosened their belts when they sat at one of the trestle tables inside the Cabaret des Trois Singes, sipped their sour wine and munched their meal of stale bread and boiled beans. They loosened their belts and talked of the slave-driving that went on in the Government workshops, the tyranny of the overseers, the ever-increasing cost of living, and the paucity of their wages, certain that Furet neither heard what they said nor would be able to repeat the little that he heard.

Inside the cabaret there were two tables that were considered privileged. They were not tables properly speaking, but just empty wine-casks, standing on end, each in a recess to right and left of the narrow doorway. A couple of three-legged stools accommodated two customers and two only in each recess, and those who wished to avail themselves of the privilege of sitting there were expected to order a bottle of Furet's best wine. This was one of those unwritten laws which no frequenter of the Three Monkeys ever thought of ignoring. Furet, though an ideal landlord in so many respects, could turn nasty when he chose.

On a sultry evening in the late August of '92, two men were sitting in one of these privileged recesses in the Cabaret des Trois Singes. They had talked earnestly for the past hour, always sinking their voices to a whisper. A bottle of Citizen Furet's best wine stood on the cask between them, but though they had been in the place for over an hour, the bottle was still more than half full. They seemed too deeply engrossed in conversation to waste time in drink.

One of the men was short and thick-set with dark hair and marked Levantine features. He spoke French fluently but with a throaty accent which betrayed his German origin. Whenever he wished to emphasise a point he struck the top of the wine-stained cask with the palm of his fleshy hand.

The other man was Bastien de Croissy. Earlier in the day he had received an anonymous message requesting a private meeting in the Cabaret des Trois Singes. The matter, the message averred, concerned the welfare of France and the safety of the King. Bastien was no coward, and the wording of the message was a sure passport to his confidence. He sent Maurice Reversac home early and kept the mysterious tryst.

His anonymous correspondent introduced himself as a representative of Baron de Batz, well known to Bastien as the agent of the Austrian Government and confidant of the Emperor, whose intrigues and schemes for the overthrow of the revolutionary government of France had been as daring in conception as they were futile in execution.

"But this time," the man had declared with complete self-assurance, "with your help, cher maître, we are bound to succeed."

And he had elaborated the plan conceived in Vienna by de Batz. A wonderful plan! Neither more nor less than bribing with Austrian gold some of the more venal members of their own party, and the restoration of the monarchy.

Bastien de Croissy was sceptical. He did not believe that any of the more influential Terrorists would risk their necks in so daring an intrigue… Other ways – surer ways – ought to be found, and found quickly, for the King's life was indeed in peril: not only the King's but the Queen's and the lives of all the Royal family. But the Austrian agent was obstinate.

"It is from inside the National Convention that M. le Baron wants help. That he must have. If he has the co-operation of half a dozen members of the Executive, he can do the rest, and guarantee success."

Then, as de Croissy still appeared to hesitate, he laid his fleshy hand on the advocate's arm.

"Voyons, cher maître," he said, "you have the overthrow of this abominable Government just as much at heart as M. le Baron, and we none of us question your loyalty to the dynasty."

"It is not want of loyalty," de Croissy retorted hotly, "that makes me hesitate."

"What then?"

"Prudence! lest by a false move we aggravate the peril of our King."

The other shrugged.

"Well! of course," he said, "we reckon that you, cher maître, know the men with whom we wish to deal."

"Yes!" Bastien admitted, "I certainly do."

"They are venal?"

"Yes!"

"Greedy?"

"Yes!"

"Ambitious?"

"For their own pockets, yes."

"Well then?"

There was a pause. A murmur of conversation was going on all round. Some of Furet's customers were munching noisily or drinking with a gurgling sound, others were knocking dominoes about. There was no fear of eavesdropping in this dark and secluded recess where two men were discussing the destinies of France. One was the emissary of a foreign Power, the other an ardent royalist. Both had the same object in view: to save the King and his family from death, and to overthrow a government of assassins, who contemplated adding the crime of regicide to their many malefactions.

"M. le Baron," the foreign agent resumed with increased persuasiveness after a slight pause, "I need not tell you what is their provenance. Our Emperor is not going to see his sister at the mercy of a horde of assassins. M. le Baron is in his council: he will pay twenty thousand louis each to any dozen men who will lend him a hand in this affair."

"A dozen?" de Croissy exclaimed, then added with disheartened sigh: "Where to find them!"

"We are looking to you, cher maître."

"I have no influence. Not now."

"But you know the right men," the agent argued, and added significantly: "You have been watched, you know."

"I guessed."

"We know that you have business relations with members of the Convention who can be very useful to us."

"Which of them had you thought of?"

"Well! there is Chabot, for instance: the unfrocked friar."

"God in Heaven!" de Croissy exclaimed: "what a tool."

"The end will justify the means, my friend," the other retorted dryly. Then he added: "And Chabot's brother-in-law Bazire."

"Both these men," de Croissy admitted, "would sell their souls, if they possessed one."

"Then there's Fabre d'Eglantine, Danton's friend."

"You are well informed."

"And what about Danton himself?"

The Austrian leaned over the table, eager, excited, conscious that the Frenchman was wavering. Clearly de Croissy's scepticism was on the point of giving way before the other's enthusiasm and certainty of success. It was such a wonderful vista that was being unfolded before him. France free from the tyranny of agitation! the King restored to his throne! the country once more happy and prosperous under a stable government as ordained by God! So thought de Croissy as he lent a more and more willing ear to the projects of de Batz. He himself mentioned several names of men who might prove useful in the scheme; names of men who might be willing to betray their party for Austrian gold. There were a good many of these: agitators who were corrupt and venal, who had incited the needy and the ignorant to all kinds of barbarous deeds, not from any striving after a humanitarian ideal, but for what they themselves could get out of the social upheaval and its attendant chaos.

"If I lend a hand in your scheme," de Croissy said presently with earnest emphasis, "it must be understood that their first aim is the restoration of our King to his throne."

"Of course, cher maître, of course," the other asserted equally forcibly. "Surely you can believe in M. le Baron's disinterested motives.

"What we'll have to do," he continued eagerly, "will be to promise the men whom you will have chosen for the purpose, a certain sum of money, to be paid to them as soon as all the members of the Royal family are safely out of France…we don't want one of the Royal Princesses to be detained as hostage, do we?... Then we can promise them a further and larger sum to be paid when their Majesties make their state re-entry into their capital."

There was no doubt by now that Maître de Croissy's enthusiasm was fully aroused. He was one of those men for whom dynasty and the right of Kings amounted to a religion. For him, all that he had suffered in the past in the way of privations and loss of wealth and prestige was as nothing compared with the horror which he felt at sight of the humiliations which miscreants had imposed upon his King. To save the King! to bring him back triumphant to the throne of his forbears, were thoughts and hopes that filled Bastien de Croissy's soul with intense excitement. It was only with half an ear that he listened to the foreign emissary's further scheme: the ultimate undoing of that herd of assassins. He did not care what happened once the great goal was attained. Let those corrupt knaves of whom the Austrian Emperor stood in need thrive and batten on their own villainy, Bastien de Croissy did not care.

"You see the idea, do you not, cher maître?" the emissary was saying.

"Yes! oh yes!" Bastien murmured vaguely.

"Get as much letter-writing as you can out of the blackguards. Let us have as much written proof of their venality as possible. Then if ever these jackals rear their heads again, we can proclaim their turpitude before the entire world, discredit them before their ignorant dupes, and see them suffer humiliation and die the shameful death which they had planned for their King."

The meeting between the two men lasted well into the night. In the dingy apartment of the Rue Picpus Louise de Croissy sat up, waiting anxiously for her husband. Maurice Reversac, whom she questioned repeatedly, could tell her nothing of Maître de Croissy's whereabouts, beyond the fact that he was keeping a business appointment, made by a new client who desired to remain anonymous. When Bastien finally came home, he looked tired, but singularly excited. Never since the first dark days of the Revolution three years ago had Louise seen him with such flaming eyes, or heard such cheerful, not to say optimistic words from his lips. But he said nothing to her about his interview with the agent of Baron de Batz, he only talked of the brighter outlook in the future. God, he said, would soon tire of the wickedness of men: the present terrible conditions could not possibly last. The King would soon come into his own again.

Louise was quickly infused with some of his enthusiasm, but she did not worry him with questions. Hers was one of those easy-going dispositions that are willing to accept things as they come without probing into the whys and wherefores of events. She had a profound admiration for and deep trust in her clever husband: he appeared hopeful for the future – more hopeful than he had been for a long time, and that was enough for Louise. It was only to the faithful Maurice Reversac that de Croissy spoke of his interview with the Austrian emissary, and the young man tried very hard to show some enthusiasm over the scheme, and to share his employer's optimism and hopes for the future. Maurice Reversac, though painstaking and a very capable lawyer, was not exactly brilliant: against that his love for his employer and his employer's family was so genuine and so great that it gave him what amounted to intuition, almost a foreknowledge of any change, good or evil, that destiny had in store for them. And as he listened to Maître de Croissy's earnest talk, he felt a strange foreboding that all would not be well with this scheme: that somehow or other it would lead to disaster, and all the while that he sat at his desk that day copying the letters which the advocate had dictated to him – letters which were in the nature of tentacles, stretched out to catch a set of knaves – he felt an overwhelming temptation to throw himself at his employer's feet and beg him not to sully his hands by contact with this foreign intrigue.

But the temptation had to be resisted. Bastien de Croissy was not the type of man who could be swayed from his purpose by the vapourings of his young clerk, however devoted he might be. And so the letters were written – half a score in all – requests by Citizen Croissy of the Paris bar for private interviews with various influential members of the Convention on matters of urgency to the State.

2

More than a year had gone by since then, and Bastien de Croissy had seen all his fondly cherished hopes turn to despair one by one. There had been no break in the dark clouds of chaos and misery that enveloped the beautiful land of France. Indeed they had gathered, darker and more stormy than before. And now had come what appeared to be the darkest days of all – the autumn of 1793. The King, condemned to death by a majority of 48 in an Assembly of over 700 members, had paid with his life for all the errors, the weaknesses, the misunderstandings of the past: the unfortunate Queen, separated from her children and from all those she cared for, accused of the vilest crimes that distorted minds could invent, was awaiting trial and inevitable death.

The various political parties – the factions and the clubs – were vying with one another in ruthlessness and cruelty. Danton the lion and Robespierre the jackal were at one another's throats; it still meant the mere spin of a coin as to which would succeed in destroying the other. The houses of detention were filled to overflowing, while the guillotine did its grim work day by day, hour by hour, without distinction of rank or sex, or of age. The Law of the Suspect had just been passed, and it was no longer necessary for an unfortunate individual to do or say anything that the Committee of Public Safety might deem counter-revolutionary, it was sufficient to be suspected of such tendencies for denunciation to follow, then arrest and finally death with but the mockery of a trial, without pleading or defence. And while the Terrorists were intent on destroying one another the country was threatened by foes without and within. Famine and disease stalked in the wake of persecution. The countryside was devastated, there were not enough hands left to till the ground and the cities were a prey to epidemics. On the frontier the victorious allied armies were advancing on the sacred soil of France. The English were pouring in from Belgium, the Prussians came across the Rhine, the Spaniards crossed the gorges of the Pyrenees, whilst the torch of civil war was blazing anew in La Vendée.

Danton's cry: "To arms!" and "*La Patrie* is in danger!" resounded from end to end of the land. It echoed through the deserted cities and over the barren fields, while three hundred thousand "Soldiers of Liberty" marched to the frontiers, ill-clothed, ill-shod, ill-fed, to drive back the foreign invader from the gates of France. An epic, what? Worthy of a holier cause.

Those who were left behind, who were old, or weak, or indispensable, had to bear their share in the defence of *La Patrie*. France was transformed into an immense camp of fighters and workers. The women sewed shirts and knitted socks, salted meat and stitched breeches, and looked after their children and their homes as best they could. France came first, the home was a bad second.

It was then that little Charles-Léon fell ill. That was the beginning of the tragedy. He had always been delicate, which was not to be wondered at, seeing that he was born during the days immediately preceding the Revolution, at the time when the entire world, such as Louise de Croissy had known it, was crumbling to dust at her feet. She never thought he would live, the dear, puny mite, the precious son, whom she and Bastien had longed for, prayed for, hoped for for five years. But he was growing sturdier year by year until this awful winter when food became scarce and poor, and milk was almost unobtainable.

Kind old Doctor Larousse said it was nothing serious, but the child must have change of air. Paris was too unhealthy these days for delicate children. Change of air? Heavens above! how was it to be got? Louise questioned old Citizen Larousse:

"Can you get me a permit, doctor? We still have a small house in the Isère district, not far from Grenoble. I could take my boy there."

"Yes. I can get you a permit for the child – at least, I think so – under the circumstances."

"And one for me?"

"Yes, one for you – to last a week."

"How do you mean to last a week?"

"Well, you can get the diligence to Grenoble. It takes a couple of days. Then you can stay in your house, say, forty-eight hours to see the child installed. Two days to come back by diligence..."

"But I couldn't come back."

"I am afraid you'll have to. No one is allowed to be absent from permanent domicile more than seven days. You know that, Citizeness, surely."

"But I couldn't leave Charles-Léon."

"Why not? There is not very much the matter with him. And country air..."

Louise was losing her patience. How obtuse men are, even the best of them!

"But there is no one over there to look after him," she argued.

"Surely a respectable woman from the village would..."

This time she felt her temper rising. "And you suppose that I would leave this sick baby in the care of a stranger?"

"Haven't you a relation who would look after him? Mother? Sister?"

"My mother is dead. I have no sisters. Nor would I leave Charles-Léon in anyone's care but mine."

The doctor shrugged. He was very kind, but he had seen this sort of thing so often lately, and he was powerless to help.

"I am afraid…" he said.

"Citizen Larousse," Louise broke in firmly, "you must give me a certificate that my child is too ill to be separated from his mother."

"Impossible, Citizeness."

"Won't you try?"

"I have tried – for others – often, but it's no use. You know what the decrees of the Convention are these days…no one dares…"

"And I am to see my child perish for want of a scrap of paper?"

Again the old man shrugged. He was a busy man and there were others. Presently he took his leave: there was nothing that he could do, so why should he stay? Louise hardly noticed his going. She stood there like a block of stone, a carved image of despair. The wan cheeks of the sick child seemed less bloodless than hers.

"Louise!"

Josette Gravier had been standing beside the cot all this time. Charles-Léon's tiny hand had fastened round one of her fingers and she didn't like to move, but she had lost nothing of what was going on. Her eyes, those lovely deep blue eyes of hers that seemed to shine, to emit light when she was excited, were fixed on Louise de Croissy. She had loved her and served her ever since Louise's dying mother, Madame de Vandeleur, confided the care of her baby daughter to Madame Gravier, the farmer's wife, Josette's mother, who had just lost her own new-born baby, the same age as Louise. Josette, Ma'me Gravier's first-born, was three years old at the time and, oh! how she took the little newcomer to her heart! She and Louise grew up together like sisters. They shared childish joys and tears. The old farmhouse used to ring with their laughter and the patter of their tiny feet. Papa Gravier taught them to ride and to milk the nanny-goats; they had rabbits of their own, chickens and runner-ducks.

Together they went to the Convent school of the Visitation to learn everything that was desirable for young ladies to know, sewing and embroidery, calligraphy and recitation, a smattering of history and geography, and the art of letter-writing. For there was to be no difference in the education of Louise de Vandeleur, the motherless daughter of the distinguished general, aide-de-camp to His Majesty, and of Josette Gravier, the farmer's daughter.

When, in the course of time, Louise married Bastien de Croissy, the eminent advocate at the Paris bar, Josette nearly broke her heart at parting from her lifelong friend.

Then came the dark days of '89. Papa Gravier was killed during the revolutionary riots in Grenoble; maman died of a broken heart, and Louise begged Josette to come and live with her. The farm was sold, the girl had a small competence; she went up to Paris and continued to love and serve Louise as she had done in the past. She was her comfort and her help during those first terrible days of the Revolution: she was her moral support now that the shadow of the guillotine lay menacing over the household of the once successful lawyer. *La Patrie* in danger claimed so many hours of her day; she, too, had to sew shirts and stitch breeches for the "Soldiers of Liberty," but her evenings, her nights, her early mornings were her own, and these she devoted to the service of Louise and of Charles-Léon.

She had a tiny room in the apartment of the Rue Picpus, but to her loving little heart that room was paradise, for here, when she was at home, she had Charles-Léon to play with, she had his little clothes to wash and to iron, she saw his great dark eyes, so like his mother's, fixed upon her while she told him tales of romance and of chivalry. The boy was only five at this time, but he was strangely precocious where such tales were concerned, he seemed to understand and appreciate the mighty deeds of Hector and Achilles, of Bayard and Joan of Arc, the stories of the Crusades, of Godfrey de Bouillon and Richard of the Lion-heart. Perhaps it was because he felt himself to be weak and puny and knew with the unexplainable instinct of childhood that he would never be big enough or strong enough to emulate those deeds of valour, that he loved to hear Josette recount them to him with a wealth of detail supplied by her romantic imagination.

But if Charles-Léon loved to hear these stories of the past, far more eagerly did he listen to those of today, and in the recounting of heroic adventures which not only had happened recently, but went on almost every day, Josette's storehouse of hair-raising narratives was well-nigh inexhaustible. Through her impassioned rhetoric he first heard of the heroic deeds of that amazing Englishman who went by the curious name of the Scarlet Pimpernel. Josette told him about a number of gallant gentlemen who had taken such compassion on the sufferings of the innocent that they devoted their lives to rescuing those who were persecuted and oppressed by the tyrannical Government of the day. She told him how women and children, old or feeble men, dragged before a tribunal that knew of no issue save the sentence of death, were spirited away out of prison walls or from the very tumbrils that were taking them to the guillotine, spirited away as if by a miracle, and through the agency of this mysterious hero whose identity had always remained unknown, but whose deeds of self-sacrifice were surely writ large in the book of the Recording Angel.

And while Josette unfolded these tales of valour, and the boy listened to her awed and silent, her eyes would shine with unshed tears, and her lips quiver with enthusiasm. She had made a fetish of the Scarlet Pimpernel: had enshrined him in her heart like a demi-god, and this hero-worship grew all the more fervent within her as she found no response to her enthusiasm in the bosom of her adopted family, only in Charles-Léon. She was too gentle and timid to speak openly of this hero-worship to Maître de Croissy, and Louise, whom she adored, was wont to grow slightly sarcastic at the expense of Josette's imaginary hero. She did not believe in his existence at all, and thought that all the tales of miraculous rescues set down to his agency were either mere coincidence or just the product of a romantic girl's fantasy. As for Maurice Reversac – well! little Josette thought him too dull and unimaginative to appreciate the almost legendary personality of the Scarlet Pimpernel, so, whenever a fresh tale got about the city of how a whole batch of innocent men, women and children had escaped out of France on the very eve of their arrest or condemnation to death, Josette kept the tale to herself, until she and Charles-Léon were alone in her little room, and she found response to her enthusiasm in the boy's glowing eyes and his murmur of passionate admiration.

When Charles-Léon's chronic weakness turned to actual, serious anaemia, all the joy seemed to go out of Josette's life. Real joy, that is; for she went about outwardly just as gay as before, singing, crooning to the little invalid, cheering Louise and comforting Bastien, who spoke of her now as the angel in the house. Every minute that she could spare she spent by the side of Charles-Léon's little bed, and when no one was listening she would whisper into his ear some of the old stories which he loved. Then if the ghost of a smile came round the child's pallid lips, Josette would feel almost happy, even though she felt ready to burst into tears.

And now, as soon as the old doctor had gone, Josette disengaged her hand from the sick child's grasp and put her arms round Louise's shoulders.

"We must not lose heart, Louise chérie," she said. "There must be a way out of this impasse."

"A way out?" Louise murmured. "Oh, if I only knew!"

"Sit down here, chérie, and let me talk to you."

There was a measure of comfort even in Josette's voice. It was low and a trifle husky; such a voice as some women have whose mission in life is to comfort and to soothe. She made

Louise sit down in the big armchair; then she knelt down in front of her, her little hands clasped together and resting in Louise's lap.

"Listen, Louise chérie," she said with great excitement.

Louise looked down on the beautiful eager face of her friend; the soft red lips were quivering with excitement; the large luminous eyes were aglow with a strange enthusiasm. She felt puzzled, for it was not in Josette's nature to show so much emotion. She was always deemed quiet and sensible. She never spoke at random, and never made a show of her fantastic dreams.

"Well, darling?" Louise said listlessly: "I am listening. What is it?"

Josette looked up, wide-eyed and eager, straight into her friend's face.

"What we must do, chérie," she said with earnest emphasis, "is to get in touch with those wonderful Englishmen. You know who I mean. They have already accomplished miracles on behalf of innocent men, women and children, of people who were in a worse plight than we are now."

Louise frowned. She knew well enough what Josette meant: she had often laughed at the girl's enthusiasm over this imaginary hero, who seemed to haunt her dreams. But just now she felt that there was something flippant and unseemly in talking such fantastic rubbish: dreams seemed out of place when reality was so heart-breaking. She tried to rise and so push Josette away, but the girl clung to her and would not let her go.

"I don't know what you are talking about, Josette," Louise said coldly at last. "This is not the time for jest, or for talking of things that only exist in your imagination."

Josette shook her head.

"Why do you say that, Louise chérie? Why should you deliberately close your eyes and ears to facts – hard, sober, solid facts that everybody knows, that everybody admits to be true? I should have thought," the girl went on in her earnest, persuasive way, "that with this terrible thing hanging over you –

Charles-Léon getting more and more ill, till there's no hope of his recovery…"

"Josette!! Don't!" Louise cried out in an agony of reproach.

"I must," Josette insisted with quiet force: "it is my duty to make you look straight at facts as they are; and I say, that with this terrible thing hanging over us, you must cast off foolish prejudices and open your mind to what is the truth and will be your salvation."

Louise looked down at the beautiful, eager face turned up to hers. She felt all of a sudden strangely moved. Of course Josette was talking nonsense. Dear, sensible, quiet little Josette! She was simple and not at all clever, but it was funny, to say the least of it, how persuasive she could be when she had set her mind on anything. Even over small things she would sometimes wax so eloquent that there was no resisting her. No! she was not clever, but she was extraordinarily shrewd where the welfare of those she loved was in question. And she adored Louise and worshipped Charles-Léon.

Since the doctor's visit Louise had felt herself floundering in such a torrent of grief that she was ready to clutch at any straw that would save her from despair. Josette was talking nonsense, of course. All the family were wont to chaff her over her adoration of the legendary hero, so much so, in fact, that the girl had ceased altogether to talk about him. But now her eyes were positively glowing with enthusiasm, and it seemed to Louise, as she gazed into them, that they radiated hope and trust. And Louise was so longing for a ray of hope.

"I suppose," she said with a wan smile, "that you are harping on your favourite string."

"I am," Josette admitted with fervour.

Then as Louise, still obstinate and unbelieving, gave a slight shrug and a sigh, the girl continued:

"Surely, Louise chérie, you have heard other people besides me – clever, distinguished, important people – talk of the Scarlet Pimpernel."

"I have," Louise admitted: "but only in a vague way."

"And what he did for the Maillys?"

"The general's widow, you mean?"

"Yes. She and her sister and the two children were simply snatched away from under the very noses of the guard who were taking them to execution."

"I did hear something about that," was Louise's dry comment; "but..."

"And what about the de Tournays?" Josette broke in eagerly.

"They are in England now. So I heard."

"They are. And who took them there? The Marquis was in hiding in the woods near his property: Mme. de Tournay and Suzanne were in terror for him and in fear for their lives. It was said openly that their arrest was imminent. And when the National Guard went to arrest them, Mme. de Tournay and Suzanne were gone, and the Marquis was never found. You've said it yourself, they are in England now."

"But Josette darling," Louise argued obstinately, "there's nothing to say in all those stories that any mysterious Englishman had aught to do with the Maillys and the Tournays."

"Who then?"

"It was the intervention of God."

Josette shook her pretty head somewhat sadly.

"God does not intervene directly these days, my darling," she said; "He chooses great and good men to do His bidding."

"And I don't see," Louise concluded with some impatience, "I don't see what the Maillys or the Tournays have to do with me and Charles-Léon."

But at this Josette's angelic temper very nearly forsook her.

"Don't be obtuse, Louise," she cried hotly. "We don't want to get in touch with the Maillys or the Tournays. I never suggested anything so ridiculous. All I meant was that they and hundreds – yes, hundreds – of others owe their life to the Scarlet Pimpernel."

Tears of vexation rose from her loving heart at Louise's obduracy. She it was who tried to rise now, but this time Louise held her down: Poor Louise! She did so long to believe – really believe. Hope is such a precious thing when the heart is full to bursting of anxiety and sorrow. And she longed for hope and for faith: the same hope that made Josette's eyes sparkle and gave a ring of sanguine expectation to her voice.

"Don't run away, Josette," she pleaded. "You don't know how I envy you your hero-worship and your trust. But listen, darling: even if your Scarlet Pimpernel does exist – see, I no longer say that he does not – even if he does, he knows nothing about us. How then can he interfere?"

Josette drew a sigh of relief. For the first time since the hot argument had started she felt that she was gaining ground. Her faith was going to prevail. Louise's scepticism was beginning to give way. The whole expression of her face had changed: the look of despair had gone and there was a light in her eyes which suggested that hope had crept at last into her heart. The zealot had vanquished the obstinacy of the sceptic, and Josette having gained her point could speak more calmly now.

She shook her head and smiled.

"Don't you believe it, chérie," she said gently.

"Believe what?"

"That the Scarlet Pimpernel knows nothing about you. He does. I am sure he does. All you have to do is just to invoke him in your heart."

"Nonsense, Josette," Louise protested. "You are not pretending, I suppose, that this Englishman is a supernatural being?"

"I don't know about that," said the young devotee, "but I do know that he is the bravest, finest man that ever lived. And I know also that wherever there is a great misfortune or a great sorrow he appears like a young god, and at once care and anxiety disappear, and grief is turned to joy."

"I wish I could have your faith in miracles, my Josette."

"You need not call it a miracle. The good deeds of the Scarlet Pimpernel are absolutely real."

"But even so, my dear, what can we do? We don't know where to find him. And if we did, what could he do for us – for Charles-Léon?"

"He can get you a permit to go into the country with Charles-Léon, and to remain with him until he is well again."

"I don't believe it. Nothing short of a miracle can accomplish that. You heard what the doctor said."

"Well, I say that the Scarlet Pimpernel can do anything! And I mean to get in touch with him."

"You are stupid, Josette."

"And you are a woman of little faith. Why don't you read your Bible, and see what it says there about faith?"

Louise shrugged. "The Bible," she said coolly, "tells us about moving mountains by faith, but nothing about finding a needle in a haystack or a mysterious Englishman in the streets of Paris."

But Josette now was proof against her friend's sarcasm. She jumped to her feet and put her arms round Louise.

"Well!" she rejoined, "my faith is going to find him, that's all I know. I wish," she went on with a comic little inflection of her voice, "that I had not wasted this past hour in trying to put some of that faith into you. And now I know that I shall have to spend at least another hour driving it into Maurice's wooden head."

Louise smiled. "Why Maurice?" she asked.

"For the same reason," the girl replied, "that I had to wear myself out in order to break your obstinacy. It will take me some time perhaps, as you say, to find the Scarlet Pimpernel in the streets of Paris. I shall have to be out and about a great deal, and if I had said nothing to any of you, you and Maurice and even Bastien would always have been asking me questions: where I had been? why did I go out? why was I late for dinner? And Maurice would have gone about looking like a bear with a sore head, whenever I refused to go for a walk with him. So of course," Josette concluded naïvely, "I shall have to tell him."

Louis said nothing more after that: she sat with clasped hands and eyes fixed into vacancy, thinking, hoping, or perhaps just praying for hope.

But Josette having had her say went across the room to Charles-Léon's little bed. She leaned over him and kissed him. He whispered her name and added feebly: "Tell me some more…about the Scarlet Pimpernel…when will he come…to take me away…to England?"

"Soon," Josette murmured in reply: "very soon. Do not doubt it, my precious. God will send him to you very soon."

Then without another word to Louise she ran quickly out of the room.

3

Josette had picked up her cape and slung it round her shoulders; she pulled the hood over her fair curls and ran swiftly down the stairs and out into the street. Thoughts of the Scarlet Pimpernel had a way of whipping up her blood. When she spoke of him she at once wanted to be up and doing. She wanted to be up and doing something that would emulate the marvellous deeds of that mysterious hero of romance – deeds which she had heard recounted with bated breath by her fellow-workers in the Government workshops where breeches were stitched and stockings knitted by the hundred for the "Soldiers of Liberty," marching against the foreign foe.

Josette on this late afternoon had to put in a couple of hours at the workshop. At six o'clock when the light gave out she would be free; and at six o'clock Maurice Reversac would of a certainty be outside the gates of the workshop waiting to escort her first for a walk along the Quai or the Cour la Reine and then home to cook the family supper.

She came out of the workshop on this late afternoon with glowing eyes and flaming cheeks, and nearly ran past Maurice without seeing him as her mind was so full of other things. She was humming a tune as she ran. Maurice was waiting for her at the gate, and he called to her. He felt very happy all of a sudden because Josette seemed so pleased to see him.

"Maurice!" she cried, "I am so glad you have come."

Maurice, being young and up to his eyes in love, did not think of asking her why she should be so glad. She was glad to see him and that was enough for any lover. He took hold of her by the elbow and led her through the narrow streets as far as the Quai and then over to Cour la Reine, where there were seats under the chestnut trees from which the big prickly burrs were falling fast, and split as they fell, revealing the lovely smooth surface of the chestnuts, in colour like Josette's hair; and as the last glimmer of daylight faded into evening the sparrows in the trees kicked up a great shindy, which was like a paean of joy in complete accord with Maurice's mood.

Nor did Maurice notice that Josette was absorbed; her eyes shone more brightly than usual, and her lips, which were so like ripe fruit, were slightly parted, and Maurice was just aching for a kiss.

Her persuaded her to sit down: the air was so soft and balmy – a lovely autumn evening with the scent of ripe fruit about; and those sparrows up in the chestnut trees did kick up such a shindy before tucking their little heads under their wings for the night. There were a few passers-by – not many – and this corner of old Paris appeared singularly peaceful, with a whole world of dreams and hope between it and the horrors of the Revolution. Yet this was the hour when the crowds that assembled daily on the *Place de la Barrière du Trône* to watch the guillotine at its dread work wandered, tired and silent, back to their homes, and when rattling carts bore their gruesome burdens to the public burying-place.

But what are social upheavals, revolutions or cataclysms to a lover absorbed in the contemplation of his beloved? Maurice Reversac sat beside Josette and could see her adorable profile with the small tip-tilted nose and the outline of her cheek so like a ripe peach. Josette sat silent and motionless at first, so Maurice felt emboldened to put out a timid hand and take hold of hers. She made no resistance and he thought of a surety that he would swoon with joy because she allowed that exquisite little hand to rest contented in his great rough palm. It felt just like a bird, soft and warm and fluttering, like those sparrows in up the trees.

"Josette," Maurice ventured to murmur after a little while, "you are glad to see me…you said so…didn't you, Josette?"

She was not looking at him, but he didn't mind that, for though the twilight was fast drawing in he could still see her adorable profile – that delicious tip-tilted nose and the lashes that curled like a fringe of gold over her eyes. The hood had fallen back from her head and the soft evening breeze stirred the tendrils of her chestnut-coloured hair.

"You are so beautiful, Josette," Maurice sighed, "and I am such a clumsy lout, but I would know how to make you happy. Happy! My God! I would make you as happy as the birds – without a care in the world. And all day you would just go about singing – singing – because you would have forgotten by then what sorrow was like."

Encouraged by her silence he ventured to draw a little nearer to her.

"I have seen," he murmured quite close to her ear, "an apartment that would be just the right setting for you, Josette darling: only three rooms and a little kitchen, but the morning sun comes pouring in through the big windows and there is a clump of chestnut trees in front in which the birds will sing in the spring from early dawn while you still lie in bed. I shall have got up by then and will be in the kitchen getting some hot milk for you; then I will bring you the warm milk, and while you drink it I shall sit and watch the sunshine play about in your hair."

Never before had Maurice plucked up sufficient courage to talk at such length. Usually when Josette was beside him he was so absorbed in looking at her and longing for her that his tongue refused him service; for these were days when true lovers were timid and *la jeune fille* was an almost sacred being, whose limpid soul no profane word dared disturb, and Maurice had been brought up by an adoring mother in these rigid principles. This cruel and godless Revolution had, indeed, shattered many ideals and toughened the fibres of men's hearts and women's sensibilities, else Maurice would never have dared thus to approach the object of his dreams – her whom he hoped one day to have for wife.

Josette's silence had emboldened him, and the fact that she had allowed her hand to rest in his all this while. Now he actually dared to put out his arm and encircle her shoulders; he was, in fact, drawing her to him, feeling that he was on the point of stepping across the threshold of Paradise, when slowly she turned her face to him and looked him straight between the eyes. Her own appeared puzzled and there was a frown as of great perplexity between her brows.

"Maurice," she asked, and there was no doubt that she was both puzzled and astonished, "are you, perchance, trying to make love to me?"

Then, as he remained silent and looked, in his turn, both bewildered and hurt, she gave a light laugh, gently disengaged her hand and patted him on the cheek.

"My poor Maurice!" she said, "I wish I had listened sooner, but I was thinking of other things…"

When a man has had the feeling that he has actually reached the gates of Paradise and that a kindly Saint Peter was already rattling his keys so as to let him in – when he has felt this for over half an hour and then, in a few seconds, is hurtled down into an abyss of disappointment, his first sensation is as if he had been stunned by a terrific blow on the head, and he becomes entirely tongue-tied.

Bewildered and dumb, all Maurice could do was to stare at the adorable vision of a golden-haired girl whom he worshipped and who, with a light heart and a gay laugh, had just dealt him the most cruel blow that any man had ever been called upon to endure.

The worst of it was that this adorable golden-haired girl had apparently no notion of how cruel had been the blow, for she prattled on about the other things of which she had been thinking quite oblivious of the subject-matter of poor Maurice's impassioned pleading.

"Maurice dear," she said, "listen to me and do not talk nonsense."

Nonsense!! Ye gods!

"You have got to help me, Maurice, to find the Scarlet Pimpernel."

Her beautiful eyes, which she turned full upon him, were aglow with enthusiasm – enthusiasm for something in which he had no share. Nor did he understand what she was talking about. All he knew was that she had dismissed his pleading as nonsense, and that with a curious smile on her lips she was just turning a knife round and round in his heart.

And, oh, how that hurt!

But she also said that she wanted his help, so he tried very hard to get at her meaning, though she seemed to be prattling on rather inconsequently.

"Charles-Léon," she said, "is very ill, you know, Maurice dear – that is, not so very ill, but the doctor says he must have change of air or he will perish in a decline."

"A doctor can always get a permit for a patient in extremis..." Maurice put in, assuming a judicial manner.

"Don't be stupid, Maurice!" she retorted impatiently. "We all know that the doctor can get a permit for Charles-Leon, but he can't get one for Louise or for me, and where is Charles-Léon to go with neither of us to look after him?"

"Then what's to be done?"

"Try and listen more attentively, Maurice," she retorted. "You are not really listening."

"I am," he protested, "I swear I am!"

"Really – really?"

"Really, Josette – with both ears and all the intelligence I've got."

"Very well, then. You have heard of the Scarlet Pimpernel, haven't you?"

"We all have – in a way."

"What do you mean by 'in a way'?"

"Well, no one is quite sure that he really exists, and…"

"Maurice, don't, in Heaven's name, be stupid! You must have brains or Maître de Croissy could not do with you as his confidential clerk. So do use your brains, Maurice, and tell me if the Scarlet Pimpernel does not exist, then how did the Maillys get away – and the Frontenacs – and the Tournays – and – and…? Oh, Maurice, I hate your being so stupid!"

"You have only got to tell me, Josette, what you wish me to do," poor Maurice put in very humbly, "and I will do it, of course."

"I want you to help me find the Scarlet Pimpernel."

"Gladly will I help you, Josette; but won't it be like looking for a needle in a haystack?"

"Not at all," this intrepid little Joan of Arc asserted. "Listen, Maurice! In our workshop there is a girl, Agnes Minet, who was at one time in service with a Madame Carré, whose son Antoine was in hiding because he was threatened with arrest. His mother didn't dare write to him lest her letters be intercepted. Well, there was a public letter-writer who plied his trade at the corner of the Pont-Neuf – a funny old scarecrow he was – and Agnes, who cannot write, used sometimes to employ him to write to her fiancé who was away with the army. She says she doesn't know exactly how it all happened – she thinks the old letter-writer must have questioned her very cleverly, or else have followed her home one day – but, anyway, she caught herself telling him all about Antoine Carré and his poor mother. Well, that very evening the English milor – that great and wonderful Scarlet Pimpernel – found Antoine Carré and took him and his mother safely out of France."

She paused a moment to draw breath, for she had spoken excitedly and all the time scarcely above a whisper, for the subject-matter was not one she would have liked some evilwisher to hear. There were so many spies about these days eager for blood-money – the forty sous which could be earned for denouncing a "suspect."

Maurice, fully alive to this, made no immediate comment, but after a few seconds he suggested: "Shall we walk?" and took Josette by the elbow. It was getting dark now: the Cour la Reine was only poorly-lighted by a very few street lanterns placed at long intervals. They walked together in silence for a time, looking like young lovers intent on amorous effusions. The few passers-by, furtive and noiseless, took no notice of them.

"Antoine Carré's case is not the only one, Maurice," Josette resumed presently. "I could tell you dozens of others. The girls in the workshop talk about it all the time when the superintendent is out of the room."

Again she paused, and then went on firmly, stressing her command: "You have got to help me, you know, Maurice."

"Of course I will, Josette," Maurice murmured. "But how?"

"You must find the public letter-writer who used to have his pitch at the corner of the Pont-Neuf."

"There isn't one there now. I went past…"

"I know that. He has changed his pitch, that's all."

"How shall I know which is the right man? There are a number of public letter-writers in Paris."

"I shall be with you, Maurice, and I shall know, I am sure I shall know. There is something inside my heart which will make it beat faster as soon as the Scarlet Pimpernel is somewhere nigh. Besides…"

She checked herself, for involuntarily she had raised her voice, and at once Maurice tightened his hold on her arm. In the fast-gathering gloom a shuffling step had glided furtively past them. They could not clearly see the form of this passer-by, only the vague outline of a man stooping under a weight which he carried over his shoulders.

"We must be careful, Josette…" Maurice whispered softly.

"I know – I was carried away. But, Maurice, you will help me?"

"Of course," he said.

And though he did not feel very hopeful he said it fervently, for the prospect of roaming through the streets of Paris in the company of Josette in search of a person who might be mythical and who certainly would take a lot of finding, was of the rosiest. Indeed, Maurice hoped that the same mythical personage would so hide himself that it would be many days before he was ultimately found.

"And when we have found him," Josette continued glibly, once more speaking under her breath, "you shall tell him about Louise and Charles-Léon, and that Louise must have a permit to take the poor sick baby into the country and to remain with him until he is well."

"And you think…"

"I don't think, Maurice," she said emphatically, "I know that the Scarlet Pimpernel will do the rest."

She was like a young devotee proclaiming the miracles of her patron saint. It was getting very dark now and at home Louise and Charles-Léon would be waiting for Josette, the angel in the house. Mechanically and a little sadly Maurice led the girl's footsteps in the direction of home. They spoke very little together after this: it seemed as if, having made her profession of faith, Josette took her loyal friend's co-operation for granted. She did not even now realise the cruelty of the blow which she had dealt to his fondest hopes. With the image of this heroic Scarlet Pimpernel so firmly fixed in her mind, Josette was not likely to listen to a declaration of love from a humble lawyer's clerk, who had neither deeds of valour nor a handsome presence wherewith to fascinate a young girl so romantically inclined.

Thus they wandered homewards in silence – she indulging in her dreams, and he nursing a sorrow that he felt would be eternal. Up above in the chestnut trees the sparrows had gone to roost. Their paean of joy had ceased, only the many sounds of a great city not yet abed broke the silence of the night.

Furtive footsteps still glided well-nigh soundlessly by; now and then there came a twitter, a fluttering of wings from above, or from far away the barking of a dog, the banging of a door, or the rattling of cart-wheels on the cobble-stones. And sometimes the evening breeze would give a great sigh that rose up into the evening air as if coming from hundreds of thousands of prisoners groaning under the tyranny of bloodthirsty oppressors, of a government that proclaimed Liberty and Fraternity from the steps of the guillotine.

And at home in the small apartment of the Rue Picpus, Josette and Maurice found that Louise had cried her eyes out until she had worked herself into a state of hysteria, while Maître de Croissy, silent and thoughtful, sat in dejection by the bedside of his sick child.

4

The evening was spent – strangely enough – in silence and in gloom. Josette, who a few hours before had thought to have gained her point and to have brought both hope and faith into Louise's heart, found that her friend had fallen back into that state of dejection out of which nothing that Josette said could possibly drag her. Josette put this down to Bastien's influence. Bastien too had always been sceptical about the Scarlet Pimpernel, didn't believe in his existence at all. He somehow confused him in his mind with that Austrian agent Baron de Batz, of whom he had had such bitter experience. De Batz, too, had been full of schemes for rescuing the King, the Royal family, and many a persecuted noble, threatened with death, but months had gone by and nothing had been done. The mint of Austrian money promised by him was never forthcoming. De Batz himself was never on the spot when he was wanted. In vain had Bastien de Croissy toiled and striven his hardest to bring negotiations to a head between a certain few members of the revolutionary government who were ready to accept bribes, and the Austrian emissaries who professed themselves ready to pay. Men like Chabot and Bazire, and Fabre d'Eglantine had been willing enough to negotiate, though their demands became more and more exorbitant as time went on and the King's peril more imminent: even Danton had thrown out hints that in these hard times a man must live, so why not on Austrian money, since French gold was so scarce? but somehow, when everything appeared to be ready, and greedy palms were already outstretched to receive the promised bribes, the money was never there, and de Batz, warned of his peril if he remained in France, had fled across the border.

And somehow the recollection of that intriguer was inextricably mixed up in de Croissy's mind with the legendary personality of the Scarlet Pimpernel.

"Josette is quite convinced of his existence," Louise had said to her husband that afternoon, when they stood together in sorrow and in tears beside the sick-bed of Charles-Leon, "and that he can and will get me the permit to take our darling away into the country."

But Bastien shook his head, sadly and obstinately.

"Don't lure yourself with false hopes, my dear," he said. "Josette is an angel, but she is also a child. She dreams and persuades herself that her dreams are realities. I have had experience of such dreams myself."

"I know," Louise rejoined with a sigh.

Hers was one of those yielding natures, gentle and affectionate, that can be swayed one way or the other by an event, sometimes by a mere word; and yet at times she would be strangely obstinate, with the obstinacy of the very weak, or of the feather-pillow that seems to yield at a touch only to regain its own shape the next moment.

A word from Bastien and all the optimism which Josette's ardour had implanted in her heart froze again into scepticism and discouragement.

"If we cannot save Charles-Léon," she said, "I shall die."

Twenty-four hours had gone by since then, and today Bastien de Croissy sat alone in the small musty office of the Rue de la Monnaie. He had sent his clerk, Maurice Reversac, off early because he was a kindly man and had not forgotten the days of his own courtship, and knew that the happiest hours of Maurice's day were those when he could meet Josette Gravier outside the gate of the Government workshop and take her out for a walk.

De Croissy had also sent Maurice away early because he wanted to be alone. A crisis had arisen in his life with which he desired to deal thoughtfully and dispassionately. His child was ill, would die, perhaps, unless he, the father, could contrive to send him out of Paris into the country under the care of his mother. The tyranny of this Government of Liberty and Fraternity had made this impossible; no man, woman or child was allowed to be absent from the permanent domicile without a special permit, which was seldom, if ever, granted; not unless some powerful leverage could be found to force those tyrants to grant the permit.

Now Bastien de Croissy was in possession of such a leverage. The question was: had the time come at last to make use of it? He now sat at his desk and a sheaf of letters were laid out before him. These letters, if rightly handled, would, he knew, put so much power into his hands that he could force some of the most influential members of the government to grant him anything he chose to ask.

"Get as much letter-writing as you can out of the blackguards," the Austrian emissary had said to him during that memorable interview in the Cabaret des Trois Singes, and de Croissy had acted on this advice. On one pretext or another he had succeeded in persuading at any rate three influential members of the existing Government to put their demands in writing. Bastien had naturally carefully preserved these letters. De Batz was going to use them for his own ends: as a means wherewith to discredit men who proclaimed their disinterestedness and patriotism from the house-tops, and not only to discredit them, "but to make them suffer the same humiliation and the same shameful death which they had planned for their King." These also had been the emissary's words at that fateful interview; and de Croissy had kept the letters up to now, not with a view to using them for his own benefit, or for purposes of blackmail, but with the earnest hope that one day chance would enable him to use them for the overthrow and humiliation of tyrants and regicides.

But now events had suddenly taken a sharp turn. Charles-Léon might die if he was not taken out of this fever-infested city, and Louise, very rightly, would not trust the sick child in a stranger's hands. And if Charles-Léon were to die, Louise would quickly follow the child to his grave.

Bastien de Croissy sat for hours in front of his desk with those letters spread out before him. He picked them up one by one, read and re-read them and put them down again. He rested his weary head against his hand, for thoughts weighed heavily on his mind. To a man of integrity, a high-minded gentleman as he had always been, the alternative was a horrible one. On one side there was that hideous thing, blackmail, which was abhorrent to him, and on the other the life of his wife and child. Honour and conscience ruled one way, and every fibre of his heart the other.

The flickering light of tallow candles threw grotesque shadows on the whitewashed walls and cast fantastic gleams of light on the handsome face of the great lawyer, with its massive forehead and nobly sculptured profile, on the well-shaped hands and hair prematurely grey.

The letter which he now held in his hand was signed "François Chabot," once a Capuchin friar, now a member of the National Convention and one of Danton's closest friends, whose uncompromising patriotism had been proclaimed on the house-tops both by himself and his colleagues.

And this is what Francois Chabot had written not much more than a year ago to Maître de Croissy, advocate:

> "My friend, as I told you in our last interview, I am inclined to listen favourably to the proposals of B. If he really disposes of the funds of which he boasts, tell him that I

> can get C out of his present impasse and put him once more in possession of the seat which he values. Further, I and the others can keep him in undisturbed possession thereof. We'll even give him a guarantee that nothing shall happen (say) for five years to disturb him again. But you can also tell B that his proposals are futile. I shall want twenty thousand on the day that C enters his house in the park. Moreover, your honorarium for carrying this matter through must be paid by B. My friends and I will not incur any expense in connection with it."

Bastien de Croissy now took up his pen and a sheet of paper, and after a moment's reflection he transcribed the somewhat enigmatic letter by substituting names for initials, and intelligible words for those that appeared un-understandable. The letter so transcribed now began thus:

> "My friend, as I told you in our last interview, I am inclined to listen favourably to the proposals of de Batz. If he really disposes of the funds of which he boasts, tell him that I can get the King out of his present impasse and put him once more in possession of his throne..."

The rest of the letter he transcribed in the same way: always substituting the words "the King" for "C" and "de Batz" for "B"; "his house in the park" Maître de Croissy transcribed as "Versailles."

The whole text would now be clear to anybody. Bastien then took up a number of other letters and transcribed these in the same way as he had done the first: then he made two separate packets of the whole correspondence; one of these contained the original letters, and these he slipped in the inside pocket of his coat, the other he tied loosely together and put it away with other papers in his desk. He then locked the desk and the strongbox, turned out the lights in the office and finally went home.

His mind was definitely made up.

The same evening Bastien made a clean breast of all the circumstances to Louise. Maurice was there and Josette of course, and there was little Charles-Léon, who lay like a half-animate bird in his mother's arms.

For Maurice the story was not new. He had known of the first interview between de Croissy and the Austrian emissary, he had watched the intrigue developing step by step, through the good offices of the distinguished advocate. As a matter of fact he had more than once acted as messenger, taking letters to and fro between the dingy offices of the Rue de la Monnaie and the sumptuous apartments of the Representatives of the People. He had spoken to Chabot, the unfrocked friar who lived in unparalleled luxury in the Rue d'Anjou, dressed in town like a Beau Brummel, but attended the sittings of the National Convention in a tattered coat and shoes down at heel, his hair unkempt, his chin unshaven, his hands unwashed, in order to flaunt what he was pleased to call his democratic ideals. He saw Bazire, Chabot's brother-in-law, who hired a mudlark to enact the part of a pretended assassin in order that he might raise the cry: "The royalists are murdering the patriots!" (As it happened, the pretended assassin did not turn up at the right moment, and Bazire had been left to wander alone up and down the dark cul-de-sac waiting to receive the stab that was to exalt him before the Convention as the victim of his ardent patriotism.) Maurice had interviewed Fabre d'Eglantine, Danton's most intimate friend, who was only too ready to see his palm greased with foreign gold, and even the ruthless and impeccable Danton had to Maurice's knowledge nibbled at the sweet biscuit held to his nose by the Austrian agent.

All these men Maurice Reversac had known, interviewed and despised. But he had also seen the clouds of bitterness and disappointment gather in Bastien de Croissy's face: he guessed more than he actually knew how one by one all the hopes born of that first interview in the Cabaret des Trois Singes had been laid to dust. The continued captivity of the Royal Family, the severance of the Queen from her children had been the first heavy blows dealt to those fond hopes. The King's condemnation and death completely shattered them. Maurice dared not ask what the Austrian was doing, or what final preposterous demands had come from the Representatives of the People, which had caused the negotiations to be finally broken off. For months now the history of those negotiations had almost been forgotten. As far as Maurice was concerned he had ceased to think of them, he only remembered the letters that had passed during that time, as incidents that might have had wonderful consequences, but had since sunk into the limbo of forgetfulness.

To Louise and Josette, on the other hand, the story was entirely new. Each heard it with widely divergent feelings. Obviously to Louise it meant salvation. She listened to her husband with glowing eyes, her lips were parted, her breath came and went with almost feverish rapidity, and every now and then she pressed Charles-Léon closer and closer to her breast. Never for a moment did she appear in doubt that here was complete deliverance from every trouble and every anxiety. Indeed the only thing that seemed to trouble her was the fact that Bastien had withheld this wonderful secret from her for so long.

"We might have been free to leave this hell upon earth long before this," she exclaimed with passionate reproach when Bastien admitted that he had hesitated to use such a weapon for his own benefit.

"It looks so like blackmail," Bastien murmured feebly.

"Blackmail?" Louise retorted vehemently. "Would you call it murder if you killed a mad dog?"

Bastien gave a short, quick sigh. The letters were to have been the magic key wherewith to open the prison door for his King and Queen: the mystic wand that would clear the way for them to their throne.

"Is not Charles-Léon's life more precious than any King's?" Louise protested passionately.

And soon she embarked on plans for the future. She would take the child into the country, and presently, if things didn't get any better, they would join the band of loyal *émigrés* who led a precarious but peaceful existence in Belgium or England; Josette and Maurice would come with them, and together they would all wait for those better times which could not now be very long in coming.

"There is nothing," she declared emphatically, "that these men would dare refuse us. By threatening to send those letters to the *Moniteur* or any other paper we can force them to grant us permits, passports, anything we choose. Oh, Bastien!" she added impetuously, "why did you not think of all this before?"

Josette alone was silent. She alone had hardly uttered a word the whole evening. In silence she had listened to Bastien's exposition of the case, and to Maurice's comments on the situation, and she remained silent while Louise talked and reproached and planned. She only spoke when Bastien, after he had read aloud some of the more important letters, gathered them all together and tied them once more into a packet. He was about to slip them into his coat pocket when Josette spoke up.

"Don't do that, Bastien," she said impulsively, and stretched out her hand for the packet.

"Don't do what, my dear?" de Croissy asked.

"Let Louise take charge of the letters," the girl pleaded, "until those treacherous devils are ready to give you the permits and safe-conducts in exchange for them. You can show your transcriptions to them at first: but they wouldn't be above sticking a knife into you in the course of conversation, and rifling your pockets if they knew you had the originals on you at the time."

Bastien couldn't help smiling at the girl's eagerness, but he put the packet of letters into her outstretched hand.

"You are right, Josette," he said: "you are always right. The angel in the house! What will you do with them?"

"Sew them into the lining of Louise's corsets," Josette replied.

And she never said another word after that.

5

Louise de Croissy stood by the window and watched her husband's tall massive figure as he strode down the street on his way to the Rue de la Monnaie. When he had finally disappeared out of her sight Louise turned to Josette.

Unconsciously almost, and certainly against her better judgment, Josette felt a strange misgiving about this affair. She hadn't slept all night for thinking about it. And this morning when Bastien had set off so gaily and Louise seemed so full of hope she still felt oppressed and vaguely frightened. There is no doubt that intense love does at times possess psychic powers, the power usually called "second sight." Josette's love for Louise and what she called her "little family" was maternal in its intensity and she always averred that she knew beforehand whenever a great joy was to come to them and also had a premonition of any danger that threatened them.

And somehow this morning she felt unable to shake off a consciousness of impending doom. She, too, had watched at the window while Bastien de Croissy started out in the direction of the Rue de la Monnaie, there to pick up the packet of transcriptions and then to go off on his fateful errand; and when he had turned the angle of the street and she could no longer see him she felt more than ever the approach of calamity.

These were the last days of September: summer had lingered on and it had been wonderfully sunny all along. In the woods the ash, the oak and the chestnut were still heavy with leaf, and thrushes and blackbirds still sang gaily their evening melodies. But today the weather had turned sultry: there were heavy clouds up above that presaged a coming storm.

"Why, what's the matter, Josette chérie?" Louise asked anxiously, for the girl, as she gazed out into the dull grey light, shivered as if with cold and her pretty face appeared drawn and almost haggard. "Are you disappointed that your mythical Scarlet Pimpernel will not, after all, play his heroic role on our stage?"

Louise said this with a light laugh, meaning only to chaff, but Josette winced as if she had been stung, and tears gathered in her eyes.

"Josette!" Louise exclaimed, full of contrition and of tenderness. She felt happy, light-hearted, proud too, of what Bastien could do for them all. Though the morning was grey and dismal, though there were only scanty provisions in the house – aye! even though Charles-Léon lay limp and listless in his little bed, Louise felt that on this wonderful day she could busy herself about her poor dingy home, singing to herself with joy. She, like Bastien himself, had never wished to emigrate, but at times she had yearned passionately for the fields and woods of the Dauphiné where her husband still owned the family château and where there was a garden in which Charles-Léon could run about, where the air was pure and wholesome so that the colour could once more tinge the poor lamb's wan cheeks.

She could not understand why Josette was not as happy as she was herself. Perhaps she was depressed by the weather, and sure enough soon after Bastien started the first lightning-flash shot across the sky, and after a few seconds there came the distant rumble of thunder. A few heavy drops fell on the cobble-stones and then the rain came down, a veritable cataract, as if the sluices of heaven had suddenly been opened. Within a few minutes the uneven pavements ran with muddy streams and the unfortunate passers-by, caught in the shower, buttoned up their coat collars and bolted for the nearest doorway. The wind howled down the chimneys and rattled the ill-fitting window-panes. No wonder that Josette's spirits were damped by this dismal weather!

Louise drew away from the window, sighing: "Thank God, I made Bastien put on his thick old coat!" Then she sat down and called Josette to her. "You know, chérie," she said, and put loving arms round the girl's shoulders. "I didn't mean anything unkind about your hero: I was only chaffing. I loved your enthusiasm and your belief in miracles; but I am more prosy than you are, chérie, and prefer to pin my faith on the sale of compromising letters rather than on deeds of valour performed by a mythical hero."

To please Louise, Josette made a great effort to appear cheerful; indeed, she chided herself for her ridiculous feeling of depression, which had no reason for its existence and only tended to upset Louise. She pleaded a headache after a sleepless night.

"I lay awake," she said, with an effort to appear light-hearted, "thinking of the happy time we would all have over in the Dauphiné. It is so lovely there in the late autumn when the leaves turn to gold."

The rest of the morning Josette was obliged to spend in the Government workshops sewing shirts for the "Soldiers of Liberty," so presently when the storm began to subside she put on her cloak and hood, gave Charles-Léon a last kiss and hurried off to her work. She had hoped to get her allotted task done by twelve o'clock, when Maurice could meet her and they could sally forth together in search of fresh air under the trees of Cour la Reine. Unfortunately, as luck would have it, she was detained in the workshop along with a number of other girls until a special consignment of shirts was ready for packing. When she was finally able to leave the shop it was past one o'clock and Maurice was not waiting at the gate.

She hurried home for her midday meal, only to hear from Louise that Bastien and Maurice had already been and gone. They had snatched a morsel of food and hurried away again, for they had important work to do at the office. Louise was full of enthusiasm and full of hope. Bastien, she said, had seen Fabre d'Eglantine, also Chabot and Bazire, and had already entered into negotiations with them for the exchange of the compromising letters against permits for himself and his family – which would, of course, include Josette and Maurice – to take up permanent domicile on his estate in the Dauphiné. Bastien and Maurice, after they had imparted this joyful news and had their hurried meal, had gone back to the office. It seems that after the three interviews were over and Bastien was back at the Rue de la Monnaie, François Chabot had called on him with a ponderous document which he desired put into legal jargon that same afternoon.

"It will take them several hours to get through with the work," Louise went on to explain, "and when it is ready Maurice is to take the document to Citizen Chabot's apartment in Rue d'Anjou; so I don't suppose we shall see either of them before supper-time. Bastien says he was so amused when Chabot called at the office. His eyes were roaming round the room all the time. I am sure he was wondering in his mind where Bastien kept the letters, and I am so thankful, Josette darling, that we took your advice and have them here in safe-keeping. Do you know, Bastien declares that if those letters were published to-morrow Chabot and the lot of them, not even excepting the great Danton, would find themselves at the bar of the accused, and within the hour their heads would be off their shoulders? And serve them right, the murdering, hypocritical devils!"

After which she unfolded to her darling Josette her plans for leaving this hateful Paris within the next twenty-four hours. Dreams and hopes! Louise was full of them just now: strange that to Josette the whole thing was like a nightmare.

6

In the late afternoon Josette had again to go back to the workshop to put in a couple of hours' more sewing. She left Louise in the apartment, engrossed in sorting out the necessary clothes required for the journey, and singing merrily like a bird. Bastien and Maurice were not expected home for some hours. Charles-Léon was asleep.

It was past eight o'clock and quite dark when Josette finally returned home to the Rue Picpus for the evening. Under the big *port-cochère* of the apartment house she nearly fell into the arms of Maurice Reversac, who apparently was waiting for her.

"Oh, Maurice!" she cried, "how you frightened me!" And then, "What are you doing here?"

Instead of replying he took her by the wrist and drew her to the foot of the main staircase, away from the *concierge*'s lodge, where in an angle of the wall they could be secure from prying ears and eyes. Here Maurice halted, but he still clung to her wrist, and leaned against the wall as if exhausted and breathless.

"Maurice, what is it?"

The staircase was in almost total darkness, only a feeble light filtrated down from an oil-lamp fixed on one of the landings above. Josette could not see her friend's face, but she felt the tremor that shook his arm and she heard the stertorous breath that struggled through his lips. The sense of doom, of some calamity that threatened them all, the nameless foreboding that had haunted her all day held her heart in an icy grip.

"Maurice!" she insisted.

At last he spoke; he murmured his employer's name.

"Maître de Croissy."

Josette could scarcely repress a cry:

"Arrested?"

He shook his head.

"Not…? Dead…? When? How? What is it, Maurice? In God's name, tell me!"

"Murdered!"

"Murd – "

She clapped her hand to her mouth and dug her teeth into it to smother the scream which would have echoed up the well of the stairs. Louise's apartment was only up two flights. She would have heard.

"Tell me!" Josette gasped rather than spoke. She did not really understand. What Maurice had just said was so impossible. Inconceivable! She had expected a cataclysm… Yes. All day she had felt like the dread hand of Doom hovering over them all. But not this! In Heaven's name, not this! Murdered? Bastien? Why, Maurice must be crazy! And she said it aloud, too.

"You are crazy, Maurice!"

"I thought I was just now."

"You've been dreaming," she insisted. For still she did not believe.

"Murdered, I tell you! Dead!"

"Where?"

"In the office…"

"Then let us go…"

She wanted to run…out…at once, but Maurice got hold of her and held her so that she could not go.

"Wait, Josette! Let me tell you first."

"Let me go, Maurice! I don't believe it. Let me go!"

Maurice had already pulled himself together. He had contrived to steady his voice, and now, with a perfectly firm grip, he pulled Josette's hand under his arm and led her out into the street. There would be no holding her back if she was determined to go. The rainstorm had turned to a nasty drizzle and it was very cold. The few passers-by who hurried along the narrow street had their coat collars buttoned closely round their necks. A very few lights glimmered here and there in the windows of the houses on either side. Street lamps were no longer lighted these days in the side streets for reasons of economy.

Out in the open Maurice put his arm round Josette's shoulder and instinctively she nestled against him. Almost paralysed with horror, she was shivering with cold and her teeth were chattering, but there was a feeling of comfort and of protection in Maurice's arm which seemed to steady her. Also she wanted to hear every word that he said, and he did not dare raise his voice above a whisper. They walked as fast as the unevenness of the cobble-stones allowed, and now and then they broke into a run; and all the while, in short jerky sentences, Maurice tried to tell the girl something of what had happened.

"Maître de Croissy," he said, "had an interview with Citizen Chabot in the morning... While he was there Chabot sent for Bazire...and after that the three of them went together to Danton's lodgings..."

"You weren't with them?"

"No... I was waiting at the office. Presently Maître de Croissy came back alone. He was full of hope...the interview had gone off very well...better than he expected... Chabot and Bazire were obviously terrified out of their lives... Maître de Croissy had left them with Danton, and come on to the office..."

"Yes! and then?"

"About half an hour later, Chabot called at the office...alone...he brought a document with him...did Madame tell you?"

"Yes! yes!..."

"He stayed a little while talking...talking...explaining the document...a very long one...of which he wanted three copies made…with additions…and so on… He wanted the papers back by evening…"

Maurice seemed to be gasping for breath. His voice was husky as if his throat were parched. It was difficult to talk coherently while threading one's way through the narrow streets, and once or twice he forced Josette to stand still for a moment or two, to rest against the wall while she listened.

"We went home to dinner after Chabot had gone…" Maurice went on presently. "I can't tell you just how I felt then…a kind of foreboding you know…"

"Yes, I know," she said, "I felt it too…last night…"

"Something in that devil's eyes had frightened me…but you know Maître de Croissy…he won't listen…once he has made up his mind…and he laughed at me when I ventured on a word of warning…you know…"

"Oh, yes!" Josette sighed, "I know!"

"We went back to the office together after dinner. Maître de Croissy worked on the document all afternoon. It was ready just when the light gave out. He gave me the paper and told me to take it to Citizen Chabot. I went. Chabot kept me waiting, an hour or more. It was nearly eight o'clock when I got back to the office. The front door was ajar. I remember thinking this strange. I pushed open the door…"

He paused, and suddenly Josette said quite firmly:

"Don't tell me, Maurice. I can guess."

"What, Josette?"

"Those devils got you out of the way. They meant to filch the letters from Bastien. They killed him in order to get the letters."

"The two rooms," Maurice said, "looked as if they had been shattered by an earthquake."

"They broke everything so as to get the letters, and they killed him first."

They had reached the house in the Rue de la Monnaie. It looked no different than it had always done. Grim, grey, dilapidated.

Inside the house there was that smell of damp and of mortar like in a vault. Apparently no one knew anything as yet about what had occurred on the second floor where Citizen Croissy, the lawyer, had his office. No one challenged the young man and the girl as they hurried up the stairs. Josette as she ran was trembling in every limb, but she knew that the time had come for calmness and for courage, and with a mighty effort she regained control over her nerves. She was determined to be a help rather than a hindrance, even though horror had gripped her like some live and savage beast by the throat so that she scarcely could breathe, and turned the dread in her heart to physical nausea.

Maurice had taken the precaution of locking the front door of the office, but he had the key in his pocket. Before inserting it in the keyhole he paused to take another look at Josette. If she had faltered the least bit in the world, if he had perceived the slightest swaying in her young firm body, he would have picked her up in his arms where she stood and carried her away – away from that awful scene behind this door.

He could not see her face, for the stairs were very dark, but through a dim and ghostly light he perceived the outline of her head and saw that she held it erect and her shoulders square. All he said was:

"Shall we go to the Commissariat first?"

But she shook her head. He opened the door and she followed him in. The small vestibule was in darkness, but the door into the office was open, and here the light from the oil-lamp which dangled from the ceiling revealed the prone figure of Bastien de Croissy on the floor, his torn clothing and the convulsive twist of his hands. A heavy crowbar lay close beside the body, and all around there was a litter of broken furniture, wood, glass, a smashed inkstand with the ink still flowing out of it and staining the bit of faded carpet; sand and debris of paper and of string and the smashed drawers of the bureau. The strongbox was also on the floor with its metal door broken open and money and papers scattered around. Indeed, the whole place did look as if it had been shattered by an earthquake.

But Josette did not look at all that. All she saw was Bastien lying there, his body rigid in the last convulsive twitching of death. She prayed to God for the strength to go near him, to kneel beside him and say the prayers for the dead which the Church demanded. Maurice knelt down beside her, and they drew the dead man's hands together over his breast, and Josette took her rosary from her pocket and wound it round the hands; then she and Maurice recited the prayers for the dead: she with eyes closed lest if she continued to look she fell into a swoon. She prayed for Bastien's soul, and she also prayed for guidance as to what she ought to do now that Bastien was gone: for Louise was not strong and after this she would have no one on whom to lean, only on her, Josette.

When she and Maurice had finished their prayers they sought among the debris for the two pewter candlesticks that used to stand on the bureau. Maurice found them presently; they were all twisted, but not broken, and close by there were the pieces of tallow candle that had fallen out of their sconces. He straightened them out, and with a screw of paper held to the lamp he lighted the candles and Josette placed them on the floor, one on each side of the dead man's head.

After which she tiptoed out of the room. Maurice extinguished the hanging lamp; he followed Josette out through the door and locked it behind him.

Then the two of them went silently and quickly down the stairs.

7

Louise de Croissy lay on the narrow horsehair sofa like a log. Since Josette had broken the terrible news to her, more than twenty-four hours ago, she had been almost like one dead: unable to speak, unable to eat or sleep. Even Charles-Léon's childish cajoleries could not rouse her from her apathy.

For twenty-four hours she had lain thus, silent and motionless, while Josette did her best to keep Charles-Léon amused and looked after his creature comforts as best she could. She adored Louise, but somehow at this crisis she could not help feeling impatient with the other woman's nervelessness and that devastating inertia. After all, there was Charles-Léon to think of; all the more now as the head of the family had gone. Josette still had her mind set on finding the Scarlet Pimpernel, who of a truth was the only person in the world who could save Louise and Charles-Leon now. Josette had no illusions on the score of the new danger which threatened those two. Bastien had been murdered by Terrorists because he would not give up the letters that compromised them without getting a quid pro quo. They had killed him and ransacked his rooms. They might have ordered his arrest – it was so easy these days to get an enemy arrested – but no doubt feared that he might have a chance of speaking during his trial and revealing what he knew. Only dead men tell no tales.

But the letters had not been found, and at this hour there was a clique of desperate men who knew that their necks were in peril if those letters were ever made public. Josette had no illusions. Sooner or later, within a few hours perhaps, those men would strike at Louise. There would be a perquisition, arrest possibly, and possibly another murder. She wanted Louise to destroy the letters, they had been the cause of this awful cataclysm, but at the slightest hint Louise had clutched at her bosom with both hands as if she would guard the letters with her life. The next evening when Josette came home she found Louise already in bed; it was the first time she had moved from that narrow horsehair sofa since the girl had broken the news to her. She had laid out her clothes on a chair, with her corsets ostentatiously spread out on the top of the other things as if to invite attention. The packet of letters was no longer inside the lining. Josette noticed this at once, also that Louise was feigning sleep and was watching her through half-closed lids.

With well-assumed indifference Josette went about her business in the house, smoothed Louise's pillow, kissed her and Charles-Léon good night, and then got into bed. But she did not get much sleep, tired to death though she was. She foresaw the complications. Louise had some fixed idea about those letters, the result of the shock no doubt, and was clinging to them with the obstinacy of the very weak. She had hidden them and meant to keep their hiding-place a secret, even from Josette. No doubt her nerves had to a certain extent given way, for in spite of her closed eyes as she lay on her bed there was that expression of cunning in her face which is peculiar to those whose minds are deranged.

Josette and Maurice had spent most of that day at the Commissariat of Police. It was a terrible ordeal from first to last. The airless room that smelt of dirt and humanity, the patient crowd of weary men and women waiting their turn to pass into the presence of the Commissary, the suspense of the present and the horror of the past nearly broke down Josette's fortitude. Nearly, but not quite; for she had Maurice with her, and it was wonderful what comfort she derived from his nearness. She had always been so self-reliant, so accustomed to watch over those she cared for, and cater for their creature comforts, that Maurice Reversac's somewhat diffident ways, his timid speech and dog-like devotion had tempered her genuine affection for him with a slight measure of contempt. She could not help but admire his loyalty to his employer and his disinterestedness and felt bound to admit that he was clever and learned in the law, else Bastien would not have placed reliance on his judgment, as he often did, but all the time she had the feeling that morally and physically he was a weakling, the ivy that clung rather than the oak that supported.

But since this awful trouble had come upon her, how different it all was. Josette felt just as self-reliant as in the past, for Louise and Charles-Léon were more dependent on her than ever before, but there was Maurice now, a different Maurice altogether, and he had become a force.

When their turn came to appear before the Commissary, Josette, having Maurice at her side, did not feel frightened. They both gave their names and address in a clear voice, showed their papers of identity, and gave a plain and sincere account of the terrible events of the day before. Citizen Croissy, the well-known advocate, had been foully murdered in his office in the Rue de la Monnaie. It was their duty as citizens of the Republic to report this terrible fact to the Commissariat of the section.

The Commissary listened, raised his eyebrows, toyed with a paper-knife; his face was a mask of complete incredulity.

"Why should you talk of murder?" he asked.

Maurice mentioned the crowbar, the ransacked room, the scattered papers, the broken strongbox. It was clearly a case of murder for purposes of robbery.

"Any money missing?" the Commissary asked.

"No!"

"Eh bien!" he remarked with a careless shrug. "You see?"

"The murder had a political motive, Citizen Commissary," Josette put in impulsively, "the assassins were not after money, but after certain papers..."

"Now you are talking nonsense," the Commissary broke in curtly. "Murder? What fool do you suppose would resort to murder nowadays?" He checked himself abruptly, for he was on the point of letting his tongue run away with him. What he had very nearly said, and certainly had implied, was that no fool would take the risk and trouble of murder these days when it was so easy to rid oneself of an enemy by denouncing him as "suspect of treason" before the local Committee of Public Safety. Arrest, trial and the guillotine would then follow as a matter of course, and one got forty sous to boot as a reward for denouncing a traitor. Then why trouble to murder?

No wonder the Commissary checked himself in time before he had said all this: men in office had been degraded before now, if not worse, for daring to criticise the decrees of this paternal Government.

"I'll tell you what I will do, Citizeness," he said, speaking more particularly to Josette because her luminous blue eyes were fixed upon his, and he was a susceptible man; "I don't believe a word of your story, mind! but I will visit the scene of that supposed murder, and listen on the spot to the depositions of witnesses. Then we'll see."

"There were no witnesses to the crime, Citizen Commissary," Josette declared.

Whereupon the Commissary swore loudly, blustered and threatened all false accusers with the utmost penalties the law could impose. Witnesses? There must be witnesses. The *concierge* of the house...the other lodgers...anyway he would see, and if in the end it was definitely proved that this tale of assassination and political crime was nothing but a cock-and-bull story, well! let all false witnesses look to their own necks...that was all.

"You will appear before me tomorrow," were the parting words with which the Commissary dismissed Maurice and Josette from his presence.

No wonder that after that long and wearisome day, Josette should have lain awake most of the night a-thinking. It was very obvious that nothing would be done to bring the murderers of Bastien to justice. Perhaps she had been wrong after all to speak of "political motives" in connection with the crime: she had only moral proofs for her assertion, and those devils who had perpetrated the abominable deed would be all the more on the alert now, and Louise's peril would be greater even than before.

"Holy Virgin," she murmured naïvely in her prayers, "help me to find the Scarlet Pimpernel!"

On the following morning, Louise, though still listless and apathetic, rose and dressed herself without saying a word. Josette with an aching heart could not help noticing that her face still wore an expression of cunning and obstinacy, and that her eyes were still dry: Louise indeed had not shed a single tear since the awful truth had finally penetrated to her brain, and she had understood that Bastien had been foully murdered because of the letters.

With endearing words and infinite gentleness Josette did her best to soften the poor woman's mood. She drew her to Charles-Léon's bedside and murmured some of the naïve prayers which when they were children together they had learned at the old Convent of the Visitation. Her own soulful blue eyes were bathed in tears.

"Don't try and make me cry, Josette," Louise said. These were the first words she had spoken for thirty-six hours, and her voice sounded rasping and harsh. "If I were to shed tears now I would go on crying and crying till my eyes could no longer see and then they would close in death."

"You must not talk of death, Louise," Josette admonished gently, "while you have Charles-Léon to think of."

"It is because I think of him," Louise retorted, "that I don't want to cry."

But of the letters not a word, though Josette, by hint and glance, asked more than one mute question.

"Bastien would rather have seen your tears, Louise," she said with a tone of sad reproach.

"Perhaps he will – from above – when I stand by his graveside…but not now – not yet."

Louise, however, never did stand by her husband's graveside; that morning when Maurice and Josette went to the Commissariat in order to obtain permission for the burial of Citizen Croissy, they were curtly informed that the burial had already taken place, and no amount of questioning, of entreaty and of petitions elicited any further information, save that the body had been disposed of by order of what was vaguely designated as "the authorities"; which meant that it had probably been thrown in the fosse commune of the Jardin de Picpus – the old convent garden – the common grave where no cross or stone could mark the last resting-place of the once brilliant and wealthy advocate of the Paris bar. The reason, curtly given, for this summary procedure was that it was the usual one in the case of suicides.

Thus was the foul murder of the distinguished lawyer classed as a case of suicide. It was useless to protest and to argue; only harm would come to Louise and Charles-Léon if either Maurice or Josette entered into any discussion on the subject. As soon as they opened their mouths they were roughly ordered to hold their peace. Maurice Reversac was commanded to accompany the Citizen Substitute to the office of the Rue de la Monnaie, there to complete certain formalities in connection with the goods and chattels belonging to "the suicide," and then officially to give up the keys of the apartment.

8

Josette in her naïve little prayers had implored the Holy Virgin to aid her in finding the Scarlet Pimpernel. She was convinced that nothing could save Louise and Charles-Léon from Bastien's awful fate save the intervention of her mysterious hero, but the last two days had been so full of events that it had been quite impossible for her to begin her quest for the one man on whom in this dark hour she could pin her faith. Maurice, on the other hand, had promised that he would do his best, and this was all the more wonderful as he had not the same faith as Josette in the existence of the heroic Englishman. Nevertheless, in order to please and cheer her, and in the intervals of running from pillar to post, from the Rue de la Monnaie to the Commissariat and back again, he did seriously set to work to get on the track of the public letter-writer who was wont to ply his trade at the corner of the Pont-Neuf and who was supposed to be in touch with the Scarlet Pimpernel himself.

Maurice knew all the highways and byways of old Paris – the small eating-houses and estaminets where it was possible to enter into casual conversation with simple everyday folk who would suspect no harm in discreet inquiries. Thus he came quite by chance on the track of what he thought might be a clue. There was, it seems, in a distant quarter of the city near the Batignolles, a funny old scarecrow who had set up his tent and carried on his trade of letter-writing for those who were too illiterate or too prudent to put pen to paper for themselves. Not that Maurice believed for a moment that the scarecrow in question had anything to do with a band of English aristos, but he thought that the running him to earth, the walk across Paris, even though the weather was at its vilest, would take Josette out of herself for an hour or so, and turn her thoughts into less gloomy channels.

Josette readily agreed, and while Maurice was away on his melancholy errand in the Rue de la Monnaie, she promised that she would wait for him at the Commissariat de Police, and then they could sally forth together in quest of the hero of her dreams.

The waiting-room of the Commissariat was large and square. The walls had at some remote time been whitewashed; now they and the ceiling were of a dull grey colour, and all around there was a dado-line of dirt and grease made by the rubbing of innumerable shoulders against the lime. On the wooden benches ranged against the walls, patient, weary-looking women sat, some with shawls over their heads, others shivering in thin bodice and kirtle, and all hugging bundles or babies. One of them made room for Josette, who sat down beside her preparing to wait. There were a number of men, too, mostly in ragged breeches and tattered coats, who hung about in groups whispering and spitting on the floor, or sitting on the table: nearly all of them were either decrepit or maimed. A few children scrambled in the dirt, getting in everybody's way. The place was almost unendurably stuffy, with a mingled odour of boiled cabbage, wet clothes and damp mortar; only from time to time when the outside door was opened for someone to go in or out did a gust of cold air come sweeping through the room. Josette wished she had arranged to meet Maurice somewhere else; she didn't think she could wait much longer in this dank atmosphere. She was very tired, too, and the want of air made her feel drowsy.

The sound of a familiar voice roused her from the state of semi-torpor into which she had fallen. Blinking and rather dazed, she looked about her. Old Doctor Larousse had just come in. He had a bundle of papers in his hand and looked fussy and hurried.

"A dog's life!" he muttered in the face of anyone who listened to him. "All these papers to get signed and more than half an hour to wait, maybe, in this filthy hole!"

Josette at sight of him jumped up and intercepted him at the moment when two or three others tried to get a word with him. All day yesterday she had wished to get in touch with the old doctor, and again this morning, not so much because of Charles-Léon, but because she was getting seriously anxious about Louise. Citizen Larousse had been away from home for the past twenty-four hours: Josette had called at his rooms two or three times during the day, but always in vain.

Now she pulled the old man by the sleeve, forced him to listen to her.

"Citizen Doctor," she demanded, "at what hour can you come to the Rue Picpus and see Citizeness Croissy, who is seriously ill?"

Larousse shook her hand off his arm with unusual roughness: he was a kindly man, but apparently very harassed this morning.

"At what hour – at what hour?" he muttered petulantly. "Hark at your impudence, Citizeness! At no hour, let me tell you – not today, anyhow! I am off to Passy as soon as I can get these cursed papers signed."

"Citizeness Croissy is in a dangerous state, Citizen Doctor," the girl insisted earnestly. "The day before yesterday her husband was murd – was found dead in his office. The shock has prostrated her – "

"I know, I know!" the doctor broke in, and did his best to shake off this pretty but tiresome petitioner, "the man committed suicide. I was called in to make the report. These papers here have to do with it. I must get them signed."

"Citizen Doctor, think of the widow! Her mind is nearly deranged. She wants – "

"Many of us want things these days, little Citizeness," the old man said more gently, for Josette's deep blue eyes were fixed upon him and they were irresistible – would have been irresistible, that is, if he, Larousse, had not been quite so worried this morning. "I, for one, want to get to Passy, where my wife is ill with congestion of the lungs, and I shall not leave her bedside until she is well or…"

He shrugged his shoulders. He was a kind-hearted man really, but for two days he had been anxious about his wife. Josette Gravier was pretty, very pretty; she had large blue eyes that looked like a midnight sky in June when she was excited or eager or distressed, and there were delicate golden curls round her ears which always made old Larousse think of the days of his youth, of those summer afternoons when he was wont to wander out in the woods around Fontainebleau with his arm round a pretty girl's waist – just such a girl as Josette. But today? No, he was not in a mood to think of the days of his youth, and he had no use for pretty girls with large blue reproachful eyes. He was much too worried to be cajoled.

"You will have to find another doctor, little Citizeness," he concluded gruffly, "or else wait a day or two."

"How can I wait a day or two," she retorted, "with Citizeness Croissy nigh to losing her reason? Can't you imagine what she has gone through?"

The old man shrugged. He had seen so much misery, so much sorrow and pain, it was difficult to be compassionate to all. There had never been but one in this world who had compassion for the whole of humanity, and humanity repaid Him by nailing Him to a cross.

"We all have to go through a lot these days, Citizeness," the old man said, "and I do not think that your friend will lose her reason. One is apt to let one's anxiety magnify such danger. I'll come as soon as I can."

"How soon?"

"Three or four days – I cannot tell."

"But in the meanwhile, Citizen Doctor, what shall I do?"

"Give her a soothing draught."

"To what purpose? She is calm – too calm – "

"Find another doctor."

"How can I? It takes days to obtain a permit to change one's doctor. You know that well enough, Citizen."

The girl now spoke with bitter dejection and the old man with growing impatience. He had freed himself quickly enough from the subtle spell of the girl's beauty: the weight of care and worry had again descended on him and hardened his heart. A queue had formed against the door which led to the Commissary's private office, and the old doctor feared that he would lose his turn if he did not immediately take his place in the queue. The papers had got to be signed and he was longing to get away to Passy, where his wife lay sick with congestion. He tried to shake off Josette's grip on his arm, but she would not let go.

"Can you get me a permit," she pleaded, "to change our doctor?"

Oh, those permits – those awful, tiresome, cruel permits, without which no citizen of this free Republic could do anything save die! Permit to move, permit for bread, permit for meat or milk, permit to call in a doctor, a midwife or an undertaker! Permits, permits all the time!

The crowd in the room, indifferent at first, had begun to take notice of this pretty girl's importunate demands. They were here, all of them, in quest of some permit or other, the granting of which depended on the mood of the official who sat at his desk the other side of the door. If the official was harassed and tired he would be disobliging, refuse permit after permit: to a sick woman to see a doctor, to an anaemic child to receive more milk, to a man to take work beyond a certain distance from his home. He could be disobliging if he chose, for full powers were vested in him. Such were the ways of this glorious Republic which had for its motto: Liberty and Fraternity. Such was the state of slavery into which the citizens of the free Republic had sunk. And as Josette insisted, still clinging to the doctor's arm, the men shrugged and some of them sneered. They knew that old Larousse could not get the permit for which she craved. It took days to obtain any kind of a permit: there were yards of red tape to measure out before anything of the sort could be obtained, even if the Commissary was in one of his best moods. They were all of them sorry for the girl in a way, chiefly because she was so pretty, but they thought her foolish to be so insistent. The women gazed on her and would have commiserated with her, only that they had so many troubles of their own. And they were all so tired, so tired of hanging about in this stuffy room and waiting their turn in the queue. It was so hard to worry over other people's affairs when one was tired and had countless worries of one's own.

Now someone came out of the inner room and the queue moved on. Josette was suddenly separated from the doctor, who was probably thankful to be rid of her; with a deep sigh of dejection she went back to her seat on the bench. A few glances of pity were still cast on her, but presently the queue was able to move on again and she was soon forgotten. No one took any more notice of her. The men whispered among themselves, the women, fagged and silent, stood waiting for their turn to go in. Only one man seemed to take an interest in Josette: a tall ugly fellow with one leg who was leaning against the wall with his crutches beside him. He was dressed in seedy black with somewhat soiled linen at throat and wrist, and his hair, which was long and lanky, was tied back at the nape of the neck with a frayed-out black ribbon. He wore no hat, his shoes were down at heel and his stockings were in holes. By the look of him he might have been a lawyer's clerk fallen on evil days.

Josette did not at first notice him, until presently she had that peculiar feeling which comes to one at times that a pair of eyes were fixed steadily upon her. She looked up and encountered the man's glance, then she frowned and quickly turned her head away, for the seedy-looking clerk was very ugly, and she did not like the intentness with which he regarded her. Much to her annoyance, however, she presently became conscious that he had gathered up his crutches and hobbled towards her. The crowd made way for him, and a few seconds later he stood before her, leaning upon his crutches.

"Your pardon, Citizeness," he said, and his voice was certainly more pleasing than his looks, "but I could not help hearing just now what you said to Citizen Larousse…about your friend who is sick…and your need of a doctor…"

He paused, and Josette looked up at him. He appeared timid and there certainly was not a suspicion of insolence in the way he addressed her, but he certainly was very ugly to look at. His face was the colour of yellow wax, and on his chin and cheeks there was a three days' growth of beard. His eyebrows were extraordinarily bushy and overshadowed his eyes, which were circled with purple as if from the effects of a blow. So much of his countenance did Josette take in at the first glance, but his voice had certainly sounded kindly, and poor little Josette was so devoured with anxiety just now that any show of kindness went straight to her heart.

"Then you must also have heard, Citizen," she said, "that Doctor Larousse could do nothing for my friend."

"That is why," the man rejoined, "I ventured to address you, Citizeness. I am not a doctor, only a humble apothecary, but I have some knowledge of medicine. Would you like me to see your friend?"

He had gradually dropped his voice until in the end he was hardly speaking above his breath. Josette felt strangely stirred. There was something in the way in which this man spoke which vaguely intrigued her and she couldn't make out why he should have spoken at all. She looked him straight in the eyes; her own were candid, puzzled, inquiring. If only he were less ugly, his skin less like parchment and his chin free from that stubby growth of beard.

"I could come now," he said again. Then added with a light shrug, "I certainly could do your friend no harm just by seeing her, and I know of a cordial which works wonders on overstrung nerves."

Josette could never have told afterwards what it was that impelled her to rise then and there and to say:

"Very well, Citizen. Since you are so kind, will you come with me and see my sick friend?"

She made her way to the door and he followed her, working his way through the crowd across the room on his crutches. It was he who, despite his infirmities, opened the door and held it for the girl to pass through. It was close on midday. It had ceased raining and the air was milder, but heavy-laden clouds still hung overhead and the ill-paved streets ran with yellow-coloured mud.

Josette thought of Maurice as she started to walk in the direction of the Rue Picpus. She walked slowly because of the maimed man who hobbled behind her on his crutches, covering the ground in her wake, however, with extraordinary sureness and speed. She thought of Maurice, wondering what he would think of this adventure of hers, and whether he would approve. She was afraid that he would not. Maurice was cautious – more cautious than she was – and that very morning he had warned her to be very circumspect in everything she said and did, for Louise's sake and Charles-Léon's.

"Those devils," he had said to her just before they left home, "are sure to have their eye on Madame de Croissy. They haven't found the letters, but they know that they exist, and will of a surety have another try at getting possession of them."

"We must try and leave Madame alone as seldom as possible," he had said later on. "Unless I am detained over this awful business I will spend most of my day with her while you are at the workshop."

Apparently Maurice had been detained by the authorities, so Josette imagined, for he should have come to meet her at the Commissariat before now, but when he got there presently and found her gone he would probably conclude that she had been tired of waiting and had already gone home – and he would surely follow.

All the while that Josette's thoughts had run on Maurice, she had heard subconsciously the tap-tap of the man's crutches half a dozen paces or so behind her; then her thoughts had gone a-roaming on the terrible past, the dismal present, the hopeless future. What, she thought, would become of Louise and Charles-Léon after this appalling tragedy? Maître de Croissy's property in the Dauphiné brought in nothing: it was administered by a faithful soul who had been bailiff on the estate for close on half a century, and he just contrived to collect a sufficiency of money by the sale of timber and agricultural produce to pay for necessary repairs and stop the buildings and the land from going to rack and ruin, but there was nothing left over to pay as much as the rent of the miserable apartment in the Rue Picpus, let alone clothes and food. Maître de Croissy had been able to make a paltry income by his profession; but now? What was to become of his widow and of his child?

And Josette's thoughts of the future had been so black, so dismal and so absorbing that she was very nearly knocked down by a passing cart. The curses of the driver and the shouts of the passers-by brought her back to present realities, and these included the nearness of her maimed companion. She turned to look for him, but he was nowhere to be seen. She stood by for quite a long time at the angle of the street, thinking perhaps that he had fallen behind and would presently overtake her. But she waited in vain. There was no sign of the strange creature in the seedy black with the one leg and the crutches, the ugly face and gentle voice.

Quite against her will and her better judgment Josette felt vaguely dismayed and disappointed. What could this sudden disappearance mean of a man who had certainly forced his companionship upon her? Why had he gone with her thus far and then vanished so unaccountably? Did he really intend to visit Louise, or was his interest in her only a blind so as to attach himself to Josette? But if so what could be his object? All these thoughts and conjectures were very disturbing. There was always the fear of spies and informers present in every man or woman's mind these days, and Josette remembered Maurice's warning to be very circumspect and she wished now that she had insisted on waiting at the Commissariat for Maurice's return before she embarked on this adventure with the mysterious stranger.

And then she suddenly remembered that just before coming up to the Pont-Neuf the maimed man had hobbled up close to her and asked:

"But whither are we going, Citizeness?"

And that she had replied:

"To No. 43, in the Rue Picpus, Citizen. My friend has an apartment there on the second floor."

And now she wished she had not given a total stranger such explicit directions.

9

The rest of the day dragged on in its weary monotony. Josette had spent an hour with Louise at dinner-time, when she had tried again, as she had done in the past ten days, to rouse the unfortunate woman from her apathy. She did not tell her about the seedy apothecary with the one leg, who had thrust himself into her company only to vanish as mysteriously as he had appeared. She was beginning to feel vaguely frightened about that man: his actions had been so very strange that the conviction grew upon her that he must be some sort of Government spy.

Maurice Reversac also came in for a hurried meal at midday, and Josette spoke to him about the man at the Commissariat who had insisted on coming with her to visit Louise and then disappeared as if the cobble-stones of the great city had swallowed him up. Maurice, who was always inclined to prudence, wished that Josette had not been quite so free in her talk with the stranger. He dreaded those Government spies who undoubtedly would be detailed to watch the family of the murdered man; but whatever fears assailed him he kept them buried in his heart and indeed did his best to reassure Josette. But he did beg her to be more than ordinarily cautious. He stayed talking with her for a little while and then went away.

It was too late now to trudge all the way to the Batignolles in search of the public letter-writer, and Maurice, well aware of Josette's impetuosity at the bare mention of the Scarlet

Pimpernel, thought it best to say nothing to her tonight on the subject. He was trying to put what order he could in the affairs of the late advocate, and to save what could possibly be saved out of the wreckage of his fortune for the benefit of the widow and the child.

"I have been promised a permit," he said, "to go down into the Dauphiné for a day or two. I can then see the bailiff and perhaps make some arrangement with him by which he can send Madame a small revenue from the estate every month. Then, if they let me carry on the practice…"

"Do you think they will?"

Maurice shrugged.

"One never knows. It all depends if lawyers are scarce now that they have killed so many. There is always some litigation afoot."

Finally he added, with a great show of confidence which he was far from feeling:

"Don't lose heart, Josette chérie. Every moment of my life I will devote to making Madame and the boy comfortable because I know that is the way to make you happy."

But Josette found it difficult not to lose heart. She was convinced in her own mind that danger greater than ever now threatened Louise entirely because of her, Josette's, indiscretion, and that the maimed man of the Commissariat whom she had so foolishly trusted was nothing but a Government spy.

The truth did not then dawn upon her, not until many hours later, after she had spent her afternoon as usual at the workshop and then came home in the late afternoon.

As soon as Josette entered the living-room she knew that the miracle had happened – the miracle to which she had pinned her faith, for which she had hoped and prayed and striven. She had left Louise lying like a log on the sofa, silent, dry-eyed, sullen, with Charles-Léon, quietly whimpering in his small bed. She found her a transformed being with eyes bright and colour in her cheeks. But it was not this sudden transformation of her friend, nor yet Louise's cry: "Josette chérie! You were right and I was wrong to doubt." It was something more subtle, more intangible, that revealed to this ardent devotee that the hero of her dreams had filled the air with the radiance of his personality, that he had brought joy where sorrow reigned, and security and happiness where unknown danger threatened. Louise had run up to Josette as soon as she heard the turn of the latchkey in the door. She was laughing and crying, and after she had embraced Josette she rank back into the living-room and picked Charles-Léon up in her arms and hugged him to her breast.

"My baby," she murmured, "my baby! He will get strong and well and we shall be delivered from this hateful country."

Then she put Charles-Léon down, threw herself on the sofa, and burying her face in her arms she burst into tears. She cried and sobbed; her shoulders quivered convulsively. Josette made no movement towards her: it was best that she should cry for a time. The reaction from a state of dull despair had evidently been terrific, and the poor woman's over-wrought nerves would be all the better for this outlet of tears. How could Josette doubt for a moment that the miracle had happened?

As soon as she was a little more calm, Louise dried her eyes, then she drew a much-creased paper from the pocket of her skirt and without a word held it out to Josette. It was a letter written in a bold clear hand and was addressed to Citizeness Croissy at No. 43, Rue Picpus, on the second floor, and this is what it said:

> "As soon as you receive this, believe that sincere friends are working for your safety. You must leave Paris and France immediately, not only for the boy's health's sake, but because very serious danger threatens you and him if you remain. This evening at eight o'clock take your boy in your arms and an empty market-basket in your hand.

> Your *concierge* will probably challenge you; say that you are going to fetch your bread ration which you omitted to get this morning because of the bad weather. If the *concierge* makes a remark about your having the child with you, say that the Citizen Doctor ordered you to take him out as soon as the rain had ceased. Do not on any account hasten downstairs or through the *porte-cochère*, just walk quietly as if in truth you were going to the baker's shop. Then walk quietly along the street till you come to the district bakery. There will probably be a queue waiting for rations at the door. Take your place in the queue and go in and get your bread. In the crowd you will see a one-legged man dressed in seedy black. When he walks out of the shop, follow him. Divest yourself of all fear. The League of the Scarlet Pimpernel will see you safely out of Paris and out of France to England or Belgium, whichever you wish. But the first condition for your safety and that of the child is implicit trust in the ability of the League to see you through, and, as a consequence of trust, implicit obedience."

The letter bore no signature, but in the corner there was a small device, a star-shaped flower drawn in red ink. Josette murmured under her breath:

"The Scarlet Pimpernel! I knew that he would come."

Had she been alone she would have raised the paper to her lips, that blessed paper on which her hero's hand had rested. As it was she just held it tight in her hot little palm, and hoped that in her excitement Louise would forget about it and leave it with her as a precious relic.

"And of course you will come with me and Charles-Léon, Josette chérie."

Louise had to reiterate this more than once before the sense of it penetrated to Josette's inner consciousness. Even after the third repetition she still looked vague and un-understanding.

"Josette chérie, of course you will come."

"But, Louise, no! How can I?" the girl murmured.

"How do you mean, how can you?"

Josette held up the precious letter.

"He does not speak of me in this."

"The English League probably knows nothing about you, Josette."

"But *he* does."

"How do you know?"

Josette evaded the direct question. She quoted the last few words of the letter:

"As a consequence of trust, implicit obedience."

"That does not mean…"

"It means," Josette broke in firmly, "that you must follow the directions given you in this letter, word for word. It is the least you can do, and you must do it for the sake of Charles-Léon. I am in no danger here, and I would not go if I were. Maurice will be here to look after me."

"You are talking nonsense, chérie. You know I would not go without you."

"You would sacrifice Charles-Léon for me?"

Then as Louise made no reply – how could she? – Josette continued with simple determination and unshaken firmness:

"I assure you, Louise chérie, that I am in no danger. Maurice cannot go away while he has Bastien's affairs to look after. He wouldn't go if he could, and it would be cowardly to leave him all alone here to look after things."

"But, Josette…"

"Don't say anything more about it, Louise. I am in no danger and I am not going. And what's more," she added softly, "I know that the Scarlet Pimpernel will look after me. Don't be afraid, he knows all about me."

And not another word would she say.

Louise, no doubt, knew her of old. Josette was one of those dear, gentle creatures whom nothing in the world could move once she was set on a definite purpose – especially if that purpose had in it the elements of self-sacrifice. The time, too, was getting on. It was already past seven o'clock. Louise busied herself with Charles-Léon, putting on him all the warm bits of garments she still possessed. Josette was equally busy warming up some milk, the little there was, over the fire in the tiny kitchen.

At eight o'clock precisely Louise was ready. She prepared to gather the child in her arms. Josette had a big shawl ready to wrap round them both: she thrust the empty market-basket over Louise's arm. Her heart ached at thought of this parting. God alone knew when they would meet again. But it all had to be done, it all had to be endured for the sake of Charles-Léon. Louise had declared her intention of going to England rather than to Belgium. She would meet a greater number of friends there.

"I will try and write to you, Josette chérie," she said. "My heart is broken at parting from you, and I shall not know a happy hour until we are together again. But you know, *ma chérie*, that Bastien was always convinced that this abominable Revolution could not last much longer; and – who knows? – Charles-Léon and I may be back in Paris before the year is out."

She was, perhaps, too excited to feel the sorrow of parting quite as deeply as did Josette. Indeed, Louise was in a high state of exultation, crying one moment and laughing the next, and the hand with which she clung to Josette was hot and dry as if burning with fever. Just at the last she was suddenly shaken with a fit of violent trembling, her teeth chattered and she sank into a chair, for her knees were giving way under her.

"Josette!" she gasped. "You do not think, perchance…"

"What, chérie?"

"That this…this letter is all a hoax? And that we – Charles-Léon and I – are walking into a trap?"

But Josette, who still held the letter tightly clasped in her hand, was quite sure that it was not a hoax. She recalled the seedy apothecary at the Commissariat and his gentle voice when he spoke to her, and there had been a moment when his steady gaze had drawn her eyes to him. She had not thought about it much at the time, but since then she had reflected and remembered the brief but very strange spell which seemed to have been cast over her at the moment. No, the letter was not a hoax. Josette would have staked her life on it that it was dictated, or perhaps even written, by the hero of her dreams.

"It is not a trap, Louise," she said firmly, "but the work of the finest man that ever lived. I am as convinced as that I am alive that the one-legged man in seedy black whom you will see in the bakery is the Scarlet Pimpernel himself."

It was Josette who lifted Charles-Léon and placed him in Louise's arms. A final kiss to them both and they were gone. Josette stood in the middle of the room, motionless, hardly breathing, for she tried to catch the last sound of Louise's footsteps going down the stairs. It was only after she had heard the opening and closing of the outside door of the house that she at last gave way to tears.

Just like this Josette had cried when Louise, after her marriage to Bastien de Croissy, left the little farm in the Dauphiné in order to take up her position as a great lady in Paris society. The wedding had taken place in the small village church, and everything had been done very quietly because General de Vandeleur, Louise's father, had only been dead a year and Louise refused to be married from the house of one of her grand relations. Papa and Maman Gravier and Josette were the three people she had cared for most in all the world until Bastien came along, and she had the sentimental feeling that she wished to walk straight out of the one house where her happy girlhood had been passed into the arms of the man to whom she had given her heart.

The wedding had been beautiful and gay, with the whole village hung about with flags and garlands of flowers; and previous to it there had been all the excitement of getting Louise's trousseau together, and of journeys up to Paris to order and try on the wedding gown. And Josette had been determined that no tears or gloomy looks from her should cast a shadow over her friend's happiness. It was when everything was over, when Louise drove away in the barouche en route for Paris, that Josette was suddenly overwhelmed with the sorrow which she had tried to hold in check for so long. Then as now she had thrown herself down on the sofa and cried out her eyes in self-pity for her loneliness. But what was the loneliness of that day in comparison with what it was now? In those days Josette still had her father and mother: there were the many interests of the farm, the dogs, the cows, haymaking, harvesting. Now there was nothing but dreariness ahead. Dreariness and loneliness. No one to look after, no one to fuss over. No Charles-Léon to listen to tales of heroism and adventure. Only the Government workshop, the girls there with their idle chatter and their reiterated complaints: only the getting up in the morning, the munching of stale food, the stitching of shirts, and the going to bed at night!

Josette thought of all this later on when bedtime came along, and she knelt beside Charles-Léon's empty cot and nearly cried her eyes out. Nearly but not quite, for presently Maurice came home. And it was wonderful how his presence put a measure of comfort in Josette's heart. Somehow the moment she heard the turn of his latchkey in the door, and his footsteps across the hall, her life no longer appeared quite so empty. There was someone left in Paris after all, who would need care and attention and fussing over when he was sick; his future would have to be planned, suitable lodgings would have to be found for him, and life generally re-ordained according to the new conditions.

And first of all there was the excitement of telling Maurice all about those new conditions.

Even before he came into the room Josette had jumped to her feet and hastily dried her eyes. But he saw in a moment that she had been crying.

"Josette!" he cried out, "what is it?"

"Take no notice, Maurice," Josette replied, still struggling with her tears, "I am not really crying…it is only because I am so…ever so happy!"

"Why? What has happened?"

"He came, Maurice," she said solemnly, "and they have gone."

Of course Maurice could not make head or tail of that.

"He? They?" he murmured frowning. "Who came, and who has gone?"

She made him sit down on the ugly horsehair sofa and she sat down beside him and told him about everything. Her dreams had turned to reality, the Scarlet Pimpernel had come to take Louise and Charles-Léon away out of all this danger and all this misery: he had come to take them away to England where Louise would be safe, and Charles-Léon would get quite well and strong.

"And left you here!" Maurice exclaimed involuntarily, when Josette paused, out of breath, after she had imparted the great and glorious news: "gone to safety and left you here to face…"

But Josette with a peremptory gesture put her small hand across his mouth.

"Wait, Maurice," she said, "let me tell you."

She drew the precious letter from under her fichu – Louise, fortunately, had not demanded its return – and she read its contents aloud to Maurice.

"Now you see!" she concluded triumphantly, and fixed her glowing eyes on the young man.

"I only see," he retorted almost roughly, "that they had no right to leave you here…all alone."

"Not alone, Maurice," she replied; "are you not here to take care of me?"

That, of course, was a heavenly moment in Maurice's life. Never had Josette – Josette who was so independent and self-reliant – spoken like this before, never had she looked quite like she did now, adorable always, but more so with that expression of dependence and appeal in her eyes. The moment was indeed so heavenly that Maurice felt unable to say anything. He was so afraid that the whole thing was not real, that he was only dreaming, and that if he spoke the present rapture would at once be dispelled. He felt alternately hot and cold, his temples throbbed. He tried to express with a glance all that went on in his heart. His silence and his looks did apparently satisfy Josette, for after a moment or two she explained to him just what her feelings were about the letter.

"The Scarlet Pimpernel demands trust and obedience, Maurice," she said with naïve earnestness. "Well! would that have been obedience if Louise had lugged me along with her? He doesn't mention me in the letter. If he had meant me to come, he would have said so."

With this pronouncement Maurice had perforce to be satisfied; but one thing more he wanted to know: what had become of the letters? But Josette couldn't tell him. Ever since Bastien's death, Louise had never spoken of them, or given the slightest hint of what she had done with them.

"Let's hope she has destroyed them," Maurice commented with a sigh.

The next day they spent in hunting for new lodgings for Maurice. Strange! Josette no longer felt lonely. She still grieved after Louise and Charles-Léon, but somehow life no longer seemed as dreary as she thought it would be.

10

Louise, in very truth, was much too excited to feel the pang of parting as keenly as did Josette. And ever since Charles-Léon had fallen sick she had taken a veritable hatred to Paris and her dingy apartment in the Rue Picpus. The horror of her husband's death had increased her abhorrence of the place, and now hatred amounted to loathing.

Therefore it was that she went downstairs with a light heart on that memorable evening of September. She had Charles-Léon in her arms and carried the empty market-basket, with her ration card laid ostentatiously in it for anyone to see. The *concierge* was in the doorway of his lodge and asked her whither she was going. These were not days when one could tell a *concierge* to mind his own business, so Louise replied meekly:

"To the bakery, Citizen," and she showed the man her ration card.

"Very late," the *concierge* remarked dryly.

"The weather has been so bad all day…"

"Too bad even now to take the child out, I imagine."

"It has left off raining," Louise said still gently, "and the poor cabbage must have some fresh air; the Citizen Doctor insisted on that."

She felt terribly impatient at the delay, but did not dare appear to be in a hurry, whilst the *concierge* seemed to derive amusement at keeping her standing beside his lodge. He knew her for an aristo, and many there were in these days who found pleasure in irritating or humiliating those who in the past had thought themselves their betters.

However, this ordeal, like so many others, did come to an end after a time; the *concierge* condescended to open the *porte-cochère* and Louise was able to slip out into the street. It had certainly left off raining, but it was very cold and damp underfoot. Louise trudged on as fast as she could, her thin shoes squelching through the mud. Fortunately the bakery was not far, and soon she was able to take her place in the queue outside the shop. There was no crowd at this hour: a score of people at the most, chiefly women. Louise's anxious glance swept quickly over them and at once her heart gave a jump, for she had caught sight of a maimed man on crutches, dressed in black as the mysterious letter had described. He was ahead of her in the queue, and she saw him quite distinctly when he entered the shop, and stood for a moment under the lantern which hung above the door. But his face she could not clearly see, for he wore a black hat with a wide brim: a hat as shabby as his clothes. Presently he disappeared inside the shop, and Louise did not see him again until she herself had been to the counter and been served with her ration of bread. Then she saw him just going out of the shop and she followed as soon as she could.

There were still a good many people in the street, and just over the road there were two men of the Republican Guard on duty, set there to watch over the queue outside the licensed bakeries. Some of the people there were still waiting their turn, others were walking away, some in one direction, some in another. But there was no sign anywhere of the one-legged man. Louise stood for a moment in the ill-lighted street, perturbed and anxious, wondering in which direction she ought to go; her heart seemed to sink into her shoes, and she was desperately tired, too, from standing so long with the child in her arms. But with those men of the Republican Guard watching her she did not like to hesitate too long and, thoroughly heart-sick now and nigh unto despair, she began to fear that the letter and all her hopes were only idle dreams. Almost faint with fatigue and disappointment she had just turned her weary footsteps towards home when suddenly she heard the distant tap-tap of crutches on the cobble-stones.

With a deep sigh of relief Louise started at once to walk in the direction whence came the welcome sound. The tap-tap kept on slightly ahead of her, so all she had to do was to follow as closely as she could. With Charles-Léon asleep in her arms she had trudged on thus for about ten minutes, turning out of one street and into another, when suddenly the tap-tap ceased. The maimed man had paused beside an open street door; when Louise came up with him he signed to her to enter.

She hadn't the least idea where she was, but from the direction in which she had gone she conjectured that it was somewhere near the Temple. There were not many people about, and though on the way she had gone past more than one patrol of the National Guard, the men had taken no notice of her; she was just a poor woman with a child in her arms and a ration of bread in her basket; nor had they paid any heed to a maimed, seedy-looking individual hobbling along on crutches.

Now as Louise passed through the open door her guide whispered rapidly to her:

"Go up two flights of stairs and knock at the door on your right."

Strangely enough, Louise had no hesitation in obeying; though she had no idea where she would find herself she felt no fear. Perhaps she was too tired to feel anything but a longing for rest. She went up the two flights of stairs and knocked at the door which her guide had indicated. It was opened by a rough-looking youngish man in ragged clothes, unshaved, unkempt, who blinked his eyes as if he had just been roused out of sleep.

"Is it Madame de Croissy?" he asked, and Louise noted that he spoke French with a foreign accent; also the word "Madame" was unusual these days. This, of course, reassured her. Her thoughts flew back to Josette and the girl's firm belief in the existence of the Scarlet Pimpernel.

The young man led the way through a narrow ill-lit passage to a room where Louise's aching eyes were greeted with the welcome sight of a table spread with a cloth on which were laid a knife and fork, a plate and a couple of mugs. There was also a couch in a corner of the room with a pillow on it and a rug. It was rather cold and a solitary tallow candle shed a feeble, vacillating light on the bare whitewashed walls and the blackened ceiling, but Louise thought little of all this; she sank down on a chair by the table, and the young man then said to her in his quaint stilted French:

"In one moment, Madame, I will bring you something to eat, for you must be very hungry; and we also have a little milk for the boy. I hope you won't mind waiting while I get everything ready for you."

He went out of the room before Louise had found sufficient energy to say "Thank you." She just sat there like a log, her purple-rimmed eyes staring into vacancy. Charles-Léon, who, luckily, had been asleep all this time, now woke and began to whimper. Louise hugged him to her bosom until the tousled young ruffian reappeared presently, carrying a tray on which there was a dish and a jug. Louise felt almost like swooning when a delicious smell of hot food and steaming milk tickled her nostrils. The young man had poured out a mugful of milk for Charles-Léon, and while the child drank eagerly Louise made a great effort to murmur an adequate "Thank you."

"It is not to me, Madame," the man retorted, "that you owe thanks. I am here under orders. You, too, I am afraid," he went on with a smile, "will have to submit to the will of my chief."

"Give me the orders, sir," Louise rejoined meekly. "I will obey them."

"The orders are that you eat some supper now and then have a good rest until I call you in the early morning. You will have to leave here a couple of hours before the dawn."

"Charles-Léon and I will be ready, sir. Anything else?"

"Only that you get a good sleep, for tomorrow will be wearisome. Good night, Madame."

Before Louise could say another word the young man had slipped out of the room.

Charles-Léon slept peacefully all night cuddled up against his mother, but Louise lay awake for hours, thinking of her amazing adventure. She was up betimes, and soon after a distant church clock struck half-past four there was a knock at the door. Her young friend of the evening before had come to fetch her; he looked as if he had been up all night, and certainly he had not taken off his clothes. Louise picked Charles-Léon up, and with him in her arms she followed her friend down the stairs. Outside she found herself in a narrow street: it was quite dark because the street lanterns had already been extinguished and there was not yet a sign of dawn in the sky. Through the darkness Louise perceived the vague silhouette of a covered cart such as the collectors of the city's refuse used for their filthy trade. A small donkey was harnessed to the cart and it was being driven apparently by a woman.

Neither the woman nor the young man spoke at the moment, but the latter intimated to Louise by a gesture that she must step into the cart. Only for a few seconds did she hesitate. The cart was indeed filthy and reeked of all sorts of horrible odours calculated to make any sensitive person sick. A kindly voice whispered in her ear:

"It cannot be helped, Madame, and you must forgive us: anyway, it is no worse than the inside of one of their prisons."

Her friend now took Charles-Léon from her, and summoning all her courage she stepped into the cart. The child was then handed back to her and she gathered herself and him into a heap under the awning. She wanted to assure her friend that not only was she prepared for anything, but that her heart was full of gratitude for all that was being done for her. But before she could speak a large piece of sacking was thrown right over her, and over the sacking a pile of things the nature of which the poor woman did not venture to guess. As she settled herself down, as comfortably as she could, she came in contact with what appeared to be a number of bottles.

A minute or two later with much creaking of wheels and many a jerk the cart was set in motion. It went jogging along over the cobble-stones of the streets of Paris at foot pace, while under the awning, smothered by a heap of all sorts of vegetable refuse, Louise de Croissy had sunk into a state of semi-consciousness.

11

She was roused from her torpor by the loud cry of "Halte!" The cart came to a standstill and Louise, with sudden terror gripping her heart, realised that they had come to one of the gates of Paris where detachments of the National Guard, officered by men eager for promotion, scrutinised every person who ventured in or out of the city.

The poor woman, crouching under a heap of odds and ends, heard the measured tramp of soldiers and a confused murmur of voices. Through a chink in the awning she could see that the grey light was breaking over this perilous crisis of her life. Presently a gruff commanding voice rose above the confused murmur around, alternating with the shrill croaky tones of a woman, whom Louise guessed to be the driver of the cart. The gruff voice when first it reached Louise's consciousness was demanding to see what there was underneath the awning. She could do nothing but hug the child closer to her breast, for she knew that within the next few seconds her life and his would tremble in the balance. She hardly dared to breathe; her whole body was bathed in a cold sweat. Heavy footsteps, accompanied by short, shuffling ones, came round to the back of the cart, and a few seconds later the end flap of the awning was thrust aside and a wave of cold air swept around inside the cart. Some of it penetrated to poor Louise's nostrils, but she hardly dared to breathe. She knew that her fate and that of Charles-Léon would be decided within the next few minutes perhaps.

The gruff voice was evidently that of one in authority.

"Anyone in there?" it demanded, and to the unfortunate woman it seemed as if the heap of rubbish on the top of her was being prodded with the point of a bayonet.

"No one now, Citizen Officer," a woman's shrill voice responded, obviously the voice of the old hag who was driving the cart: "that's my son there, holding the donkey's head. He can't speak, you know, Citizen…never could since his birth…tongued-tied as the saying is. But a good lad…can't gossip, you see. And here's his passport and mine!"

There was some rustle of papers, one or two muttered words and then the woman spoke again:

"I'm picking up my daughter and her boy at Champerret presently," she said: "their passports and permits are all in order too, but I haven't got them here."

"Where are you going then all of you?" the gruff voice asked, and there was more rustle of papers and a tramping of feet. The passports were being taken into the guard-room to be duly stamped.

"Only as far as Clichy, Citizen Officer. It says so on the permit. See here, Citizen. 'Permit for Citizeness Ruffin and her son Pierre to proceed to Clichy for purposes of business!' That's all in order is it not, Citizen Officer?"

"Yes! yes! that's all in order all right. And now let's see what you have got inside that cart."

"All in order…of course it is…" the old woman went on, cackling like an old hen; "you don't catch Mère Ruffin out of order with the authorities. Not her. Passports and permits, everything always in order, Citizen Officer. You ask any captain at the gates. They'll tell you. Mother Ruffin is always in order…always…in order…"

And all the while the old hag was shifting and pushing about the heap of rubbish that was lying on the top of the unfortunate Louise.

"It's not a pleasant business, mine, Citizen Officer," she continued with a doleful sigh; "but one must live, what? Citizen Arnould – you know him, don't you, Citizen? Over at the chemical works – he buys all my stuff from me."

"Filthy rubbish, I call it," the officer retorted; "but don't go wasting my time, mother. Just shift that bit of sacking, and you can take your stuff to the devil for aught I care."

Louise, trembling with fear and horror, still half-smothered under the pile of rubbish, was on the point of losing consciousness. Fortunately Charles-Léon was still asleep and she was able to keep her wits sufficiently about her to hold him tightly in her arms. Would the argument between the soldier and the old hag never come to an end?

"I am doing my best, Citizen Officer, but the stuff is heavy," the woman muttered; "and all my papers being in order I should have thought... Mother Ruffin's papers always are in order, Citizen Officer... Ask any captain of the guard...he'll tell you..."

"Nom d'un nom," the soldier broke in with an oath, "are you going to shift that sacking or shall I have to order the men to take you to the guard-room?"

"The guard-room? Me? Mère Ruffin, known all over the country as an honest patriot? You'd get a reprimand, Citizen Officer – that's what you would get for taking Mère Ruffin to the guard-room. Bien! bien! don't lose your temper, Citizen Officer...no harm meant... Here! can't one of your men give me a hand?... But... I say..."

A click of glass against glass followed: Louise remembered the bottles that were piled up round her. After this ominous click there was a moment's silence. Sounds from the outside reached Louise's consciousness: men talking, the clatter of horses' hoofs, the rattle of wheels, challenge from the guard, cries of "Halte!" distant murmurs of people talking, moving, even laughing, whilst she, hugging Charles-Léon to her breast, marvelled at what precise moment she and her child would be discovered and dragged out of this noisome shelter to some equally noisome prison. The woman had ceased jabbering: the click of glass seemed to have paralysed her tongue; but only for a moment: a minute or so later her shrill voice could be heard again.

"You won't be hard on me will you, Citizen Officer?" she said dolefully.

"Hard?" the soldier retorted. "That'll depend on what you've got under there."

"Nothing to make a fuss over, Citizen Officer: a poor widow has got to live, and..."

There was another click of glass – several clicks, then a thud, the bottles tumbling one against the other, then the officer's harsh voice saying with a laugh:

"So! that's it! is it? Absinthe? What? You old reprobate! No wonder you didn't want me to look under that sacking."

"Citizen Officer, don't be hard on a poor widow..."

"Poor widow indeed? Where did you steal the stuff?"

"I didn't steal it, Citizen Officer... I swear I didn't."

"How many bottles have you got there?"

"Only a dozen, Citizen..."

"Out with them."

"Citizen Officer..."

"Out with them I say..."

"Yes, Citizen," the old woman said meekly with an audible snuffle.

She sprawled over the back of the cart, pushed some of the rubbish aside and Louise was conscious of the bottles being pulled out from round and under her. She heard the soldier say:

"Is that all?"

"One dozen, Citizen Sergeant. You can see for yourself." The woman dropped down to the ground. Louise could hear her snuffling the other side of the awning. After which there came a terrible moment, almost the worst of this awful and protracted ordeal. The officer appeared to have given an order to one of the soldiers, who used the end of his bayonet for the purpose of ascertaining whether there were any more bottles under the sacking. What he did was to bang away with it on the pile of rubbish that still lay on the top of Louise; some of these bangs hit Louise on the legs: one blow fell heavily on one of her ankles. The courage with which she endured these blows motionless and in silence was truly heroic. Her life and Charles-Léon's depended on her remaining absolutely still. And she did remain quite still, hugging the child to her breast, outwardly just another pile of rubbish on the floor of the cart. The boy was positively wonderful, he seemed to know that he must not move or utter a sound. Though he must have been terrified, he never cried, but just clung to his mother, with eyes tightly closed. Louise in fact came to bless the very noisomeness of the refuse which lay on the top of her, for obviously the soldier did not like to touch it with his hands.

"I get most of my stuff from the hospitals," Louise could hear the old hag talking volubly to the officer; "you can see for yourself, Citizen, it is mostly linen which has been used for bandages…sore legs you know and all that… Citizen Arnould over at the chemical works gives me good money for it. It seems they make paper out of the stuff. Paper out of linen I ask you…brown or red paper I should say, for you should see some of it…and all the fever they've got in the wards now…yellow fever if not worse…"

"There! that'll do, Mother Ruffin," the officer broke in roughly: "all your talk won't help you. You've got to pay for taking the stuff through, and you know it…and there'll be a fine for trying to smuggle…"

There followed loud and long-winded protests on the part of the old hag; but apparently the officer was at the end of his tether and would listen to none of it, although he did seem to have a certain measure of tolerance for the woman's delinquency.

"You come along quietly, Mother," he said in the end, "it will save you trouble in the end."

He called to his men, and snuffling, cackling, protesting, the old woman apparently followed them quietly in the direction of the guard-room. At any rate Louise heard nothing more. For a long, long time she did not hear anything. The reaction after the terror of this past half-hour was so great that she fell into a kind of torpor; the noises of the street only came to her ears through a kind of fog. The only feeling she was conscious of was that she must hold Charles-Léon closely to her breast.

How long this state of numbness lasted she did not know. She had lost count of time; and she had lost the use of her limbs. Her ankle where she had been hit with the flat of the soldier's bayonet had ached furiously at first: now she no longer felt the pain. Charles-Léon, she thought, must have gone to sleep, for she could just feel his even breathing against her breast.

Suddenly she was aroused by the sound, still distant, of the woman's shrill voice. It drew gradually nearer.

"Now then, Pierre, let's get on," the old hag was shrieking as she came along.

Pierre, whoever he was, had apparently remained at the donkey's head all this time. Louise from the first had suspected that he was none other than her friend of the tousled head; but who that awful old hag with the snuffle and the cackling voice was she could not even conjecture. But she was content to leave it at that. Apparently those wonderful and heroic Englishmen employed strange tools in their work of mercy. At the moment she felt far too tired and too numb even to marvel at the amazing way in which that old woman had hoodwinked the officer of the guard. As Louise returned to consciousness she could hear vaguely in the distance the soldiers laughing and chaffing and the woman muttering and grumbling:

"Making a poor woman pay for honest trading…a scandal I call it…"

"Ohé, la mère!" the soldiers shouted amidst loud laughter, "bring us some more of that absinthe tomorrow."

"Robbers! thieves! brigands!" the woman ejaculated shrilly, "catch me again coming this way…"

She apparently busied herself with putting the bottles – or some of them at any rate – back into the cart: after which the flap of the awning was again lowered: there was much creaking and shaking of the cart; soon it was once more set in motion; to the accompaniment of more laughter and many ribald jokes on the part of the soldiers, who stood watching the departure of the ramshackle vehicle and its scrubby driver.

Anon the creaking wheels resumed their jolting, axle-deep in mud, over the country roads riddled with ruts. But of this Louise de Croissy now knew little or nothing. She had mercifully once more ceased to think or feel.

12

Days of strange adventures followed, adventures that never seemed real, only products of a long dream.

There was that halt on the wayside in the afternoon of the first day, with Paris a couple of leagues and more behind. The end flap of the awning was pulled aside and the horrible weight lifted from Louise's inert body. Glad of the relief and of the breath of clean air, she opened her eyes, then closed them again quickly at sight of the hideous old woman whose scarred and grimy face was grinning at her from the rear of the cart. A dream figure in very truth, or a nightmare! But was she not the angel in disguise who, by dint of a comedian's art, had hoodwinked the sergeant at the gate of Paris and passed through the jealously guarded barriers with as much ease as if her passengers in that filthy cart had been provided with the safest of passports?

Yet, strive how she might, Louise could see nothing in that ugly and ungainly figure before her that even remotely suggested a heroine or an angel. She gave up the attempt at fathoming the mystery, and allowed herself and Charles-Léon to be helped out of the cart and, with a great sigh of gladness, she sank down on the mossy bank by the roadside, and ate of the bread and cheese which the hag had placed beside her, together with a bottle of milk for the boy.

When she and Charles-Léon had eaten and drunk and she had taken in as much fresh country air as her lungs would hold, she looked about her, intending to thank that extraordinary old woman for her repeated kindness, but the latter was nowhere to be seen; also the donkey was no longer harnessed to the cart. Somewhere in the near distance there was a group of derelict cottages and, chancing to look that way, Louise saw the woman walking towards it and leading the donkey by the bridle.

She never again set eyes on that old hag. Presently, however, a rough fellow clad in a blue smock, who looked like a farm labourer, appeared upon the scene; he was leading a pony, and as soon as he caught Louise's glance he beckoned to her to get back into the cart. Mechanically she obeyed, and the man lifted Charles-Léon and placed him in his mother's arms. He harnessed the pony to the cart, and once more the tumble-down vehicle went lumbering along the muddy country lanes. Fortunately, though the sky was grey and the wind boisterous, the rain held off most of the time. For three days and nights they were on the road, sleeping when they could, eating whatever was procurable on the way. They never once touched the cities, but avoided them by circuitous ways; always a pony, or sometimes a donkey, was harnessed to the cart, but the same rough-looking farm labourer held the reins the whole time. Two or three times a day he would get down, always in the vicinity of some derelict building or other into which he would disappear, and presently he would emerge once more leading a fresh beast of burden. Once or twice he would be accompanied on those occasions by another man as rough-looking as himself, but for the most part he would attend to the pony or donkey alone.

There were some terrible moments during those days, moments when Louise felt that she must choke with terror. Her heart was in her mouth, for patrols of soldiers would come riding or marching down the road, and now and again there would be a cry of "Halte!" and a brief colloquy would follow between the Sergeant in command and the driver of the cart. But apparently – thank God for that – the cart and its rustic driver appeared too beggarly and insignificant to arouse suspicion or to engage for long the attention of the patrols.

The worst moment of all occurred in the late afternoon of the third day. The driver had turned the cart off the main road into a narrow lane which ran along the edge of a ploughed field. It was uphill work and the pony had done three hours' work already, dragging the rickety vehicle along muddy roads. Its pace got slower and slower. The wind blew straight from the north-east, and Louise felt very sick and cold, nor could she manage to keep Charles-Léon warm: the awning flapped about in the wind and let in gusts of icy draught all round.

When presently the driver pulled up and came round to see how she fared, she ventured to ask him timidly whether it wouldn't be possible to find some sheltered spot where they could all spend the night in comparative warmth for the child. At once the man promised to do his best to find some derelict barn or cottage. He turned into the ploughed field and soon disappeared from view. Louise remained shivering in the cart with Charles-Léon hugged closely to her under her shawl. She had indeed need of all her faith in the wonderful Scarlet Pimpernel to keep her heart warm, while her body was racked with the cold.

She had no notion of time, of course; and sundown meant nothing when all day the sky had been just a sheet of heavy, slate-coloured clouds. A dim grey light still hung over the dreary landscape, while slowly the horizon veiled itself in mist. The driver had been gone some time when Louise's sensitive ears caught the distant sound of horses' hoofs splashing in the mud of the road. It was a sound that always terrified her. Up to now nothing serious had happened, but it was impossible to know when some meddlesome or officious Sergeant might with questions and suspicions shatter at one fell swoop all the poor woman's hopes of ultimate safety. The patrol – for such it certainly was – was coming at a fair speed along the main road.

Perhaps, thought Louise, the soldiers would ride past the corner of the lane and either not see the cart or think it not worth investigating. Bitterly she reproached herself for her want of endurance. If she had not sent the driver off to go in search of a shelter for the night, he would have driven on at least another half kilometre and then surely the cart would not have been sighted from the road. And, what's more, she would not have been alone to face this awful contingency.

For contingency it certainly was. Anything – the very worst – might happen now, for the man was not there to answer harsh questions with gruff answers, he was not there with his ready response and his amazing knack of averting suspicions. Louise was alone and she heard the squad of soldiers turn into the lane. Her heart seemed to cease beating. A moment or two later the man in command cried "Halte!" and himself drew rein close to the rear of the cart.

"Anyone there?" he queried in a loud voice.

Oh! for an inspiration to know just what to say in reply! "There's someone under there," the soldier went on peremptorily; "who is it?"

More dead than alive, Louise was unable to speak.

The Sergeant then gave the order! "Allons! just see who is in there; and," he added facetiously, "let's hear where the driver of this elegant barouche has hidden himself."

There was some clatter and jingle of metal: the sound of men dismounting, the pawing and snorting of horses. Through the chinks in the awning Louise could perceive the dim light of a couple of dark lanterns like two yellow eyes staring. Then the awning in the rear of the cart was raised, the lantern lit up the interior and Louise was discovered crouching in the distant corner on a pile of sacking, hugging Charles-Léon.

"Ohé! la petite mère!" the Sergeant called out not unkindly: "come out and let's have a look at you."

Louise crawled out of the darkness, still hugging Charles-Léon. The evening was drawing in. She wondered vaguely if anything in her appearance would betray that she was no rustic, but an unfortunate, fleeing the country. She looked wearied to death, dishevelled and grimy. The Sergeant leaning down from his saddle peered into her face.

"Who is in charge of your barouche, petite mère?" he asked.

"My – my – husband," Louise contrived to stammer through teeth that were chattering.

"Where is he?"

"Gone to the village…to see if we can get…a bed…for the night…"

"Hm!" said the Sergeant. And after a moment or two: "Suppose you let me see your papers."

"Papers?" Louise murmured.

"Yes! Your passports, what?"

"I haven't any papers."

"How do you mean you haven't any papers?" the Sergeant retorted, all the kindliness gone out of his voice.

"My husband…" Louise stammered again.

"Oh! you mean your husband has got your papers?"

Louise, no longer able to utter a sound, merely nodded.

"And he's gone to the village?"

Another nod.

"Where is the village?"

Louise shook her head.

"You mean you don't know?"

The man paused for a moment or two. Clearly there was something unusual in this helpless creature stranded in the open country with a child in her arms, and no man in sight belonging to her.

"Well!" he said after a moment or two, during which he vainly tried to peer more closely in Louise's face, "you'll come along with us now, and when your husband finds the barouche gone he will know where to look for you."

"You get into your carriage, petite mère," he added; "one of the men will drive you."

So shaken and frightened was Louise that she could not move. Her knees were giving way under her. Two men lifted her and Charles-Léon into the cart. They were neither rough nor unkind – family men perhaps with children of their own – or just machines performing their duty. Louise could only wonder what would happen next. Crouching once more in the cart, she felt it give a lurch as one man scrambled into the driver's seat. He took the reins and clicked his tongue, and the pony had just answered to a flick of the whip when from the ploughed field there came loud cries of "Ohé!" coming right out of the evening mist. Louise didn't know if she could feel relief or additional terror when she heard that call. It was her rustic friend coming back at full speed. He was running, and came to a halt in the lane breathless and obviously exhausted.

"Sergeant," he cried, gasping for breath, "give a hand...on your life give a hand...a fortune, Sergeant, if we get him now."

The soldier, taken aback by the sudden appearance of this madman – he thought of him as such – fell to shouting:

"What's all this?" and had much ado to hold his horse, which had shied and reared at the strident noise. The other soldiers – there were only four of them – were in a like plight, and for a moment or two there was a good deal of confusion which the quickly gathering darkness helped to intensify.

"What's all this?" the Sergeant queried again as soon as the confusion subsided. "Here! you!" he commanded: "are you the owner of this aristocratic vehicle!"

"I am," the man replied.

"And is that your wife and child inside?"

"They are. But in Satan's name, Sergeant..."

"Never mind about Satan now. You just get into your stylish vehicle and turn your pony's head round; you are coming along with me."

"Where to?"

"To Abbeville, parbleu. And if your papers are not in order..."

"If you go to Abbevile, Sergeant," the man declared, still panting with excitement, "you lose the chance of a lifetime... there's a fortune for you and me and these honest patriots waiting for us in the middle of this ploughed field."

"The man's mad," the Sergeant declared. "Allons, don't let's waste any more time. En evant!"

"But I tell you I saw him, Citizen Sergeant," the man protested.

"Saw whom? The devil?"

"Worse. The English spy."

It was the Sergeant's turn to gasp and to pant.

"The English spy?" he exclaimed.

"Him they call the Scarlet Pimpernel!" the man asserted hotly.

"Where?" the Sergeant cried. And the four men echoed excitedly! "Where?"

The man pointed towards the ploughed field.

"I went to look for a shelter for the night for my wife and child. I came to a barn. I heard voices. I drew near. I peeped in. Aristos I tell you. A dozen of them. All talking gibberish. English, what? And drinking. Drinking. Some of them were asleep on the straw. They mean to spend the night there."

He paused, breathless, and pressed his grimy hands against his chest as if every word he uttered caused him excruciating pain. The words came from his throat in short jerky sentences. Clearly he was on the verge of collapse. But now the Sergeant and his men were as eager, as excited as he was.

"Yes! yes! go on!" they urged.

"They are there still," the man said, trying to speak clearly: "I saw them. Not ten minutes ago. I ran away, for I tell you they look like devils. And one of them is tall...tall like a giant...and his eyes..."

"Never mind his eyes," the Sergeant broke in gruffly: "I am after those English devils. There's a reward of ten thousand livres for the capture of their chief...and promotion..." he added lustily.

He turned his horse round in the direction of the field, and called loudly "Allons!"

The driver halloed after him.

"But what about me, Citizen Sergeant?"

"You can follow. In what direction did you say?"

"Straight across," the man replied. "See that light over there...keep it on your right...and then follow the track...and there's a gap in the hedge..."

But the Sergeant was no longer listening. No doubt visions of ten thousand livres and fortune rising to giddy heights rose up before him out of the fast-gathering gloom. He was not going to waste time. The men followed him, as eager as he was. Louise with an inexpressible sense of relief heard the jingle of their accoutrements, the creaking of damp leather, the horses snorting and pawing the wet earth. The flap of the awning had been lowered again: she couldn't see anything, but she heard the welcome sounds, and no longer felt the cold.

"My baby, my baby," she murmured, crooning to Charles-Léon, "I do believe that God is on our side."

The cart moved along. She didn't know in which direction. The pony was going at foot-pace: probably the driver was leading it, for the darkness now was intense – the welcome darkness that enveloped the wanderers as in a black shroud. At first Louise could not help thinking of that Sergeant and the soldiers. What would they do when they found that they had been hoodwinked? They would scour the countryside of course to find traces of the cart. Would they succeed in the darkness of the night? She dared not let her thoughts run on farther. All she could do was to press Charles-Léon closer and closer to her heart and to murmur over and over again: "I do believe that God is on our side."

He was indeed, for the night passed by and there was no further sign of the patrol. After a time the cart came to a standstill and the driver came round, and helped her and Charles-Léon to descend. They all sheltered in the angle of a tumble-down wall which had once been part of a cottage. The man wrapped some sacking round Louise and the child and she supposed that she slept, for she remembered nothing more until the light of dawn caused her to open her eyes.

The next day they came in sight of Calais. The driver pulled up and bade Louise and the child descend. Louise knew nothing of this part of France. It appeared to her unspeakably dreary and desolate. The earth was of a drab colour, so different to the rich reddish clay of the Dauphiné, and instead of the green pastures and golden cornfields, stiff scrubby grass grew in irregular tufts here and there. The sky was grey and there was a blustering wind which brought with it a smell of fish and salt water. The stunted trees, with their branches all tending away from the sea, had the mournful appearance of a number of attenuated human beings who were trying to run away and were held back by their fettered feet. Calais lay far away on the right, and there was only one habitation visible in this desolate landscape. This was a forlorn and dilapidated-looking cottage on the top of the cliff to the west: its roof was all crooked on the top like a hat that has been blown aside by the wind. The driver pointed to the cottage and said to Louise:

"That is our objective now, Madame, but I am afraid it has to be reached on foot. Can you do it?"

This was the first time that the man spoke directly to Louise. His voice was serious and kindly, nevertheless she was suddenly conscious of a strange pang of puzzlement and doubt – almost of awe: for the man spoke in perfect French, the language of a highly educated man. Yet he had the appearance of a rough country boor: his clothes were ragged, he wore neither shirt nor stockings: of course his unshaved cheeks and chin added to his look of scrubbiness and his face and hands were far from clean. At first, when he replaced the horrible old hag on the driver's seat of the cart, Louise had concluded that he was one of that heroic band of Englishmen who were leading her and Charles-Léon to safety, but this conclusion was soon dispelled when the man spoke to the several patrols of soldiers who met them on the way. She had heard him talk to them, and also the night before, during those terrible moments in the lane; and he had spoken in the guttural patois peculiar to the peasantry of Northern France.

But now, that pleasant, cultured voice, the elegant diction of a Parisian! Louise did not know what to make of it. Had she detected the slightest trace of a foreign accent she would have understood, and gone back to her first conclusion, that here was one of those heroic Englishmen of whom Josette was wont to talk so ecstatically. But a French gentleman, masquerading in country clothes, what could it mean?

The poor woman's nerves were so terribly on edge that one emotion would chase away another with unaccountable speed. For the past few hours she had felt completely reassured – almost happy – but now, just a few words uttered by this man whom she had learned to trust sent her back into a state of panic, and the vague fears which she had experienced when first she left her apartment in the Rue Picpus once more reared their ugly heads. It was stupid of course! A state bordering on madness! But Louise had not been quite normal since the tragic death of Bastien.

And suddenly she clutched at her skirt, in the inner pocket of which she had stowed the packet of letters which already had cost Bastien de Croissy his life. But the letters were no longer there. She searched and searched, but the packet had indubitably gone. Then she was seized with wild panic. Pressing the child to her bosom she turned as if to fly. Whither she knew not, but to fly before the hideous arms of those vengeful Terrorists were stretched out far enough to get hold of Charles-Léon.

But before she had advanced one step in this wild career a strange sound fell upon her ear, a sound that made her pause and look vaguely about her to find out how it was that *le bon Dieu* had sent this heaven-born protector to save her and the boy. The sound was just a pleasant mellow laugh, and then the same kindly voice of a moment ago said quietly:

"This is yours, I believe, Madame."

Instinctively she turned like a frightened child, hardly daring to look. Her glance fell first on the packet of letters which she had missed and which was held out to her by a very grimy yet strangely beautiful hand: from the hand her eyes wandered upwards along the tattered sleeve and the bent shoulder to the face of the driver who had been the silent companion of her amazing three days' adventure. And out of that face a pair of lazy deep-set blue eyes regarded her with obvious amusement, whilst the aftermath of that pleasant mellow laugh still lingered round the firm lips.

With her eyes fixed upon that face, which seemed like a mask over a mystical entity, Louise took the packet of letters. Her trembling lips murmured an awed "Who are you?" whereat the strange personage replied lightly, "For the moment your servant, Madame, only anxious to see you safely housed in yonder cottage. Shall we proceed?"

All Louise could do was to nod and then set off as briskly as she could, so as to show this wonderful man how ready she was to follow him in all things. He had already taken the pony out of the cart and set Charles-Léon on its back. The cart he left by the roadside, and he walked beside the pony steadying Charles-Léon with his arm. Thus the little party climbed to the top of the cliff. It was very heavy going, for the ground was soft and Louise's feet sank deeply into the sand; but she dragged herself along bravely, although she felt like a somnambulist, moving in a dream walk to some unknown, mysterious destination, a heaven peopled by heroic old hags and rough labourers with unshaven cheeks and merry, lazy eyes. The cottage on the cliff was not so dilapidated as it had appeared in the distance. The man brought the pony to a halt and pushed open the door. Louise lifted Charles-Léon down and followed her guide into the cottage. She found herself in a room in which there was a table, two or three chairs and benches, and an iron stove in which a welcome fire was burning. Two men were sitting by the fire and rose as Louise, half-fainting with fatigue, staggered into the room. Together they led her to an inner room where there was a couch, and on this she sank breathless and speechless. Charles-Léon was then laid beside her: the poor child looked ghastly, and Louise, with a pitiable moan, hugged him to her side. One of the men brought her food and milk, whilst the other placed a pillow to her head. Louise, though only half-conscious at this moment, felt that if only she had the strength she would have dragged herself down on her knees and kissed the hands of those rough-looking men in boundless gratitude.

She remained for some time in a state of torpor, lying on the couch holding the boy closely to her. The door between the two rooms was ajar: a welcome warmth from the iron stove penetrated to the tired woman's aching sinews. A vague murmur of voices reached her semi-consciousness. The three men whom she regarded as her saviours were talking together in whispers. They spoke in English, of which Louise understood a few sentences. Now and again that pleasant mellow laugh which she had already heard came to her ears, and somehow it produced in her a sense of comfort and of peace. One of the three men, the one with the mellow laugh, seemed to be in command of the others, for he was giving them directions of what they were to do with reference to a boat, a creek and a path down the side of a cliff, and also to a signal with which the others appeared to be familiar.

But the voices became more and more confused; the gentle murmur, the pleasant roar of the fire acted as a lullaby, and soon Louise fell into a dreamless sleep.

13

A pleasant, cultured voice, speaking French with a marked foreign accent, roused Louise out of her sleep. She opened her eyes still feeling dazed and not realising for the moment just where she was. One of the young men whom she had vaguely perceived the night before was standing under the lintel of the door.

"I hope I haven't frightened you, Madame," he now said, "but we ought to be getting on the way."

It was broad daylight, with a grey sky heavy with clouds that threatened rain, and a blustering wind that moaned dismally down the chimney. From the distance came the regular booming of the breakers against the cliffs. It was a sound Louise had never heard in her life before and she could not help feeling alarmed at the prospect of going on the sea with Charles-Léon so weak and ill, even though salvation and hospitable England lay on the other side. But she had made up her mind that however cowardly she felt in her heart of hearts, she would bear herself bravely before her heroic friends. As soon as the young man had gone, she made herself and the boy ready for the journey – the Great Unknown as she called it with a shudder of apprehension.

There was some warm milk and bread for her and Charles-Léon on the table in the other room. She managed to eat and drink and then said bravely: "We are quite ready now, Monsieur."

The young man guided her to the front door of the house. Here she expected to see once more the strange and mysterious man who had driven her all the way from Paris in the ramshackle vehicle and who throughout four long wearisome days and nights had never seemed to tire, and never lost his ready wit and resourcefulness in face of danger from the patrols of the National Guard.

Not seeing him or the cart she turned to her new friend. "What has happened to our elegant barouche?" she asked with a smile, "and the pony?"

"They wouldn't be much use down the cliff-side, Madame," he replied; "I hope you are not too tired to walk..."

"No, no! of course not, but..."

"And one of us will carry the boy."

"I didn't mean that," she rejoined quickly.

"What then?"

"The...driver who brought us safely here...he was so kind...so...so wonderful... I would love to see him again...if only to thank him..."

The young man remained silent for a minute or two, then when Louise insisted, saying: "Surely I could speak to him before we go?" he said rather curtly, she thought: "I am afraid not, Madame."

She would have liked to have insisted still more urgently, thinking it strange that this young man should speak so curtly of one who deserved all the eulogy and all the recognition that anyone could give for his valour and ingenuity, but somehow she had the feeling that for some obscure reason or other the subject of that wonderful man was distasteful to her new friend, and that she had better not inquire further about him. Anyway, she was so surrounded by mysteries that one more or less did not seem to matter.

Just then she caught sight of another man who was coming up the side of the cliff. He kept his head bent against the force of the wind, which was very boisterous and made going against it very difficult. Soon he reached the top of the cliff. He greeted Louise with a pleasant "Bonjour, Madame," uttered with a marked English accent. Indeed to Louise he looked, just like the other, a fine, upstanding young foreigner, well-groomed despite the inclemency of the weather and the primitiveness of his surroundings. The two men exchanged a few words together which Louise did not understand, after which one of them said, "En route!" and the other added in moderately good French, "I hope you are feeling fit and well, Madame; you have another tiring day before you."

Louise assured him that she was prepared for any amount of fatigue; he then took Charles-Léon in his arms; his friend took hold of Louise by the elbow, and led the way down the cliff, carefully guiding her tottering footsteps.

At the foot of the cliff the little party came to a narrow creek, and Louise perceived a boat hidden in a shallow cave in the rock. Guided by her friends Louise crept into the cave, and stepped into the boat. The young men made her as comfortable as they could and gently laid Charles-Léon in her arms. Except for gentle words of encouragement to the little boy now and then, they spoke very little, and Louise, who by now was in a kind of somnambulistic state, could only nod her thanks when one or the other of them asked if she felt well, or offered her some scanty provisions for herself and Charles-Léon.

The party sat in the boat during the whole of the day, until it was quite dark. In the distance far out at sea Louise's aching eyes perceived from time to time ships riding on the waves. Charles-Léon was frightened at first, and crouched against his mother, and when the waves came tumbling against the rocks and booming loudly he hid his little head under her shawl. But after a time the reassuring voices of the young Englishmen coupled with boyish curiosity induced him to look at the ships; he listened to childish seafaring yarns told by one or the other of them: soon he became interested and, like his mother, felt no longer afraid.

Poor Louise, was, of course, terribly ignorant of all matters connected with the sea, as she had never been as much as near it in her life. She only knew vaguely the meaning of the word tide, and when the young men spoke of "waiting for the tide" before putting out to sea, she did not know what they meant. She fell to wondering whether they would all presently cross La Manche in the tiny rowing boat which was not much bigger than those in which she and Josette with papa and maman Gravier were wont in the olden days to go out for picnics on the Isère. But she asked no questions. Indeed by now she felt that she had permanently lost the use of her tongue.

Soon evening began to draw in. A long twilight slowly melted into the darkness of a moonless night. Looking towards the sea it seemed to Louise that she was looking straight at a heavy black curtain – like a solid mass of gloom. The wind continued unabated, and now that she could no longer see the sea, and only heard its continuous roar, Louise once more felt that hideous, cold fear grinding at her heart. Those terrifying waves seemed to come nearer and nearer to the sheltering cave, while the breakers broke on the stony beach with a sound like thunder. As was quite natural, her terror communicated itself to the child. He refused to be comforted, and though the two men did all they could to soothe him, and one of them knelt persistently beside Louise, whispering words of encouragement in the child's ear, poor little Charles-Léon continued to shiver with terror.

Through the dismal howling of the wind and the booming of the waves no other sound penetrated to Louise's ears. After a while the young men too remained quite silent: they were evidently waiting for the signal of which they had spoken together the night before.

What that signal was Louise did not know. She certainly heard no strange sound, but the men did evidently hear something, for, suddenly and without a word, they seized their oars and pushed the boat off and out of the cave. This was perhaps on the whole the most terrifying moment in Louise's extraordinary adventure. The boat seemed to be plunging straight into a wall of darkness. It rocked incessantly, and poor Louise felt horribly sick. Presently she felt that she was being lifted to her feet and held in a pair of strong arms which carried her upwards through the darkness, whither she knew not at the time, but a little while later it occurred to her that perhaps she had died of fright, and that as a matter of fact she had now awakened in Paradise. She was lying between snow-white, lavender-scented sheets, her aching head rested on a downy pillow, and a kindly voice was persuading her to sip some hot spiced wine, which she did. It certainly proved to be delicious.

And there was Charles-Léon sitting opposite to her on the knee of a ruddy-faced, tow-haired sailor who was holding a mug of warm milk to the child's trembling lips. All that and more did indeed confirm Louise's first impression that this was not the cruel, hard world with which she was all too familiar, but rather an outpost of Paradise – if not the blessed heavens themselves.

The movement of the ship, alas! made Louise feel rather sick after a time, and this was an unpleasant and wholly earthly sensation which caused her to doubt her being in the company of the angels. But indeed she was so tired that soon she fell asleep, in spite of the many strange noises around and above her, the creaking of wood, the soughing of the wind and the lashing of the water against the side of the ship.

When she woke after several hours' sleep the pale rosy light of dawn came creeping in through the port-hole. It was in very truth a rosy dawn, an augury of the calm and beauty that was now in store for the long-suffering woman. She was in England at last, she and her child: together they were safe from those assassins who had done Bastien to death and would probably have torn Charles-Léon from her breast before they sent her to the guillotine.

Le Bon Dieu had indeed been on her side.

14

And while Louise lived through the palpitating events of those fateful days Josette Gravier was quietly taking up the threads of life again. They were not snapped; they had only slipped for a few hours out of her hands, and life, of course, had to go on just the same. She would be alone after this in the apartment of the Rue Picpus: the small rooms, the tiny kitchen seemed vast now that all those whom Josette cared for had gone. Strangely enough she was not anxious about Louise's fate; her faith was so immense, her belief in the Scarlet Pimpernel so absolute that she was able to go through the days that followed in comparative peace of mind whilst looking forward to Maurice's return.

He had obtained a permit lasting six or seven days to visit the de Croissy estates in the Dauphiné. The permit had been granted before Louise's departure was known to the authorities, or probably she and Charles-Léon, as sole heirs of Bastien de Croissy, would have been classed as *émigrés:* all their property would then be automatically confiscated and no one but Government officials allowed to administer it. Maurice spent five days of his leave in the diligence between Paris and Grenoble, and one in consultation with the old bailiff on the Croissy estate, trying to extract from him a promise that he would send to Mademoiselle Gravier on behalf of Madame de Croissy a small sum of money every month for rent and the bare necessities of life. Maurice hoped that after Josette had paid the rent out of this money she would contrive to send the remainder over to England as soon as she knew where to find Louise.

Josette had a little money of her own which she kept in her stocking, and she also received a few sous daily pay for the work which she did in the Government shops – stitching, knitting, doing up parcels for the "Soldiers of Liberty" who were fighting on the frontiers against the whole of Europe and keeping the great armies of Prussia and Austria at bay. If the rent of the apartment could be paid with monies sent from the Croissy estate, Josette was quite sure that she could live on her meagre stipend. Penury in the big cities, and especially in Paris, was appalling just now. Sugar and soap were unobtainable, and the scarcity of bread was becoming more and more acute. Queues outside the bakeries began to assemble as early as four o'clock in the morning to wait for the distribution of two ounces of bread, which was all that was allowed per person per day; and the two ounces consisted for the most part of bran and water. The baker favoured Josette because of her pretty face, but she was obliged to go for her ration very early in the morning because she had to be at the workshop by eight o'clock, and if she queued up later in the day Citizen Loquin would sometimes run out of bread before all his customers were served.

When Maurice came back from Grenoble life for Josette became more cheerful. He had found a tiny room for himself under the roof of another house in the Rue Picpus and had at once fallen back into his old habit of calling for Josette in the late afternoon at the Government shop when her day's work was done, and together the two of them would go arm-in-arm for a walk up the Champs Elysées or sometimes as far as the Bois. Maurice would bring what meagre provisions they could afford for their supper, and they would sit under the chestnut trees, now almost shorn of leaves and munch sour bread and dig their young teeth into an apple. Sometimes they would stroll into the town to see the illuminations, for there were illuminations on more than one day every week. What the wretched poverty-stricken, tyrant-ridden citizens of Paris rejoiced for on those evenings heaven alone knew! Certain it is that though tallow and grease were scarce, innumerable candles and lamps were lit, time after time, on some pretext or other, such as the passing of some decree which had a momentary popularity, or the downfall of a particular member of the Convention who had – equally momentarily – become unpopular with the mob. Such occasions were marked, in addition to the brilliant lighting of the city, by a great deal of noise and cheering, as an ill-clad, ill-fed mob thronged the streets, cheering their Robespierre or their Danton, and booing all the poor wretches who had been decreed traitors to the Republic on that day, and whose trial, condemnation and death on the guillotine would – just as night inevitably follows day – follow within twenty-four hours.

Maurice and Josette, jostled by the crowd, neither booed nor cheered: they seldom knew what the rejoicings and illuminations were for, but the movement, the lights and the noise took them out of themselves and caused them to forget for an hour or two the ever-growing problem of how to go on living. Once or twice when Maurice had carried through successfully a bit of legal business, he would buy a couple of tickets for the theatre, and he and Josette would listen enthralled to the sonorous verses of Corneille or Racine as declaimed by Citizen Talma, or laugh their fill over the drolleries of Mascarille or Monsieur Jourdain.

Sunday had been officially abolished by decree of the Convention in the new calendar, but Decadi came once every ten days with a half-holiday for Josette; then, if the day was fine, the two of them would hire a boat and Maurice would row up the river as far as Suresnes, and he and Josette would munch their sour bread and their apples under the trees by the towpath, and watch the boats gliding up and down the Seine and long for the freedom to drift downstream away from the noise and turmoil of the city, and away from the daily horrors of the guillotine and countless deaths of innocents which would for ever remain a stain on the fair fame of the country which they loved.

Maurice had never spoken again of love to Josette. He was not an ordinary lover, for he had intuition, and his love was entirely unselfish. So few lovers have a direct apprehension of the right moment for declaring their feelings; those that have this supreme gift will often succeed where others less sensitive will fail because they have not approached the loved one when she was in a receptive mood. Maurice knew that his hour had not yet come. Josette was still in a dream-state of adoration for a hero whom she had never seen. She was too young and too unsophisticated to analyse her own feelings; too ignorant of men and of life to take Maurice altogether seriously. As a friend or a brother she cared for him more than she had ever cared for another living soul, not excepting Louise; she trusted him, she relied on him: had she not said on that never-to-be-forgotten occasion: "Are you not here to take care of me?" But for the time being her thoughts were too full of that other man's image to add idealism to her affection. And so even though these autumn days were balmy and sweet, though the wood-pigeons still cooed in the forests and the blackbirds whistled in the chestnut trees, Maurice did not speak of love to Josette; although at times he suffered so acutely from her ingenuousness that tears would well up to his eyes and the words which he forced himself not to utter nearly choked him; yet he did not tell her how he loved her, and how he ached with the longing to take her in his arms, to bury his face in her golden curls, or press his burning lips on her sweet, soft mouth.

He was happy in this, that he was in a measure working for her; all her little pleasure, all the small delicacies which he brought her, and which she munched with the relish of a young animal, came to her through his exertions. He had automatically slipped into his late employer's practice. It did not amount to much, but he was a fully qualified advocate, and as clerk to Citizen Croissy, had become known to the latter's clients. A part of the money which he earned he put by for Madame because he considered that it was her due, but there was always a little over which Maurice set aside for the joy of giving Josette some small treat – tickets at the theatre, an excursion into the country, or an intimate little dinner at one of the cheap restaurants. Strange, indeed, that in the midst of the most awful social upheaval the world has ever known, life for many, like Josette Gravier and Maurice Reversac, could go on in such comparative calm.

Three weeks and more went by before Josette had any news of Louise. But one evening when she came home after her walk with Maurice she found that a letter had been thrust under the door of the apartment. It was from Louise.

> "MY JOSETTE CHÉRIE (it said),
>
> "We are in England, Charles-Léon and I, and the man who has wrought this miracle is none other than the mysterious hero of whom you have so often dreamed. I have received word that this letter will reach you. That word was signed with the device which stands for courage and self-sacrifice – a small scarlet flower, my Josette, the Scarlet Pimpernel. I am completely convinced now that I owe my salvation and that of Charles-Léon to your English hero. Here in England no one doubts it. He is the national hero, and people speak of him with bated breath as of a godlike creature, whom only the elect have been privileged to meet in the flesh. It is generally believed that he is a high-born English gentleman who devotes his life to saving the weak and the innocent from the murderous clutches of those awful Terrorists in France. He has a band of followers, nineteen

in number, who obey his commands without question, and under his leadership constantly risk their precious lives in the cause of humanity. It is difficult to understand why they do this: some call it the sublimity of self-sacrifice, others the love of sport and adventure, innate in every Englishman. But God alone can judge of motives.

"My darling Josette, you will be happy to know that we are at peace and comfortable now, my poor lamb and I, though my heart is filled with sorrow at being parted from you. Daily do I pray to God that you may come to me some day soon. Remember me to Maurice. He is a brave and loyal soul. I will not tell you of the hopes which I nurse for your future and his. You will have guessed these long ago. I am afraid that he would refuse to come away from Paris just yet, but if you, Josette, would join me here in England – and you can do that any day with the aid of the Scarlet Pimpernel – we could bide our time quietly until the awful turmoil has subsided, which, by God's will, it soon must, and then return to France, when you and Maurice could be happily united.

"As to my adventures from the moment when I left our apartment with Charles-Léon in my arms until the happy hour when we landed here in England I can tell you nothing. My lips are sealed under a promise of silence, and implicit obedience to the wishes of my heroic rescuers is the only outward token of my boundless gratitude that I can offer them.

"But I can tell you something of our arrival in Dover. I was still very sea-sick, but the feeling of nausea left me soon after I had set foot on solid ground. We walked over to a delightful place, a kind of tavern it was, though not a bit like our cafés or restaurants. Later on when I was rested, I made a note of the sign which was painted on a shield outside the door; it was '*The Fisherman's Rest,*' and, in English, such places are called inns. I have prayed God ever since I crossed that threshold that you, my Josette chérie might see it one day.

"Here for the first time since I left Paris I came in contact with people of my own sex. The maid who showed me to a room where I could wash and rest was a sight for sore eyes: so clean, so fresh, so happy! So different to our poor girls in France nowadays – under-fed, ill-clothed, in constant terror of what the near future might bring. These little maids over here go about their work singing – singing, chérie! Just think of it! Of late I have never heard anyone sing except you!

"We spent the best part of the day at '*The Fisherman's Rest*.' In the afternoon we posted to Maidstone, where we now are the guests of some perfectly charming English people. I cannot begin to tell you, chérie, of the kindness and hospitality of these English families who take us in, poor *émigrés*, feed us and clothe us and look after us until such time as we get resources of our own. I wish our good Maurice could send me a remittance from time to time, but that, I know, is impossible. But I will try to get some needlework to do; you know how efficient I was always considered, even at the convent, in sewing and embroidery. I do not wish to be a burden longer than I can help to my over-kind hosts.

"How this letter will reach you I know not, but I know that it will reach you, because a day or two ago the post brought me a mysterious communication saying that any letter of mine sent to the Bureau des Émigrés, Fitzroy Square, London, will be delivered to any address in France. This is only one of the many wonderful happenings that have occurred since I left Paris. It seems such a long time ago now, and our little apartment in the Rue Picpus seems so far, so very far away. I have forgotten nothing, Josette chérie, even though my memory has been over clouded by all the strange events which have befallen me. So little have

I forgotten that many a time and very bitterly have I reproached myself that I lent such an inattentive ear when you spoke to me about the mysterious English hero who goes by the name of the Scarlet Pimpernel, and of his no less heroic followers. Had I believed in you and them sooner, my Bastien might be beside me even now. The Scarlet Pimpernel, my Josette, is real, very real indeed. He and his nineteen lieutenants have saved the lives of hundreds of innocents: his name here is on everybody's lips, but no one knows who he is. He works in the dark, under that quaint appellation, and those of us who owe our lives to him have, so far as we know, never set eyes on him.

"Well! it is a problem the solution of which I shall probably never know. All I can do is to keep sacred in my heart the memory of all that that man has done for me.

"That is all, my Josette. I hope and pray to Almighty God that some day soon it may be your good fortune to come to me – to come to England under the tender care of the man whom you have almost deified. When that happy day comes you will find your Louise's arms stretched out in loving welcome.

"Your devoted friend,

"LOUISE.

"PS – I still have the letters."

Josette could scarcely read the welcome missive to the end. Her eyes were dim with tears. She loved Louise as she had always done, and she adored Charles-Léon, and somehow this letter, coming from far-off England, quickened and accentuated the poignancy of parting: she spent many hours sitting at the table under the lamp with Louise's letter spread out before her. One sentence in it she read over and over again, for it expressed just what she herself felt in her heart for the hero of her dreams: "All I can do," Louise had written, "is to keep sacred the memory of all that that man has done for me."

25

Josette had read on so late into the night and been so excited over what she read that sleep had quite gone out of her eyes. She could not get to sleep for thinking of Louise and her adventures, of the Scarlet Pimpernel, and also of Maurice Reversac. Poor Maurice! Whatever happened he would have his burden to bear here in Paris. For the sake of the dead, and because of Louise and Charles-Léon, he must carry on his work and trust to God to see him safely through.

That day, for the first time since his return from the Dauphiné, Maurice was not at his usual place outside the gate of the workshop, waiting for Josette to come out. Josette, slightly disappointed, knew, of course, that it must be the exigencies of business that had kept him away. But when the evening hour came and again no Maurice at the gate, Josette was anxious. Before she went home she went over to Maurice's lodgings down the street to inquire from the *concierge* if, perchance, Maurice was ill. She knew that nothing but illness could possibly have kept him from his evening walk with her, or from sending her a message. But the *concierge* had seen and heard nothing of Maurice since morning when he started off as usual for the office.

Nothing would do after that but Josette must go off, then and there, to the Rue de la Monnaie. She had not been near the place since that awful day when she saw Maître de Croissy lying dead in his devastated office; and when she turned the angle of the street and saw at a hundred paces farther along the *porte-cochère* of the house where the terrible tragedy had occurred, she was suddenly overcome with an awful prescience of doom. So powerful was this sense of forewarning that she could no longer stand on her feet, but was obliged to lean against the nearest wall while trying to conquer sheer physical nausea. A horrible, nameless terror assailed her: she was trembling in every limb. However, after a few moments she regained control over herself, chided herself for her weakness, and walked with comparative coolness to the *porte-cochère*, which had not yet been closed for the night.

Again that awful feeling of giddiness and nausea. The house had always worn that dismal air of desolation and decay with a pervading odour of damp mortar and putrid vegetables. Josette knew its history: she knew that it had once been the fine abode of a rich foreign banker who had fled the country at the first outbreak of the Revolution, that it had stood empty for two or three years, then been appropriated by the State, a *concierge* put in office, and the house let out in apartments and offices. She had often been to the house and always disliked the sight of it, its air of emptiness despite the fact that most of the apartments were inhabited: the courtyard and stairs looked to her as if they were peopled by ghosts.

Josette went up to the *concierge*'s lodge and asked if Citizen Reversac were still in his office. The *concierge* eyed her with a quizzical glance. He had seen the pretty girl in the company of Citizen Reversac before now. His sweetheart, no doubt – ah, well! these things were of everyday occurrence these days. Mothers lost their sons, wives their husbands: it was no good grieving over other people's troubles or commiserating over their misfortunes.

"Citizen Reversac was here this morning, little Citizeness," the *concierge* said in response to Josette's reiterated question, "but…you know…"

"What?"

"He was arrested this morning – "

"Arr – ?"

"Easy, easy, little Citizeness," the *concierge* rejoined quickly, and with outstretched hand steadied Josette, who looked as if she would measure her length outside his lodge. "These things," he added with a shrug, "happen every day. Why, my own sister less than a week ago…"

Josette did not hear what he said. He went rambling on about his sister whose only son had been arrested, and who was breaking her heart this very day because the boy had been guillotined.

"He was not a bad lad either, my nephew; and a good patriot; but there! one never knows."

"One never knows!" Josette murmured mechanically, stupidly, staring at the *concierge* with great unseeing eyes. The man felt really sorry for the girl. She was so very pretty, that mouth of hers had been fashioned for smiles, those blue eyes made only to shine with merriment, and those chestnut curls to tempt a man to sin. Ah, well, one never knows! These things happened every day!

26

How Josette reached home that evening she never knew. She seemed to have spent hours and hours in repeating to herself: "It cannot be true!" and "It must be a mistake."

"He has done nothing!" she murmured from time to time, and then: "In a few days they will set him free again! They must! He has done nothing! Such an innocent!"

But in her heart she knew that innocents suffered these days as often as the guilty. Only a short time ago she had been called on to fill the role of comforter. She could not help thinking of Louise and of that awful tragedy which was the precursor of the present cataclysm. But now she had to face this trouble alone: there was no one in whom she could confide, no one who could give her a word of advice or comfort. And when she found herself alone at last in the apartment of the Rue Picpus, where every stick of furniture, every door and every wall reminded her of those whom she loved and proclaimed her present loneliness, she realised the immensity of that cataclysm. She felt that with Maurice gone she had nothing more to live for. The dreariness of days without his kindly voice to cheer her, his loving arm to guide her, was inconceivable. It loomed before her like a terrifying nightmare. And she pictured to herself Maurice's surprise and indignation at his arrest, his protestations of innocence, his final courage in face of the inevitable. She thought of him in one of the squalid overcrowded prisons, thinking of her, linking his hands tightly together in a proud attempt to appear unconcerned, indifferent to his fate before his fellow-prisoners.

Maurice! Josette never knew till now how she cared for him. Love?… No! She did not know what love was, nor did she believe that the desperate ache which she had in her heart at thought of Maurice had anything to do with the love that poets and authors spoke about. On the contrary, she thought that what she felt for Maurice was far stronger and deeper than the thing people called "love." All she knew was that she suffered intensely at this moment, that his image haunted her in a way it had never done before. She recalled every moment that of late she had spent with him, every trick of his voice, every expression of his face: his kind grey eyes, the gentle smile around his lips, the quaint remarks he would make at times which had often made her laugh. Above all, she was haunted at this hour with the remembrance of a mellow late summer's evening when she chaffed him because he had spoken to her of love. How sad he was that evening, whilst she never thought for a moment that he had been serious.

"Maurice! Maurice!" she cried out in her heart; "if those devils take you from me I shall never know a happy hour again."

But it was not in Josette's nature to sit down and mope. Her instinct was to be up and doing, whatever happened and however undecipherable the riddle set by Fate might be. And so in this instance also. The arrest of Maurice was in truth the knock-down blow: at this juncture Josette could not have imagined a more overwhelming catastrophe. As she was alone in the apartment she indulged in the solace of tears. She cried and cried till her eyes were inflamed and her head ached furiously: she cried because of the intense feeling of loneliness and desolation that gave her such a violent pain in her heart which nothing but a flood of tears seemed able to still. But having had her cry, she pulled herself together, dried her tears, bathed her face, then sat down to think or, rather, to remember.

With knitted brows and concentrated force of will she tried to recall all that Bastien de Croissy had said to Louise the evening when first he spoke of the letters and she, Josette, suggested stitching the packet in the lining of Louise's corsets. These letters were more precious than any jewels on earth, for they were to be the leverage wherewith to force certain influential members of the Convention to grant Louise a permit to take her child into the country, to remain with him and nurse him back to health and strength. The possession of those letters had been the cause of Bastien de Croissy's terrible death. They were seriously compromising to certain influential representatives of the people, proofs probably of some black-hearted treason to their country. The possession of them was vitally important to their writers, so important that they chose the way of murder rather than risk revelation. A man on trial, a man condemned to death might have the chance of speaking. It is only the dead who cannot speak.

So now for the knowledge of who were the writers of the letters. And Josette, her head buried in her hands, tried to recall every word which Bastien had spoken the night before his death, while she, Josette, sat under the light of the lamp, stitching the precious packet into the lining of Louise's corsets. But unfortunately at one moment during the evening her mind, absorbed in the facts themselves, had been less retentive than usual. Certain it is that at this desperately critical moment she could not recall a single name that Bastien had mentioned, and after his death, Louise, with the obstinacy of the half-demented, had guarded the letters with a kind of fierce jealousy; she had taken them to England with her, with what object God only knew – probably none! Just obstinacy and without definite consciousness.

It was in the small hours of the morning that Josette had an inspiration. It was nothing less, and it so comforted her that she actually fell asleep, and as soon as she was washed and dressed ran out into the street. She ran all the way to the corner of the

Pont des Arts, where vendors of old books and newspapers had their booths. She bought a bundle of back numbers of *Le Moniteur* and, hugging it under her cape, she ran back to the Rue Picpus.

The *Moniteur* gave the reports of the sittings of the Convention day by day, the debates, the speeches. Josette, whilst sitting by herself the night before with her mind still in a whirl with the terrible news of Maurice's arrest, had not been able to recall a single name mentioned by Bastien in connection with the letters, but with the back numbers of the *Moniteur* spread out before her, with the names of several members of the Convention staring at her in print, the task of reconstructing the conversation of that night became much easier. For instance, she did remember Louise exclaiming at one moment: "But he is Danton's most intimate friend!" and Bastien saying then: "All three of them are friends of Danton."

And shrewd little Josette concentrated on the *Moniteur* until she came upon the report of a debate in the Convention over a proposition put forward by Citizen Danton. Who were his friends? Who his supporters? He had a great number, for he was still at the height of his popularity: they agreed and debated and perorated, and Josette, while she read, murmured their names repeatedly to herself: "Desmoulins, Desmoulins, Desmoulins – no! that wasn't it. Hérault, Hérault de Séchelles – no! Delacroix – no, again no! Chabot?… Chabot…?" And slowly memory brought the name back to her mind – Chabot! That was one of the names! Chabot, Danton's friend. "Yes!" Bastien had said at one moment, "an unfrocked Capuchin friar!" and Louise had uttered an exclamation of horror. Chabot! that certainly was one of the names. And Josette read on; taxed her memory, forced it to serve her purpose. More names which meant nothing, and then one that stood out! Fabre d'Eglantine – Danton's most intimate friend! Chabot and Fabre – two names! And then a third one – Bazire! Josette had paid no attention at the time. She had heard Bastien mention those names, but only vaguely, and her brain had only vaguely registered them; but now they came back. Memory had served her a good turn.

Fabre, Chabot, Bazire! Josette had no longer any doubt as to who the men were who had written the letters, letters that were the powerful leverage wherewith to force them to grant whatever might be asked of them: a permit for Louise, freedom for Maurice Reversac.

Josette had not been sufficiently care-free up to now to note what the weather was like, but now, with a sense almost of gladness in her heart, she threw open the window and looked up at the sky. She only had a small glimpse of it because the Rue Picpus was narrow and the houses opposite high, but she did have a glimpse of clear blue, the blue of which Paris among all the great cities of Europe can most justifiably boast, translucent and exhilarating. The air was mild. There was no trace of wintry weather, of rain or of cold. The sun was shining and she, Josette, was going to drag Maurice out of the talons of those revolutionary birds of prey.

From far away came the dismal sound of the bell of St Germain, booming out the morning hour. Another day had broken over the unfortunate city, another day wherein men waged a war to the death one against the other, wherein they persecuted the innocent, heaped crime upon crime, injustice upon injustice, flouted religion and defied God; another day wherein ruled the devils of hate and dolour, of tribulation and of woe. But Josette did no longer think of devils or of sorrow. She was going to be the means of opening the prison gates for Maurice.

27

Since the day when Charlotte Corday forced her way into the apartment of Citizen Marat and plunged a dagger into the heart of that demagogue, the more prominent members of the revolutionary government were wont to take special precautions to guard their valuable lives.

Thus the *conventionnel* François Chabot in his magnificent apartment in the Rue d'Anjou made it a rule that every person desirious of an interview with him must be thoroughly searched for any possible concealed weapon before being admitted to his august presence. The unfrocked friar proclaimed loudly his patriotism, declared his readiness to die a martyr like Marat, but he was taking no risks. He had married a very rich and very beautiful young wife. Whilst professing in theory the most rigid *sans-culottism,* he lived in the greatest possible luxury, ate and drank only of the best, wore fine clothes, and surrounded himself with every comfort that his wife's money could buy.

Josette did indeed appear as a humble suppliant when, having mounted the carpeted stairs which led up to the first floor of that fine house in the Rue d'Anjou, she found herself face to face with a stalwart janitor at the door of François Chabot's apartment.

"Your business?" he demanded.

"To speak with Citizen Chabot," Josette replied.

"Does the Citizen expect you?"

"No, but when he knows of the business which has brought me here he will not refuse to see me."

"That is as it may be, but you cannot pass this door without stating your business."

"It is private, and for Citizen Chabot's private ear alone."

The stalwart looked down on the dainty figure before him. Being a man he looked down with considerable pleasure, for Josette in her neat kirtle and well-fitting bodice, her frilled muslin cap perched coquettishly on her chestnut curls, was exceedingly pleasant to look on. Her blue eyes did not so much plead as demand that her wish to speak with Citizen Chabot should not be peremptorily denied.

The janitor pulled himself up and his waistcoat down, passed his hand over his bristly cheek, hemmed and hawed and cleared his throat, then, unable apparently to resist the command of those shining eyes any longer, he said finally:

"I will see what can be done, Citizeness."

"That is brave of you," Josette said demurely, and then added: "Where shall I wait?" which translated into ordinary language meant: "You would not surely allow me to wait outside the door where any passer-by might behave in an unseemly manner towards me?"

At any rate this was how the janitor interpreted Josette's simple query. He opened the door on the thickly carpeted, richly furnished vestibule and said: "Wait here, Citizeness."

Josette went in. It was years since she had seen such beautiful furniture, such tall mirrors and rich gildings, years since she had trodden on such soft carpets, and these were the days when women had to go shoeless, and children died for want of nourishment, whilst men like Chabot preached equality and fraternity, and loudly proclaimed the simplicity and abnegation of their lives. Josette's astonishment at all this luxury caused her to open wide her eyes, and when those blue eyes were opened wide, men, even the most stalwart, became like putty.

"Sit down there, Citizeness," the magnificent janitor said, "whilst I go and inquire if the Citizen Representative will see you."

Josette sat down and waited. Two or three minutes later the janitor returned. As soon as he caught sight of Josette he shook his head, then said:

"Not unless you will state your business. And," he added, "you know the rule: no one is admitted to speak with any Representatives of the People without being previously searched."

"Give me pen and paper," Josette rejoined, "that I may state my business in writing."

When the man brought her pen and paper she wrote:

"Dead men tell no tales, but the written words endure."

She folded the paper, then demanded wax and a seal. Presumably the man couldn't read, but one never knew. A seal was safer and Chabot himself would be grateful to her for having thought of it. A few moments later she found herself in a small room, bare of furniture or carpet, into which the janitor had ushered her after he had taken her written message to the Citizen Representative. A middle-aged woman, who was probably the housekeeper, passed her rough hands all over Josette's young body, dived into her shoes, under her muslin fichu, and even under her cap. Satisfied that there was no second Charlotte Corday intent on assassination, she called the janitor back and handed an indignant if silent Josette back to him. The audience could now be granted with safety.

Such were the formalities attendant upon a request for an audience with one of the representatives of the people in this glorious era of Equality and Fraternity.

28

François Chabot was at this time about forty years of age. A small, thin, nervy-looking creature with long nose, thick lips, arched eyebrows above light brown eyes, and a quantity of curly hair which swept the top of his high coat-collar at the back, covering it with grease. He was dressed in the height of fashion, with a very short waist and long tails to his coat. His neck was swathed in a high stock collar, and his somewhat receding chin rested on a voluminous jabot of muslin and lace.

Josette, who had been ushered into his presence with so much ceremony, eyed him with curiosity, for she had heard it said of Representative Chabot that he affected to attend the sittings of the Convention in a tattered shirt, with bare legs and wearing a scarlet cap. In fact, it was said of him that he owed most of his popularity to this display of cynicism: also, that he, like his brother-in-law Bazire, had before now paid a hired assassin to dig a knife between his ribs in order to raise the cry among his friends in the Convention: "See! the counter-revolutionists are murdering the patriots. Marat first, now the incorruptible Chabot. Whose turn will it be next?"

But Josette, though remembering all this, was in no mood to smile. Did not this damnable hypocrite hold Maurice's life in his ugly hands? Those same hands – large, bony, with greyish nails and spatulated fingers – were toying with the written message which Josette had sent in to him. They were perhaps the hands that had dealt the fatal blow to Bastien de Croissy.

Josette glanced on them with horror and then quickly drew her eyes away.

The janitor had motioned her to a seat, then he retired, closing the door behind him. Josette was alone with the Citizen Representative. He was sitting at a large desk which was littered with papers, and she sat opposite to him. He now raised his pale, shifty eyes to her, and she returned his searching glance fearlessly. He was obviously nervous; cleared his throat to give himself importance, and shifted his position once or twice. The paper which he held between two fingers and pointed towards Josette rustled audibly.

"Your name?" he asked curtly after a time.

"Josephine Gravier," she replied.

"And occupation?"

"Seamstress in the Government workshops. I was also companion and housekeeper in the household of Maître Croissy…"

"Ah!"

"…until the day of his death."

There was a pause. The man was as nervous as a cat. He made great efforts to appear at ease, and above all to control his voice, which after that first "Ah!" had sounded hoarse and choked.

The handsome Boule clock on the mantelpiece, obviously the spoils of a raid on a confiscated château, struck the hour with deliberate majesty. Chabot shifted his position again, crossed and uncrossed his legs, pushed his chair farther away from the bureau, and went on fidgeting with Josette's written message, crushing it between his fingers.

"Advocate Croissy," he said at last with an effort, "committed suicide, I understand."

"It was said so, Citizen."

"What do you mean by that?"

"Nothing beyond what I said."

They were like duellists, these two, measuring their foils in a preliminary passage of arms. Chabot's glance had in it now something malevolent, cruel…the cruelty of a coward who is not sure yet of what it is he has to fear.

Suddenly he said, holding up the crumpled bit of paper:

"Why did you send me this?"

"To warn you, Citizen," Josette replied quite quietly.

"Of what?"

"That certain letters of which you and others are cognisant have not been destroyed."

"Letters?" Chabot demanded roughly. "What letters?"

"Letters written by you, Citizen Representative, to Maître de Croissy, which prove you to be a shameless hypocrite and a traitor to your country."

She had shot this arrow at random, but at once she had the satisfaction of knowing that the shaft had gone home. Chabot's sallow cheeks had become the colour of lead, his thick lips quivered visibly. A slight scum appeared at the corner of his mouth.

"It's all a lie!" he protested, but his voice sounded forced and hollow. "An invention of that traitor Croissy."

"You know best, Citizen Representative," Josette retorted simply.

Chabot tried to put on an air of indifference.

"Croissy," he said as calmly as he could, "told you a deliberate lie if he said that certain letters of mine were anything but perfectly innocent. I personally should not care if anybody read them…"

He paused, then added: "If that is all you wished to tell me, my girl, the interview can end here."

"As you desire, Citizen," Josette said, and made as if to rise.

"Stay a moment," Chabot commanded. "Merely from idle curiosity I would like to know where those famous letters are. Can you perchance tell me?"

"Oh, yes," she replied. "They are in England and out of your reach, Citizen Representative."

"What do you mean by 'in England'?"

"Just what I say. When the widow of Maître de Croissy went to England with her boy she took the packet of letters with her."

"She fled from Paris, I know," Chabot retorted, still trying to control his fury. "I know it. I had the report. That cursed English spy…!" He checked himself; this girl's slightly mocking glance was making a havoc of his nerves.

"The letters, such as they are, are probably destroyed by now," he said as coolly as he could.

"They are not destroyed."

"How do you know?"

Josette shrugged. Would she be here if the letters had been destroyed?

"Why did the woman Croissy run away like a traitor?"

"Her child was sick. It was imperative he should leave Paris for a healthier spot."

"I know. Croissy told me that tale. I didn't then believe a word of it. It was just blackmail, nothing more." Then as Josette was once more silent he reiterated roughly: "Why did the woman Croissy leave Paris in such haste? Why should she have taken the letters with her? You say she did, but I don't believe it."

"Perhaps she was afraid, Citizen."

"Afraid of what? Only traitors need be afraid."

"Afraid of…committing suicide like her husband."

This shaft, too, went straight home. Every drop of blood seemed to ebb from the man's face and left it ashen grey. His pale eyes wandered all round the room as if in search of a hiding-place from that straight accusing glance. For the next minute or two he affected to busy himself with the papers on his desk, whilst the priceless Boule clock on the mantelshelf ticked away several fateful seconds.

Then he said abruptly, with an attempt at unconcern:

"Ah, bah! little woman. You think yourself very shrewd, what? No doubt you have some nice little project of blackmail in that pretty head of yours. But if you really did know all about the letters you speak of so glibly, you would also be aware that I am the man least concerned in them. There are others whose names apparently are unknown to you and who…"

"Their names are not unknown to me, Citizen Representative," Josette broke in with unruffled calm.

"Then why the hell haven't you been to them! Is it because you know less than you pretend?"

"If you, Citizen, do not choose to bargain with me I will certainly go to Citizen Bazire and Fabre d'Eglantine, but in that case…"

At mention of the two names Chabot had given a visible start: a nervous twitching of his lips showed how severely he had been hit. He still tried to bluster by reiterating gruffly:

"In that case?"

"I am treating separately with the writers of each individual letter," Josette said firmly. "Those who do not choose to bargain with me must accept the consequences."

"Which are?"

"Publication of the letters in the *Moniteur*, in *Père Duchesne* and other newspapers. They will make good reading, Citizen Representative."

"You little devil!"

He had jumped to his feet, and with clenched fists resting upon the bureau he leaned across, staring into her face. His pale brown eyes had glints in them now of cold, calculating cruelty. Had he dared he would have seized this weak woman by the throat and torn the life out of her, slowly, brutally, with hellish cunning until she begged for death.

"You devil!" he reiterated savagely. "You forget that I can make you suffer for this."

Josette gave her habitual shrug.

"You certainly can," she said calmly. "You can do the same to me as you did to Maître de Croissy. But not even a second murder will put you in possession of the letters."

Never for a moment had the girl lost her presence of mind. She knew well enough what she risked when she came to beard this hyena in his lair; but it was the only way to save Maurice. She had thought it all out and had deliberately chosen it. Throughout the interview she had remained perfectly calm and self-possessed; and now, when for the first time she had the feeling that she was winning the day, she still remained demure and apparently unmoved. But Chabot was pacing up and down the room like a caged beast, kicking savagely at anything that was in his way. At one moment it seemed as if he was on the point of giving way to his fury, of being willing to risk everything, even his own neck, for the satisfaction of his revenge. During that fateful moment Josette's life did indeed hang in the balance, for already the man's hand was on the bell-pull. Another second and he was ready to send for his stalwart and to order him to summon the men of the National Guard who were always on duty in the streets outside the dwellings of the Representatives of the People: to summon the guard and order this woman to be thrown into the most noisome prison of the city, where mental and physical torture would punish her for her presumption.

With his hand on the bell-pull Chabot looked round and encountered the cool, unconcerned glance of a pair of eyes as deeply blue as is the midnight sky in June, and other thoughts and desires, more foul than the first, distorted his ugly face. Had he read aught in those eyes but contempt and self-confidence the dark spirits that haunted this house of evil would have had their way with him. But it was the girl's evident complete self-assurance that made him pause…pause long enough to gauge the depth of the abyss into which he would fall if those compromising letters were by some chance given publicity.

He let go the bell-pull and came back to his place by the bureau. He sat down and, leaning back in his chair, he allowed a minute or two to go by while he regained control over himself. Knitting his bony hands together he twisted them until all the finger-joints cracked. He took a handkerchief from his pocket and wiped the cold sweat from his brow.

Then at last he spoke:

"You said just now, Citizeness," he rejoined with enforced calm, trying to emulate the girl's self-assurance and her show of contempt, "that when the widow Croissy ran away to England she took certain letters with her. Is that it?"

"Yes. She did."

"How do you know that?"

"She has told me so…in a letter?"

"A letter from England?"

"Yes."

"And that's a lie! How could you get a letter from England? We are at war with that accursed country, and…"

"Do not let us discuss the point, Citizen Representative. Let me assure you that the letters in question are in England: the Citizeness Croissy has not destroyed them – she has told me so. If you agree to my terms I will bring you the letters, otherwise they will be sent to the *Moniteur* and other newspapers for publication. And that," Josette added firmly, "is my last word."

"What are your terms?"

"First, a safe-conduct to enable me to travel to England without molestation…"

Chabot gave a harsh, ironical laugh.

"To travel to England? Fine idea, in very truth! Go to England and stay in England, what? And from thence make long noses at François Chabot, what? who was fool enough to let you hoodwink him!"

"Had you not best listen to me, Citizen Representative, before you jump to conclusions?"

"I listen. Indeed, I am vastly interested in your naïve project, my engaging young friend."

"My price for placing letters, which you would give your fortune to possess, in your hands, Citizen, is the liberty and life of one, Maurice Reversac, who was clerk to Maître de Croissy."

Chabot sneered. "Your lover, I suppose."

"What you choose to suppose is nothing to me. I have named my price for the letters."

Chabot, his elbow resting on the table, his chin cupped in his hand, was apparently wrapped in thought. He was contemplating that greatly daring woman who had delivered her ultimatum with no apparent consciousness of her danger. He could silence her, of course: send her to the guillotine, her and her lover, Reversac; but she seemed so sure that he would not do this that her assurance became disconcerting. The same reason which had stayed his and his friends' hands when they discussed the advisability of having Bastien de Croissy summarily arrested held good in this girl's case also. There was always the possibility of her getting a word in during her trial – a word which might prove the undoing of them all. How far was she telling the truth at this moment? How far was she lying in order to save her lover? These were the questions which François Chabot was putting to himself while he contemplated the beautiful woman before him.

And whilst he gazed on her she seemed slowly to vanish from his vision, both she and his luxurious surroundings, the costly furniture, the carpets, all the paraphernalia of his sybaritic life. Instead of this there appeared to his mental consciousness the Place de la Barrière du Trône, with the guillotine towering above a sea of faces. He saw himself mounting the fatal steps; he saw the executioner, the glint on the death-dealing knife, the horrible basket into which great and noble heads had often rolled at his, Chabot's, bidding. He heard the roll of drums ordered by Sauterre, the cries of execration of the mob, the strident laugh of those horrible hags who sat knitting and jabbering while the knife worked up and down, up and down… A hoarse cry nearly escaped him. He passed his bony fingers under his choker for he felt stifled and sick….

The vision vanished. The girl was still sitting opposite to him, demure and silent – curse her! – waiting for him to speak. And looking on her he knew that he must have those letters or he would never know a moment's peace again. Once he had them, once he felt entirely safe, he would have his revenge. Let her look to herself, the miserable trollop! She will have brought her fate upon herself.

He said "I'll give you the safe-conduct. You can start for England today."

"I will start tomorrow," she rejoined coolly. "I still must speak with Citizens Fabre and Bazire."

"I can make that right with them. You need not see them."

"I must have their signatures on the safe-conduct as well as yours, Citizen Chabot."

"You shall have them."

He was searching among the litter on his desk for the paper which he wanted. These men always had forms of safe-conduct made out with blank spaces for the name of a relation or friend who happened to be in trouble and hoped to leave the country before trouble materialised. Chabot found what he wanted. The paper was headed:

"COMMISSARIAT DE POLICE DE LA VIII^{ieme}
SECTION DE PARIS,"

and

"Laissez passer."

"Your name?" he asked once more.

"Josephine Madeleine Marie Gravier."

And Chabot, with a shaking hand, wrote these names in the blank space left for the purpose.

"Your residence?"

"Forty-three Rue Picpus."

"Your age?"

"Twenty."

"The colour of your eyes?"

She looked at him and in the blank space he wrote the word "Blue"; and farther on he made note that the hair was burnished copper, her chin small, her teeth even.

When he had filled in all the blank spaces he strewed the writing with sand; then he said, "You can come and fetch this this evening."

"It will be signed?"

"By myself and by Citizens Fabre and Bazire."

"Then I will start tomorrow."

"You have money?"

"Yes, I thank you."

"When do you return?"

"It will take me a week probably to get to England and a week or more to come back. It will be close on three weeks, Citizen Representative, before your mind is set at rest."

He shrugged and sneered:

"And in the meanwhile, your lover…"

"In the meanwhile, Citizen," Josette broke in firmly, "see to it that Maurice Reversac is safe and well. If on my return he is not there to greet me, if, in fact, you play me false in any way, it is the *Moniteur* who will have the letters, not you."

Chabot rose slowly from his chair. He stood for a moment quite still beside the desk, his spatulated fingers spread out upon the table-top. All his nervousness, his fury, his excitement seemed suddenly to drop away from him. His ugly face wore an air of cunning, almost of triumph, and there was a hideous leer around his thick lips. He appeared to be watching Josette intently while she rose, shook out her kirtle, smoothed down her fichu and straightened her cap. As she turned towards the door he said slowly:

"We shall see!" And added with mock courtesy, "*Au revoir*, little Citizeness."

A few minutes later Josette was speeding up the street on her way home.

19

Later in the day a meeting took place in the bare whitewashed room of the Club des Cordeliers between three members of the National Convention – François Chabot, Claude Bazire and Fabre d'Eglantine – and an obscure member of the Committee of Public Safety named Armand Chauvelin. This man had at one time been highly influential in the councils of the revolutionary government; before the declaration of war he had been sent to England as secret envoy of the Republic; but conspicuous and repeated failures in various missions which had been entrusted to him had hopelessly ruined his prestige and hurled him down from his high position to one of almost ignoble dependence. Many there were who marvelled how it had come to pass that Armand Chauvelin had kept his head on his shoulders: "The Republic," Danton had thundered more than once from the tribune, "has no use for failures." It is to be supposed, therefore, that the man possessed certain qualities which made him useful to those in power: perhaps he was in possession of secrets which would have made his death undesirable. Be that as it may, Chauvelin, dressed in seedy black, his pale face scored with lines of anxiety, his appearance that of a humble servant of these popular Representatives of the People, sat at one end of the deal table, listening with almost obsequious deference to the words of command from the other three.

He only put in a word now and again, for he had been summoned in order to take orders, not to give advice.

"The girl," Chabot said to him, "lives at No. 43 in the Rue Picpus. She will leave Paris tomorrow. You will shadow her from the moment that she leaves the house: never lose sight of her as you value your life. She is going to England; you will follow her. You have been in England before, Citizen Chauvelin," he added with a sarcastic grin, "so I understand, and are acquainted with the English tongue."

"That is so, Citizen Representative."

Chauvelin's eyes were downcast; not one of the three caught the feline gleam of hate that shot through their pale depths.

"Your safe-conduct is all in order. The wench will probably make for Tréport and take boat there for one of the English ports. It is up to you to board the same ship as she does. You must assume what disguise seems most suitable at the time. Our friend here, Fabre d'Eglantine, has been the means of finding you an English safe-conduct which was taken from one of that accursed nation who was trying to cross over our frontier from Belgium: he was an English spy. Our men caught and shot him; his papers remained in their hands: one of these was a safe-conduct signed by the English Minister of Foreign Affairs. Those stupid English don't usually trouble about passports or safe-conducts. They welcome the *émigrés* from France, and often among those traitors one or other of our spies have got through. Still, this document will probably serve you well, and you can easily make up to appear like the description of the original holder. Here are the two passports. Examine them carefully first, then I or one of my friends will give you further instructions."

Chabot handed two papers to Chauvelin across the table. Chauvelin took them, and for the next few minutes was absorbed in a minute examination of them. One bore the signature of Fabre d'Eglantine, who was representative for a section of Paris: it was counter-signed by François Chabot (Seine et Loire) and by Claud Bazire (Côte d'Or). The second paper bore the seal of the English Foreign Office and was signed by Lord Greville himself. It was made out in the name of Malcolm Russell Stone, and described the bearer of the safe-conduct as short and slight, with brown hair and pale face – a description, in fact, which could apply to twenty men out of a hundred. It had the advantage of not being a forgery, but was a genuine passport issued to an unfortunate Secret Service man since dead. As Chabot had said, the English authorities cared little, if anything, about passports; nevertheless, the present one might prove useful.

Chauvelin folded the two papers and put them in the inside pocket of his coat.

"So far, so good," he said dryly. "I await your further instructions, Citizen Representative."

Chabot was the spokesman of the party. He was, perhaps, sunk more deeply than the other two in the morass of treachery and veniality which threatened to engulf them all. He it was who had summoned this conference and who had thought of Armand Chauvelin as the man most likely to be useful in this terrible emergency.

"He has a character to redeem," he had said to his friends when first the question was mooted of setting a sleuth-hound on the girl's tracks: "he speaks English, he knows his way about over there..."

"He failed signally," Bazire objected, "over that affair of the English spies."

"You mean the man they call the Scarlet Pimpernel?"

"Yes!"

"Chauvelin has sworn to lay him by the heels."

"But has never succeeded."

"No; but Robespierre tells me that he is the most tenacious tracker of traitors they have on the Committees – a real bloodhound, what!"

Thus it was that Chauvelin had been called in to confer on the best means of circumventing a simple girl in the fateful undertaking she had in view. Four men to defeat one woman in her purpose! What chance would she have to accomplish it?

"It is on the return journey, my friend," Chabot was saying, "that your work will effectually begin. This wench, Josette Gravier, is going to England for the sole purpose of getting hold of a certain packet of letters – seven in all – which are now in the possession of a woman named Croissy, the widow of the lawyer Croissy who – er – committed suicide a month or so ago. You recollect?"

"I do recollect perfectly," Chauvelin remarked blandly.

Chabot cleared his throat, fidgeted in his usual nervous manner, but took good care not to encounter Chauvein's quizzical glance.

"Those letters," he said after a moment or two, "were written by me and my two friends here in the strictest confidence to Croissy, who was acting as our lawyer at the time. None of us dreamed that he would turn traitor. Well, he did, and no doubt was subsequently stricken either with remorse or fright, for after threatening us all with the betrayal of our confidence he took his own miserable life."

Chabot paused, apparently highly satisfied with his peroration. Chauvelin, silent and with thin white hands folded in front of him, waited calmly for him to continue. But his pale steely eyes were no longer downcast: their glance, bitterly ironical, was fixed on the speaker, and there was no mistaking the question which that glance implied. "Why do you take the trouble to tell me those lies?" those eyes seemed to ask. No wonder that none of the three blackguards dared to look him straight in the face!

"I think," Chabot resumed after a time with added pompousness, "that I have told you enough to make you appreciate the importance of the task which we propose to entrust to you. My friends and I must regain possession of those confidential letters, but we look to you, Citizen Chauvelin, to put us in possession of them and not to the wench Gravier – you understand?"

"Perfectly."

"She is nothing but a trollop and a baggage who has shamelessly resorted to blackmail in order to save her gallant from justice. She has put a dagger at my throat – at the throat of my two friends here – and her dagger is more deadly than the one with which the traitor Charlotte Corday pierced the noble heart of Marat…"

He would have continued in this eloquent strain had not his brother-in-law, Bazire, put a restraining hand on his shoulder. Armand Chauvelin, with his arms tightly clasped over his chest, his thin legs crossed, his pale eyes looking up at the ceiling, presented a perfect picture of irony and contempt. The others dared not resent this attitude. They had need of this man for the furtherance of their schemes. Revenge was what they were looking for now. The wench had indeed put a dagger to their throats, and for this they were determined to make her suffer; and there was no man alive with such a marvellous capacity for tracking an enemy and bringing him to book as Armand Chauvelin, in spite of the fact that he had failed so signally in bringing the greatest enemy of the revolutionary government to the guillotine. In this he certainly had failed. Not one of his colleagues, not one of the three who had need of his services now, knew how the recollection of that failure galled him. He was thankful for this mission which would take him to England once more. He had had heart-breaking ill luck over his adventures with the Scarlet Pimpernel, but luck might take a turn at any time, and, anyway, he was the only man in his own country who had definitely identified the mysterious hero with that ballroom exquisite Sir Percy Blakeney. Given a modicum of luck it was still on the cards that he, Chauvelin, might yet be even with his arch-enemy whilst he was engaged in dogging the footsteps of Josette Gravier. That wench was just the type of "persecuted innocent" that would appeal to the chivalrous nature of the elusive Sir Percy.

Yes! on the whole Chauvelin felt satisfied with his immediate prospects, and as soon as Chabot had ceased perorating he put a few curt questions to him.

"When does the girl start?" he asked.

"Tomorrow," Chabot replied. "I have told her to call at my house this evening for her safe-conduct."

"It is made out in the name of...?"

"Josephine Gravier."

"Josephine Gravier," Chauvelin iterated slowly; "and the safe-conduct is signed?"

"By myself, by my friend Fabre and my brother-in-law Claude Bazire."

Chauvelin then rose and said: "That is all I need know for the moment." He paused a moment as if reflecting and then added: "Oh! by the way, I may need a man by me whom I can trust – a man who will give me a hand in an emergency, you understand; who will be discreet and above all obedient."

"I see no objection to that," Chabot said and turned to his colleagues: "do you?"

"No. None," they all agreed.

"Do you know the right sort of man?" one of them asked.

"Yes! Auguste Picard," was Chauvelin's reply: "a sturdy fellow, ready for any adventure. He is attached to the gendarmerie of the VIIIth section at the moment, but he can be spared – Picard would suit me well: he is never troubled with unnecessary scruples," he added with a curl of the lip.

"Auguste Picard. Why not?"

They all agreed as to the suitability of Auguste Picard as a satellite to their friend Chauvelin.

"So long as he is told nothing," one of them remarked.

"Why, of course," Chauvelin hastened to reassure them all. He then concluded with complacency: "You may rest assured, my friends, that in less than a month the letters will be in your hands."

Chabot and the others sighed in unison: "The devil speed you, friend Chauvelin." One of them said: "Not one of us will know a moment's peace until your return."

On which note of mutual confidence they parted. Chauvelin went his way; the other three stayed talking for a little while at the club; other members strolled in from time to time, Danton among them. The great man himself was none too easy over this affair of the letters which had been recounted to him by his satellite Fabre d'Eglantine. He was not dead sure whether his own name was mentioned or not in the correspondence between de Batz and Croissy. He had at the time been unpleasantly mixed up in those Austrian intrigues, and it was part of de Batz's game to compromise as many patriots as he could, to incite the mob against them and thus bring about the downfall of the revolutionary Government and the restoration of the King. Chabot, Fabre and Bazire were in it up to the neck, but the moment mud-slinging began, any of their friends might get spattered with the slime. Robespierre, the wily jackal, was only waiting for an opportunity to be at Danton's throat, to wrest from him that popularity which for the time being made him the master of the Convention. It would indeed be a strange freak of Destiny if the downfall of the great Danton – the lion of the Revolution – were brought about through the intervention of a woman, a chit of a girl more feeble even than Charlotte Corday, whose dagger had put an end to Marat's career.

"But we can leave all that with safety in Armand Chauvelin's hands," was the sum-total of the confabulation between the four men before they bade one another goodnight.

20

The small diligence which had left Les Andelys in the early morning rattled into the courtyard of the *Auberge du Cheval Blanc* in Rouen soon after seven o'clock in the evening. It had encountered bad weather the whole of the way: torrential rain lashed by gusty north-westerly winds made going difficult for the horses. The roads were fetlock-deep in mud: on the other hand, the load had been light – two passengers in the front compartment and only four in the rear, and very little luggage on top.

In the rear of the coach the four passengers had sat in silence for the greater part of the journey, the grey sky and dreary outlook not being conducive to conversation. The desolation of the country, due to lack of agricultural labour, was apparent even along the fertile stretch of Normandy. The orchard trees were already bare of leaves and bent their boughs to the fury of the blast; their naked branches, weighted with the rain, were stretched out against the wind like the great gaunt arms of skinny old men suffering from rheumatism and doing their best to run away.

Of the two female travellers one looked like the middle-aged wife of some prosperous shopkeeper. She had rings on her fingers and a gold brooch was pinned to her shawl. Her hands were folded above the handle of a wicker basket out of which she extracted, from time to time, miscellaneous provisions with which she regaled herself on the journey. At one moment when the other woman who sat next to her, overcome with sleep, fell up against her shoulder, she drew herself up with obvious disgust and eyed the presumptuous creature up and down with the air of one unaccustomed to any kind of familiarity.

This other woman was Josette Gravier, *en route* for England, all alone, unprotected, ignorant of the country she was going to, of the districts she would have to traverse, of the sea which she had never seen and of which she had a vague dread; but her courage kept up by the determination to get to England, to wrest the letters from Louise de Croissy and, with them in her hand, to force those influential Terrorists into granting life and liberty to Maurice. It was Josette Gravier who, overcome with sleep, had fallen against the shoulder of her fellow-traveller, but it was a very radically transformed Josette; not disguised, but transformed from the dainty, exquisite apparition she always was into an ugly, dowdy, uncouth-looking girl unlikely to attract the attention of those young gallants who are always ready for an adventure with any pretty woman they might meet on the way. She had dragged her hair out of curl, smeared it with grease till it hung in lankish strands down her cheeks and brows; over it she wore a black cap, frayed and green with age, and this she had tied under her chin with a tired bit of black ribbon. She had rubbed her little nose and held it out to the blast till the tip was blue: she hunched up her shoulders under a tattered shawl, and forced her pretty mouth to wear an expression of boredom and discontent. What she could not hide altogether was the glory of her eyes, but even so she contrived to dim their lustre by appearing to be half asleep the whole of the way. Like the other woman she kept her basket of provisions on her lap, and at different times she munched bits of stale bread and cheese and drank thin-looking wine out of a bottle, after which she passed the back of her hand over her mouth and nose and left marks of grease on her chin and cheeks.

Altogether she looked a most unattractive bit of goods, and this, apparently, was the opinion of the two male travellers who sat opposite, for after a quick survey of their fellow-passengers they each settled down in their respective corners and whiled away the dreary hours of the long day by sleep. They did not carry provisions with them, but jumped out of the diligence for refreshments whenever the driver pulled up outside some village hostelry on the way.

At the *Auberge du Cheval Blanc* in Rouen everyone had to get down. The diligence went no farther, but another would start early the next morning and, in all probability, would reach Tréport in the late afternoon. Josette, like the other travellers, was obliged to go to the Commissariat of the town for the examination of her papers before she could be allowed to hire a bed for the night. Her safe-conduct was in order, which seemed greatly to astonish the Chief Commissary, for he eyed with some curiosity this bedraggled, uncouth female who presented a permit signed by three of the most prominent members of the National Convention.

> "Laissez passer la citoyenne Josephine Gravier agée de vingt ans demeurant a Paris VIII[ieme] section Rue Picpus No. 43, etc., etc..."

It was all in order; the Commissary countersigned the safe-conduct, affixed the municipal seal to it and handed it back to Josette. She had been the last of the travellers to present her papers at the desk; she took them now from the Commissary and turned to go out of the narrow stuffy room when a man's voice spoke gently close to her:

"Can I direct you to a respectable hostelry, Citizeness?" Josette glanced up and encountered a pair of light-coloured eyes that looked kindly and in no way provokingly at her: they were the eyes of one of her fellow-travellers who had entered the diligence at Les Andelys and had sat in the corner opposite to her, half asleep, taking no notice of anything or anybody. He was a small, thin man with pale cheeks and a sad, or perhaps discontented, expression round his thin lips: his hair was lank and plentifully streaked with grey. He was dressed in seedy black and looked quite insignificant and not at all the kind of man to scare a girl who was travelling alone.

Josette thanked him for his kindness:

"I have engaged a bed at the *Cheval Blanc*," she said, "which I am assured is a model of respectability: I shall be sharing a room with some of the maids at the hostelry, and the charge for this accommodation is not high. All the same," she added politely, "I thank you, sir, for your kind offer."

She was about to turn away when he spoke again:

"I am journeying to England, and if I can be of service there I pray you to command me."

It did not occur to Josette at the moment to wonder how this stranger came to know that she was journeying to England, but she could not help asking him who he was and why he should trouble about her.

"Before the war," he replied, "my business used often to take me to England and I was able to master its difficult language. Now, alas! my business is at an end, but I have friends over the water and, like yourself, I was lucky enough to obtain a permit to visit them."

Once more Josette thanked him: he seemed so very kind; but at the outset of her journey she had made up her mind very firmly not to enter into conversation with anyone, not to trust anyone, least of all one of her own nationality. She had no idea as yet of the difficulties which she might encounter when she landed in a strange country. Indeed, she had undertaken this journey without any thought of possible failure, but wariness and discretion were the rules of conduct which she had imposed on herself and to which she was determined to adhere rigidly. Having thanked her amiable friend, she bade him Good-night and hastened back to the hostelry.

She didn't see him again on the following morning when she took ticket for the diligence that was to take her to Tréport. An altogether different set of people were her fellow-travellers on this stage of her journey: they were a noisy crowd – three men and two women besides herself in the rear compartment of the coach; so they were rather crowded and jammed up against one another. Josette, being small and unobtrusive, was pushed into a corner by the other women, who were large and stout and took up a lot of room. Talk was incessant, chiefly on the recent incidents at Nantes. Carrier, the abominable butcher, had been recalled, but his successors had carried on his infamous work. The war in the Vendée had drawn to its close: those who took part in it fell victims to their loyalty to the throne; their wives and children were murdered wholesale. Travellers who had come from those parts spoke of this with bated breath. Only a few had escaped butchery, and this through the agency of some English spies – so 'twas said – whose activities throughout Brittany had baffled the revolutionary government. One man especially, who went, it seems, by the strange name of a small scarlet flower, had been instrumental in effecting the escape of a number of women and children out of the plague-ridden prisons of Nantes, where such numbers of them died of disease and inanition even while the guillotine was being prepared for them.

Josette, huddled up in the corner of the compartment, listened to these tales with a beating heart. Ever since she had started on this fateful journey she had wondered in her mind whether somewhere or other, in a moment of distress or difficulty, she would suddenly find that an unseen hand was there to succour or to help, whether she would hear a comforting voice to cheer her on her way, or catch unexpectedly a glance from eyes that, whilst revealing nothing to the uninitiated, would convey a world of meaning to her.

Now the tales that she heard dispelled any such hope. Women and children in greater distress than herself were claiming the aid and time of the gallant Scarlet Pimpernel. It was sad and terribly disappointing that she would not see him as she had so confidently hoped. Only in her dreams would she see him as she had done hitherto. The rumble of the coach-wheels, the heavy atmosphere made her drowsy: she shrank farther still into her corner and slept and dreamed; she dreamed of the gallant English hero and also of Maurice – Maurice who was so unselfish, so self-effacing, who was suffering somewhere in a clingy prison, pining for his little friend Josette, wondering, perhaps, what had become of her, and eating his heart out with anxiety on her account. And somehow in her dream Josette saw the English hero less clearly than she used to do; his imaginary face and form slowly faded and grew dim and were presently merged in the presentment of Maurice Reversac, who looked sad and ill – so sad and ill that Josette's heart ached for him in her sleep, and that her lips murmured his name "Maurice!" with exquisite longing and tenderness.

21

Whenever Josette's thoughts in after years reverted to her memorable journey to England, she never felt that it had been real. It was all so like a dream: her start from Paris in the early morning; the diligence; the first halt at the barrier; the examination of passports; and then the incessant rumble of wheels, the rain beating against the windows, the gusts of wind, the atmosphere reeking of stale provisions, of damp cloth and of leather; the murmur of voices; the halts outside village hostelries; the nights in the *auberge* at Meulan and Les Andelys, at Rouen and Tréport; and her fellow-travellers. They were nothing but dream figures, and it was only when she closed her eyes very tight that Josette could vaguely recall their faces: the prosperous shopman's wife with her rings and her gold brooch and her wicker basket; the crowd in the diligence between Rouen and Tréport who chattered incessantly about the English spy and the horrors of Nantes; her neighbour, who squeezed her into a corner until she could hardly breathe; and then the small, thin man – he, surely, was nothing but a figure in a dream!

Dreams, dreams! they must all have been dreams! All those events, those happenings which memory had never properly recorded, they were surely only dreams; and all the way across the Channel she sat as in a dream: she saw other travellers being very seasick, and there was, indeed, a nasty gale blowing from the south-west, but it was a favourable wind for the packet-boat to Dover and she made excellent going, whilst to Josette the fresh sea air, the excitement of seeing the white cliffs of England looming out of the mist, the sense of contentment that she was nearing the end of her journey and that her efforts on behalf of Maurice would surely be crowned with success were all most welcome after the stuffiness and dreariness of those days passed in the diligence.

And how bright and lovely England seemed to her! It was indeed a dream world into which she had drifted. People looked happy and free! Yes, free! There was no look of furtiveness or terror on their faces; even children had shoes and stockings on their feet, and not one of them had that look of disease and hunger so prevalent – alas! – in revolutionary France. Peace and contentment reigned everywhere; ay! in spite of the war-clouds that hung over the land. And Josette's heart ached when she thought of her own beautiful country, her beloved France, which was all the more dear to all her children for the terrible time she was going through.

Poor little Josette! She felt very forlorn and very much alone when she stood on the quay at Dover with her modest little bundle and her wicker basket which contained all her worldly possessions. For the first time she realised the magnitude of the task which she had imposed on herself when all around her people talked and talked and she could not understand one word that was said. Never before had she been outside France, never before had she heard a language other than her native one. She felt as if she had been dropped down from somewhere into another world and knew not yet what would become of her, a stranger among its denizens. Frightened? Only a little, perhaps, was she frightened, but firm, nevertheless, in her resolve to succeed. But what had seemed such a simple proposition in Paris looked distinctly complicated now.

She was forlorn and alone – and all round her people bustled and jostled; not that anyone was unkind – far from it – but they were all of them busy coming and going, collecting luggage, meeting friends, asking for information. She, Josette, was the only one who, perforce, was tongue-tied – a pathetic little figure in short kirtle, shawl and frayed-out black cap, with lanky hair and a red nose and a smear across one cheek, for much against her will tears would insist on coming to her eyes and they made the smear when they would roll down her face.

The crowd presently thinned out a bit: Josette could see these or those fellow-passengers hurrying hither and thither, either followed by a porter carrying luggage or shouldering their own valise. They all seemed to know where they were going; she alone was doubtful and ignorant. Indeed, she had never thought it would be as bad as this.

And suddenly a kind voice reached her ear:

"Can I be of service now, Mademoiselle? We all have to report at the constable's office, you know."

Just for the moment it seemed to Josette as if *le bon Dieu* had taken pity on her and sent one of His angels to look after her. And yet it was only the thin little man in seedy black who had spoken, and there was nothing angelic about him. He had his papers in his hand and quite instinctively she took hers out from inside her bodice and gave them to him.

"Will you come with me, Mademoiselle," he went on to say, "in case there is a little difficulty about your safe-conduct being entirely made out by the French Government, with which the English are at war! They welcome the *émigrés* as a matter of course; still, there might be a little trouble. But if you will come with me I feel sure I can see you through."

Josette gave him a look of trust and of gratitude out of her blue eyes. How could she help fancying that here was one of those English heroes of whom she had always dreamed and who were known in the remotest corners of France as angels of rescue to those unfortunates who were forced to flee from their own country and take refuge in hospitable England? Dreams! dreams! Could Josette Gravier be blamed for thinking that here were her dreams coming true? When she felt miserable, helpless and forlorn, a hand was suddenly stretched out to help her over her difficulties. Of course she did not think that this pale-faced little man was the hero of her dreams – she had always thought of the Scarlet Pimpernel as magnificently tall and superbly handsome; but then she had also thought of him as mysterious and endowed with mystic powers that enabled him to assume any kind of personality at will. There was enough talk about him among the girls in the government workshops: how he had driven through the barriers of Paris disguised as an old hag in charge of a refuse-cart in which the Marquis de Tournay and his family lay hidden: and there were other tales more wonderful still. Then why could he not diminish his stature and become a pale-faced little man who spoke both English and French and conducted her, Josette, to an office where he exhibited an English passport which evidently satisfied the official in charge not only as to his own identity, but also as to that of the girl with him?

Who but a hero of romance would have the power so to protect the weak as to smooth out every difficulty that beset Josette Gravier's path after her landing in England, from the finding her a respectable hostelry where she could spend the night to guiding her the next morning to the *Bureau des émigrés Français* in Dover, where he obtained for her all the information she wanted about her beloved Louise? Louise, indeed, lived and worked not very far from Dover, in a town called Maidstone, to which a public coach plied that very day. And into this coach did Josette Gravier step presently in the company of her new guardian angel, the thin-faced, pale-eyed little man with the soft voice, whose mysterious hints and utterances, now that she fell into more intimate conversation with him, clearly indicated that if he was not actually the Scarlet Pimpernel himself, he was, at any rate, very closely connected with him.

22

Louise de Croissy was sitting in the bow-window of the small house in Milsom Street in the city of Maidstone when, looking up from her embroidery frame, she saw Josette Gravier coming down the street in the company of a little man in black who was evidently pointing out the way to her. Louise gave one cry of amazement, jumped up from her chair, and in less than half a minute was out in the street, with arms outstretched and a cry of "Josette! My darling one!" on her lips.

The next moment Josette was in her arms.

"Josette! My little Josette! I am not dreaming, am I? It really is you?"

But Josette, overcome with fatigue and emotion, could not yet speak. She let Louise lead her to the house. She appeared half-dazed; but when they came to the door she turned to look for the guiding angel who had brought her safely within sight of her beloved Louise. All she could see of him was his back in the seedy black coat a hundred yards away, hurrying down the street.

Louise was devoured with curiosity; question after question tumbled out of her mouth.

"Josette chérie, how did you come? And all alone? And who was that funny little man in black? What made you come? Why, why didn't you let me know?"

Josette had sunk into the armchair which Louise had dragged for her beside the fire – a lovely fire glowing with coal, the flames dancing as if with joy and putting life and warmth into the girl's stiffened limbs. And Louise, kneeling beside her, holding her little cold hands, went on excitedly:

"Of course you mustn't talk now, chérie, and you must not heed my silly questions. But imagine my amazement! I thought I was dreaming. I had been thinking of you, too, all these days…and to think of you here and now… What will Charles-Léon say when he sees you?… He is getting so strong and well and…"

Then she jumped to her feet, struck her forehead with her hand and exclaimed:

"But what a fool I am to keep on chattering when you are so weary and cold, my darling!… Just wait a few minutes and close your eyes and I will get you some lovely hot tea. Everyone here in England drinks tea in the afternoon… At first I couldn't get used to it… I hadn't drunk tea for years, and then not often – only when I had a headache…but I soon got in the way of it… No, no! I won't chatter any more… Just sit still, chérie, and I'll bring you something you'll like."

She trotted off, eager, excited and longing desperately to hear how Josette had come to travel alone all the way to England; through the instrumentality of that marvellous Scarlet Pimpernel, she decided within herself; and her active brain worked round and round, conjecturing, imagining all sorts of possibilities. "I wonder what has become of poor Maurice Reversac?" she mused at one moment.

She delighted on preparing the tea for Josette and prided herself in the way she made it – one spoonful of tea for each cup and one for the pot – and in the English way of making toast with butter on it. How Josette will love that! Darling, darling Josette! Life from now on would be just perfect; no more loneliness; no more anxiety for Charles-Léon. The angel of the house was present once more.

And in the little sitting-room, ensconced in the big winged chair, Josette Gravier sat with eyes closed, still living in her dream. Was it not marvellous how *le bon Dieu* had brought her safely to Louise. The events of her journey passed before her mental vision like a kaleidoscope of many shapes and colours. It seemed almost impossible to realise that all these things had truly happened to her, Josette Gravier, and that she was really here in England instead of in the dingy Rue Picpus or stitching away at the Government workshops. And thoughts of the workshop brought back a vision of Maurice, and terror gripped her heart because of what might be happening to him – terror, and then a great feeling of joy because she remembered what she was able to do for him. Maurice to her had become as a child, as Charles-Léon was to Louise, a being dependent on her for love and, in a sense, for protection.

It was a wonderful thing, in very truth, to be sitting in a large, comfortable easy-chair beside a lovely fire here in England, and to be drinking tea and eating *pain grillé* with delicious butter on it; and, above all, to have Louise sitting beside her and watching her with loving eyes whilst she ate and drank. Tea was lovely! Like Louise, she had not tasted it for years; it was a luxury unknown in France these terrible times, and even in the happy olden days in the farm by the Isère or in the convent school of the Visitation Josette had only been given tea when she had a headache.

After a little while she felt wonderfully comforted; she knew that Louise was consumed with curiosity and, in all conscience, she could not delay satisfying her.

"Can you not guess why I am here, Louise?" she asked abruptly.

"Of course I can, chérie!" Louise replied. "You came to England for the same reason that I did – to get away from those abominable murderers."

But Josette shook her head.

"Should I have run away," she asked, "and left Maurice out there alone?"

"I don't understand, chérie. Where is Maurice?"

"In prison."

"In…?"

"He was arrested two days before I left Paris."

"But on what grounds?"

Josette gave a sigh and a shrug; she stared dreamily into the fire.

"Does one ever know?" she murmured, and then added: "I suppose that Maurice's connection with Bastien disturbed the complacency of some of those devils. They didn't know how much he knew – about those letters."

"The letters?"

"Yes – the letters. You have still got them, Louise?"

"Of course."

A deep sigh of relief came from little Josette's anxious heart. She turned her large, luminous eyes on her friend.

"That is why I came to England, chérie – to fetch those letters."

"Josette!" Louise exclaimed, "what do you mean?"

"Just that. Maurice has been arrested – you know what that means: a week or a fortnight in some dank prison, then the mockery of a trial, and, finally, the guillotine…"

"But…"

"…so *le bon Dieu* inspired me and gave me courage. I thought of the letters. In order to try and get hold of them, men like Chabot and Fabre went to the length of murder. Fortunately you had taken them away with you. I thought and thought until I remembered the names of those blackguards who had written them and who had murdered Bastien. Then I went to call on them."

"You – my little timid Josette?"

"Yes. I went and I was no longer timid. I went, first of all, to that horrible man Chabot. I told him that those compromising letters of his were still in existence and that I knew where they were. Then I proposed my bargain: complete immunity for

Maurice with a safe-conduct to enable him to leave France as soon as I had retrieved the letters and placed them in the hands of their writers."

"You did that, Josette?"

"I did it for Maurice."

"But that was just the bargain which my poor Bastien proposed to those same men, and in consequence of it…"

"…they murdered him in cold blood. I know that."

"Then how could you…?"

"I ran that risk, I know," Josette replied calmly; "but I also knew by then that possession of those letters had become a question of life and death to those assassins. I threatened them with the immediate publication of the letters in the *Moniteur* if anything happened to Maurice or to me. They didn't know where the letters were; all I told them was that they were in England and that you had kept them. Anyway, they gave me a safe-conduct to go to England and come back. And here I am, my Louise, and if you will give me the letters I will start on my journey back the day after tomorrow."

Louise made no immediate reply: she was staring at her little friend – the frail, modest girl who all alone and sustained only by her own courage had undertaken such a dangerous task for the sake of the man she loved. For, in truth, Louise was forced to the conclusion that Josette's heart, unbeknown to herself, had been touched at last by Maurice Reversac's devotion. Only a woman in love could accomplish what Josette Gravier had done, could so calmly face difficulties and dangers and be ready to face them again without rest or respite. Neither did Josette speak; she was once more staring into the fire, and the dancing flames showed her visions of Maurice suffering in prison and longing for her.

"Josette darling," Louise said after a time, "you cannot possibly start on another long journey just yet."

"Why not?"

"You must have a few days' rest. You are so tired…"

Josette gave a slight shrug.

"Oh! – tired..."

"I cannot imagine how you ever found me – I mean, so quickly. Did you go to London?"

"No, I didn't have to."

"Then, how..."

"A kind friend helped me."

"A friend? Who was it?"

"I don't know. He was a fellow-passenger first in the diligence and then on board ship."

"A stranger?"

"Why, yes! but you cannot imagine how kind he was. When I landed on the quay at Dover I felt terribly lonely and helpless; indeed, I don't know what was to become of me. Everything was horribly strange, and then I couldn't understand a word anyone said..."

"I know. I felt just like that at first, although, of course, I was in the hands of friends. I told you – in my letter..."

"I thought of you, Louise, and of the wonderful friends who were looking after you. What were they like, darling?"

"It is not easy to describe people, and I was terribly overwrought at the time, but the two friends whom we met in the cottage on the cliffs and who took us across the sea in that beautiful ship were good-looking young English gentlemen. One was fair, the other had brown hair, and..."

"Was not one of them quite small and thin, with a very pale face and light-coloured eyes...?"

"No, dear, nothing like that."

"That was what my friend looked like. He spoke to me first at Rouen, and then again at Dover when I felt so lost I didn't know what to do. He took me to a nice hostelry where I could hire a bed for the night. Then the next morning he went with me to the *Bureau des émigrés,* where they spoke French and where they looked up your name and told me where to find you. After that we took the coach for this town. My thin friend with the pale face arranged everything, and when we arrived in this city he walked through the streets with me to show me where you lived; and then – and then, while I ran to embrace you, darling, he hurried away. But I hope and pray that I may meet him again so that I can thank him properly for all the help he gave me."

"Do you think you will?"

"I think so. He told me that he would be in Dover for a couple of days and that a packet-boat would be leaving for Tréport on Thursday at two o'clock in the afternoon. That is the day after tomorrow. He said he would look out for me on the quay. So you see…"

"Josette darling," Louise exclaimed impulsively, "you must be wary of strangers!"

"But of course, Louise, I am wary – very wary. Whenever I spent the night in a hostelry, although I really had enough money to pay for a private room, I always chose to share one with other women or girls. I wouldn't sleep alone in a strange room for anything, although I did so long for privacy sometimes. But if you saw that insignificant little man, Louise, you would know that I had nothing to fear from him."

"I wonder who he is?"

"Sometimes I think…" Josette murmured.

"What, darling?"

"Oh, you will only laugh!"

"Not I. And I know what you were going to say."

"What?"

"That you think he has some connection with the Scarlet Pimpernel."

"Well, don't you?"

"I don't know, dear. You see the members of the League of the Scarlet Pimpernel with whom I came in contact were all English."

"My thin friend with the pale face might be a French member of the League. How otherwise can you explain his kindness to me?"

"I cannot explain it, chérie. Everything that happened to me was so wonderful that I am ready to accept all your theories of the supernatural powers of the mysterious Scarlet Pimpernel. But now, darling, we have chatted quite long enough. You are tired and you must have a rest. After that we'll have supper and you shall go to bed early, if you must leave me again so soon…"

"I must, Louise, I must. And you understand, don't you?"

"I suppose I do; but it will break my heart to part from you again."

"I have to think of Maurice," Josette said softly.

"You love him, Josette?"

"I don't know," the girl replied with a sigh. "At one time I thought that my heart and soul belonged to the mysterious hero whom perhaps I would never see; but since Maurice has been in danger I have realised…"

"What, chérie?"

"That he is dear, very dear to me."

23

It seemed so strange to be back in France once more, to hear again one's own tongue spoken and to understand everything that was said.

Josette, standing in the queue outside the Commissariat of Police at Rouen with the same little bundle and the same wicker basket in her hand, waiting to have her safe-conduct examined and stamped, was a very different person to the forlorn young creature who had felt so bewildered and so terribly lonely at Dover.

She had had two very happy days with Louise. Her arrival, her first sight of the beloved friend had been unalloyed joy; sitting by a cosy fire with Louise quite close to her and holding her hand brought back memories of the happiest days of her childhood. Then there was Charles-Léon looking so bright and bonny, with colour in his cheeks and all his pathetic listlessness gone. In a way, Josette had not altogether liked England; the grey clouds, the misty damp atmosphere were so unlike the brilliant blue skies of France and the sparkling clear air of her native Dauphiné that went to the head like wine; but, then, that atmosphere was pure and wholesome, Charles-Léon's bright eyes testified to that: he no longer suffered from the poisonous air of Paris; and Louise, even in this short time, seemed to have recovered the elasticity of youth.

Yes! it had been a happy, a very happy time, brightened still further by thoughts of what she, Josette, was doing for Maurice.

On the very first evening Louise had given her the sealed packet containing the precious letters: the precious, precious packet which would purchase Maurice's life and liberty. Josette turned it over and over in her hands, and gazed down on the seals and on the wrapper as if her eyes could pierce them.

"What are you looking at so intently, darling?" Louise asked with a smile.

"I didn't recognise the seals," Josette replied.

"It must be one that Bastien used at the office. I never looked closely at the impress before."

"You've never opened the packet?"

"Never. And it never left me since the moment I left our apartment."

"You had it inside your corsets?"

"In the big pocket inside my skirt; and at night I always slipped it under my pillow, or under whatever happened to be my pillow."

"That is what I will do, of course."

"Only once," Louise resumed after a moment or two, "I had a bad scare: one of the last days of our journey. We had reached the desolate region of the Artois and I was terribly, terribly tired. I remembered that the night before I had slipped the letters into my pocket as usual, nevertheless, when we halted the next day and the driver helped me out of the cart, I felt for the packet and imagine my horror when I found it was gone! A wild panic seized me: I don't know why, but I just turned ready to run away. I was suddenly convinced that I had been lured to this lonely spot for the sake of the letters and that Charles-Léon and I would now be murdered. However, I hadn't gone far when the kindest voice imaginable, accompanied by a delicious soft laugh, called me back and, my dear Josette, imagine my joy and surprise when I saw our driver coolly holding the packet out to me!"

"The driver?"

"Yes! I will leave you to guess who he was, just as I did."

They talked by the fire half the day and late into the night, dreaming dreams of happy times to come when that awful revolutionary government would be forced to give way to a spirit of good-will, charity and order – the true birthright of the French nation. Indeed, it had all been a very happy time, and those two days at Maidstone went by like a dream. And now Josette was back, in France on the last stage but one of her journey to Paris. Within three, at most four days, Maurice would be free, and together they would come out to this fair land of England, for it would not be safe to remain in France any longer. Here they would wait for the happy days that were sure to come: Maurice would find work to do, for he was clever and brave, and he would surely earn enough to support himself; then, just as they had always done in Paris, they would wander together in the English woods, those lovely woods about Maidstone of which Josette had had a passing glimpse. In a few short months spring would come and the birds in England, just like those in France, would all be nesting, and under the trees the ground would be carpeted with snowdrops and anemones just as it was at Fontainebleau. And if Maurice's heart was still unchanged, if the same words of love came to his lips which he had spoken before that awful tragedy had darkened both their lives, then she, Josette, would no longer laugh at him. She would listen silently and reverently to an avowal which she knew now would give her infinite happiness; and then she would say "Yes!" to his request that she should become his wife, and together they would steal away in the very early morning to some little English church, and here before God's altar they would swear love and fealty to one another.

Dreams, dreams, which now of a surety would soon become a glowing reality; and all the way since she had left Maidstone in the coach and after she had cried her fill over parting from Louise, Josette had thoughts only of Maurice; and now and then her little hand went up to her bosom, where inside her corsets rested that precious packet; whereupon a look of real joy would gleam out of her eyes, and not even the devices wherewith she had contrived to make her pretty face seem almost ugly could altogether mar its beauty then.

24

The little man with the pale sad face whom Josette looked on as a friend had been most kind and helpful at Dover. He had met Josette on the quay, helped her with her safe-conduct, saw her on the boat for Tréport, and promised that he would meet her again on the journey, probably at Rouen; he himself was bound for Calais, but he would be posting from there to Rouen, and if he was lucky he would get the diligence there for Paris.

Many a time during the next forty-eight hours had Josette longed for his company, not so much because she was lonely, but because the whole way from Dover she had been somewhat worried with the attentions of a stranger, and those attentions had filled her with vague mistrust. She had first caught sight of him on the packet-boat, striding up and down the deck with a swaggering, rolling gait. He was clad like a sailor and ogled all the women as he strode past them – Josette especially – and when he caught a woman's eye a hideous squint further disfigured his ugly face. Somehow she had felt uncomfortable under his glance. Then at Tréport he had seemed to keep an eye on her, and when she boarded the diligence he took a seat in the same compartment and sat opposite to her. He certainly did not molest her in any way, but she felt all the time conscious of his presence. He was very big and fat and entered into conversation with any of the other passengers who were willing to listen to him, telling tall sea yarns and expatiating on his own prowess in various adventures of which, according to his own showing, he was the hero. Oddly enough, he was a native of Nantes – so he informed one of his fellow-travellers – and had been in port there quite recently. Josette, at this, pricked up her ears, and, sure enough, the sailor had something to say about those English spies and their activity in helping aristos and other traitors to evade justice.

"Citizen Carrier," the man had gone on with a dry laugh which revealed some ugly gaps between his teeth, "grows livid with rage at the bare mention of English spies, and lashes about him with a horse-whip like an infuriated tiger with its tail. Only the other day…"

And there followed a long and involved story of how a whole family of aristos – an old man and his grand-children – were spirited away out of the prison of Le Bouffay, how and when nobody ever knew; and Carrier was in such a rage that he had an epileptic fit on the spot. To all this Josette listened eagerly; but all the same she couldn't bear that ugly fat sailor and was vaguely afraid of him.

Josette felt quite happy and relieved when at Rouen she caught sight once more of her pale-faced little friend. She had been lucky enough to fall in on the way with two pleasant women – a mother and daughter – who were ready to share a room with her in the *Taverne du Cheval Blanc*, and thither the three women repaired after the necessary visit at the Commissariat. It was here that Josette saw her friend again. He was standing in the little hall talking to a rough-looking fellow to whom he appeared to be giving instructions.

When he encountered Josette's glance, he gave her a nod and an encouraging smile.

Josette and the two women went into the public dining-room, where several of the smaller tables were already occupied. In the centre of the room there was one long table, and round it two people were sitting, waiting for supper to be served. They were for the most part a rough-looking crowd of men who were making a good deal of noise. The three women, however, were fortunate enough to find an unoccupied small table in a quiet corner where they could have their meal in comfort.

From where Josette sat she could see the door and watch the people coming in and going out. Two diligences had arrived in Rouen within the hour: the one from Tréport and the other from Paris, and a great number of weary and hungry travellers trooped into the public room, demanding supper. The big fat sailor was among these, and Josette was thankful that there was no seat available at her own table, for already she had seen the glance wherewith he had sought to catch her eye, and she had felt quite a cold wave of dread creep down her spine at sight of that ugly face with the leer and the hideous squint.

However, after that first searching glance round the room the fat sailor took no more notice of her; he lolled up to the centre table and sat down. He ate a hearty supper and continued to regale the rest of the company with his ridiculous tall yarns.

Halfway through supper Josette had the joy of seeing her small, pale-faced friend come into the room. He, too, gave a searching glance all round the room, and when he caught sight of Josette he gave her another of his pleasant smiles. Somehow at sight of him she felt comforted. Later on she could not help noticing with what deference everyone at the *Cheval Blanc* had welcomed the insignificant-looking little man. The landlord, his wife and daughter all came bustling into the room and, in a trice, had prepared and laid a separate table for him in a corner by the hearth. Though the *table d'hôte* supper was practically over by then, they brought him steaming hot soup and after that what was obviously a specially prepared dish. Some of the travellers remarked on this and whispered among themselves, but quite unconsciously, no doubt, the deference shown by the landlord and his family communicated itself to them, and the rowdy hilarity of awhile ago gave place to more sober and less noisy conversation.

Only the fat sailor tried for a time to foist his impossible tales on the company, but as no one appeared eager now to listen to him he subsided presently and remained silent and sulky, squinting at the newcomer and moodily picking his teeth. Josette could not help watching him – he was so very ugly and so very large, with his great loose paunch pressed against the table and the hideous black gaps in his mouth; and then those eyes which seemed to be looking both ways at once, one across the other and in no particular direction.

Presently he rose. Josette could not help watching him. She saw him pick up the pepper-pot and toy with it for a moment or two; then, with it in his hand, he lolled across to where Josette's little friend was quietly eating his supper. The latter didn't look up; continued to eat, even while that impudent sailor man stood looking down on him for a moment or two. On the part of a person of consideration this indifference would have seemed strange in the olden days, but now when mudlarks such as this ugly sailor were the virtual rulers of France it was never safe to resent their familiarity or even their impertinence.

The next moment, with slow deliberation, the sailor put the pepper-pot down in front of the stranger, and Josette saw her friend's pale eyes travel upwards from the pepper-pot to the ugly face leering down on him, and she could have sworn that he gave a start and that his thin hands were suddenly clenched convulsively round his knife and fork; also that his pale cheeks took on a kind of grey, ashen hue. No one apparently noticed any of this except Josette, who was watching the two men. She could only see the broad back of the sailor, saw him give a shrug and heard something like a mocking laugh ring across the room.

A second or two later the sailor had lolled out of the door, and Josette might have thought that she had imagined the whole scene but for the expression on her little friend's face. It still looked ghastly, and suddenly he put down his knife and fork and strode very quickly out of the room. What happened after that she didn't know, as her friend did not come back to finish his supper, and very soon the two women who were sharing a room with her gave the signal to go upstairs to bed.

The room which the three of them had secured for the night was at the top of the house under the roof. There were two beds in it: a large one in the far corner of the room which the mother and daughter claimed for themselves and a very small truckle bed for Josette which stood across the embrasure of the dormer window between it and the door. Josette, as was her wont, took the precaution of placing the precious packet of letters underneath her pillow; having said her prayers she slid between the coarse sheets and composed herself for sleep. Her room companions, who had the one and only candle by the side of their bed, soon put the light out, and presently their even breathing proclaimed that they had already travelled far in the land of Nod. At first it seemed pitch-dark in the room, for outside the weather was rough and no light whatever came through the dormer window; but presently a tiny gleam became apparent underneath the door. It came from the lamp which was kept alight all night in the vestibule down below for the convenience of belated travellers. Josette welcomed the little gleam; her eyes soon became accustomed to what had become semi-gloom; she felt secure and comforted, and after a few minutes she, too, was fast asleep.

What woke her so suddenly she did not know, but wake she did, and for a while she lay quite still, with eyes wide open, her heart pounding away inside her and her hand seeking the precious packet underneath her pillow. At the far end of the room the two women were obviously asleep: one of them snoring lustily. And suddenly Josette perceived that the narrow streak of light under the door had considerably widened and had become triangular in shape; indeed, it was widening even now; she also perceived that there was now an upright shaft of light which also widened and widened as slowly, very slowly, the door swung open.

Josette in an instant sat straight up in bed and gave a cry which roused her room mates out of their sleep. From where they lay they couldn't see the door, but they called out: "What is it?"

"The door!" Josette gasped in a hoarse whisper, and then, "The light! the light!"

The women had a tinder-box on a chair near their bed: they fumbled for it whilst Josette's wide, terror-filled eyes remained fixed on the door. It was half-open now, but by whose hand? Impossible to say, for there was no one to be seen. But it seemed to Josette's terrified senses as if she heard a furtive footstep making its way across the narrow landing and down the rickety stairs.

The older woman from her bed asked rather crossly:

"What is it frightened you, little Citizeness?"

Her daughter was still trying to get a light from the tinder-box, which, as was very usual these days, refused to work.

Josette gave a gasp and murmured under her breath: "The door…someone opened it… I heard…"

"Did you see anyone?"

"I don't know…but the door is open and I heard…"

"The latch didn't go home," the woman said more testily. "That's what it was. I noticed last night it didn't look very safe. The draught blew the door open…"

She settled herself back on her pillow. Her daughter gave up trying to get a light and said as testily as her mother:

"Go and shut it, Citizeness; put a chair to hold it if you are frightened and let's get to sleep again."

For a few moments after that Josette remained silent, sitting up in bed, staring at the door. Some evil-doer, she was sure, had tried it and perhaps, scared by her cry and by the women talking, had slunk away again. Certainly there was no one behind the door now. For a time it remained half-open just as it was and then it swayed gently in the draught and creaked on its rusty hinges. The two women had already turned over and were snoring peaceably once more. What could Josette do but chide herself for her fears? But impossible, of course, to go to sleep again with one's nerves on edge and that door swinging and creaking all the time; so Josette crept out of bed and tiptoed across the floor with the intention of closing the door. She moved about as softly as she could so as not to wake the others again. With her hand on the latch she ventured to peep out on the landing. The feeble glimmer emitted by the lamp down below cast a dim yellowish light up the well of the stairs. The house appeared very still, save for the sounds of the stertorous breathings which came from one or other of the rooms on the various floors where tired travellers were sleeping. Outside a dog barked. Josette listened for a moment or two for that furtive footstep which she had heard before, but everything appeared perfectly peaceful and very still. She closed the door very gently and then she groped for a chair to prop against it, when suddenly there came a loud bang right behind her and a terrific current of air swept across the room; the door was once more torn open, quite wide this time, and continued to rattle and to creak. The chair fell out of Josette's hand and she remained standing in her shift, shivering with cold and fright, with her kirtle flapping about her bare legs and her hair blowing into her eyes. The women woke and grumbled, asked with obvious irritation why the Citizeness didn't go to bed and let others sleep in peace.

Josette's heart was beating so fast that she could neither speak nor move; the weather outside was fairly rough and the draught took her breath away.

"Close the window!" the younger woman shouted to Josette. "The wind has blown it open."

At last Josette was able to get her bearings; she turned to the window and saw that in effect it was wide open and that wind and rain were beating in. She had to climb over her bed in order to get to the window and to secure it.

"I call it sheer robbery," the older woman muttered, half-asleep, "to put honest women in such a ramshackle hole."

But neither she nor her daughter offered to lend a hand to Josette, who, buffeted by the rough weather, had great difficulty in fastening the window. When she had done that she had to climb over her bed again in order to close the door; thus several minutes went by before peace reigned once more in the attic room. Josette crept back to bed. Her first thought was for the precious packet: she slid her hand under the pillow to feel for it, but the packet was no longer there.

With an agonising sinking of the heart, in a state not so much of panic as of despair, she turned and ran just as she was in shift and kirtle and without stockings or shoes out of the room and down the stairs, crying: "Thief! thief! thief!" She reached the bottom of the stairs without meeting anyone: she ran across the passage and the vestibule to the front door, tried to open it, but it was locked and bolted. She tore at the handle and at the bolts, still calling wildly: "Thief! thief!" in a voice broken by sobs.

Gradually the whole house was aroused. Doors were heard to open, testy voices wanted to know what all this noise was about. The night watchman came out of the public room, blinking his eyes. Mine host came along from his room down the passage, cursing and swearing at all this disturbance.

"Name of a name! Who is the miscreant who dares to disturb the peace of this highly respectable hostelry?"

Then he caught sight of Josette, who was still fumbling with the door and crying, "Thief! thief!" in a tear-choked voice. Her bare arms and her shoulders were wet, her clothes were wet, her wet hair fell all over her face.

"Name of a dog, wench!" the landlord thundered, and seized the disturber of the peace by the wrist, "what are you doing here? And pray why aren't you in bed where every respectable person should be at this hour?"

It was a blessing in disguise that Josette should be held so firmly by the wrist else she would certainly have measured her length on the floor. Her senses were reeling. Through the gloom she saw angry faces glowering at her. Quite a small crowd had collected in the vestibule: a crowd of angry men roused from their slumbers, clad in whatever garments they happened to have slept in; the women for the most part did not venture beyond the doorway of their rooms, and peeped out thence with eyes heavy with sleep to see what was happening. At sight of Josette most of them murmured:

"A trollop no doubt, caught in some turpitude."

The irate landlord gave Josette's arm a shake: "What were you doing here?" he demanded, "little str – "

He was going to say an ugly word, but just at the moment Josette raised her eyes to his, and Josette's eyes were bathed in tears and they had such an expression of childlike innocence in them that the worthy landlord could think of nothing but of the Madonna whose lovely image had been banished from the village church where he had been baptised and had made his first Communion, and which was now closed because the good *curé* of the village had refused to conform to the mockery of religion which an impious Government was striving to force upon the people: and looking into Josette's eyes, the landlord's thoughts flew back to the Madonna, before whose picture he had worshipped as a child. How, then, could he speak an ugly word in this innocent angel's ear?

"You have got to tell me, you know," he said somewhat sheepishly, "why you are not in your room and asleep." He paused a moment while Josette made a great effort to collect her scattered senses; ashamed of her bare legs and shoulders she tried to get farther back into the gloom.

Someone in the crowd remarked: "Perhaps she is a sleep-walker and had a nightmare."

But at this suggestion Josette shook her head.

"Did something frighten you, little Citizeness?" the landlord asked quite kindly.

Josette now found her voice again.

"Yes!" she said slowly, swallowing hard, for the last thing she wanted to do was to cry before all these people. "I woke very suddenly. I could see the door. It was being pushed open slowly from outside. I cried out. Then I heard footsteps shuffling down the stairs."

"Impossible!" the landlord said.

"I heard nothing," commented someone.

"Nor I," added another.

"I did hear a bang," remarked a third, "not many minutes ago."

"There was a bang," Josette went on slowly. "While I was closing the door the window flew open behind me. I went to shut it. Then the door flew open, and I went to shut it too. When I crept back to bed I found – oh, *mon Dieu! mon Dieu!*"

"What is it? What happened?" they all asked.

"A packet of letters," she replied, "more precious to me than life itself…"

"Not stolen?"

"Yes – stolen."

"Where were they?"

"Underneath my pillow."

"And you say that when you went back to bed those letters…"

"Were not there."

"Impossible!" the landlord reiterated obstinately.

One of the men said, "The thief, whoever he was, must still be in the house then, since the front door is bolted on the inside."

"What about the back door?" another suggested.

Several of them, under the lead of the night watchman, went to investigate the back door. It was bolted and barred the same as the front door.

"I knew it was," the night watchman said somewhat illogically. "I pushed all the bolts in myself all over the house and saw to all the windows."

He felt that Josette's story reflected adversely upon his zeal.

"The thief must still be in the house," Josette murmured mechanically.

"Impossible!" the landlord reiterated for the third time.

The glances cast on Josette became anything but kind, and though the landlord and some of the men were under the influence of her innocent blue eyes, the women from their respective doorways had a good deal to say. One of them started the ball rolling by muttering:

"It's all a pack of lies."

After which the others went at it hammer and tongs. Women are like that. Let some vixen give a lead and there is no stopping the flow of evil tongues. Poor Josette felt this hostility growing around her. It added poignancy to her distress over the letters. Indeed, the little crowd had as usual behaved like sheep; after the first doubt had been cast on Josette's story hardly anyone believed her. The theory of her being a sleep-walker was incontinently rejected: she was just a little strumpet roaming through the house at night in search of adventure. In vain did she weep and protest; in vain did she beg that her room mates be questioned as to the truth of her story: those two women refused to leave their bed, where they lay with their heads smothered under the blanket, wishing to God they had never set foot in this abominable hostelry. Josette, overcome with misery and with shame, had shrunk back into a dark angle of the vestibule, trying with all her might to overcome her terror of all these angry faces, and, above all, to swallow her tears. In her heart she prayed as she had never prayed before that *le bon Dieu*, her patron saint and her guardian angel might guide her with safety out of this awful pass. The landlord stood by, undecided, scratching his head.

"It is a matter for the police, I say." It was a woman who made this suggestion. It was quickly taken up by others, for, indeed, this seemed the easiest solution to the present difficulty; after which everybody would be able to go back to bed and go through the rest of the night in peace.

"I agree," one of the men said. "Let the wench be taken to the nearest Commissariat of Police."

And then a funny thing happened.

The suggestion that the disturber of the peace should be taken to the Commissariat of Police was received with approval, especially by the women. Some of the men were rather doubtful, and there ensued quite a considerable hubbub and a good deal of argument: the women holding to their opinion with loud, shrill voices, the men muttering and cursing.

The landlord stood by scratching his head, not knowing what to do: the casting vote as to Josette's fate would of course rest with him.

And suddenly a quiet vote broke in on the hubbub, saying authoritatively:

"Certainly not. Never shall it be said that a respectable citizeness of the Republic had been put to the indignity of being dragged before the police in the middle of the night."

It was the voice of one accustomed to command and to being obeyed – very quiet and low but peremptory. A small, thin man with pale face and hard penetrating eyes pressed his way through the small crowd. Unlike the rest of them he had slipped on his coat over his shirt, he had stockings on and shoes, and his hair was brushed back tidily. Under his coat and round his waist he wore a tricolour sash. The landlord gave a big sigh of relief: he was truly thankful that decision in this difficult case was taken out of his hands. The girl's story certainly sounded very lame...but, then, she had such lovely blue eyes...and her little mouth – well, well! Anyway, he would not have the unpleasant task of taking her to the police on an ugly charge. The others were all deeply impressed by the little man's authority and by his tricolour sash – badge of service under the Government. As for Josette, she just clasped her tiny hands together and gazed on that insignificant, pale-faced little man as would a devotee upon her favourite saint; her eyes were bathed in tears, her lips already murmured words of gratitude, but actually she was not yet able to speak.

"Where is your wife, landlord?" the little man went on to say in the same peremptory tone.

"At your service, Citizen," the woman replied for herself. She had slipped her bare feet into her shoes and she had on her kirtle and a shawl round her shoulders. Unlike the female guests of the hostelry, she felt that this matter concerned her, and she had dressed herself ready in case of an emergency.

"You will give Citizeness Gravier a bed in your daughter's room, where she will, I hope, spend the rest of the night in peace." So spake the little man with the tricolour sash, and it was marvellous with what alacrity his orders were obeyed. That tricolour sash did indeed work wonders! And now he added curtly: "Remember that the Citizeness is under the special protection of the Central Committee of Public Safety."

Josette could only stare at him with wide-open eyes that looked of a deep luminous blue in this half-light. The little man caught her glance and came over to her. He took her limp, moist hand in his and patted it gently:

"Try and get a little rest now, little woman," he said kindly. "You shall have your letters back, I promise you, even if," he added with a curious smile, "even if we have to set the whole machinery of the law going in order to recover them for you."

He said this so lightly and with so much confidence that Josette felt comforted and almost reassured; indeed, her unsophisticated heart was so full of gratitude that instinctively like a child she raised the thin, clawlike hand which patted her own to her lips. She was on the point of imprinting a kiss upon it when from somewhere in the house there resounded a tremendous crash as of falling furniture. It was immediately followed by loud and prolonged laughter. All the heads were turned towards the stairs as the noise seemed to have come from somewhere above.

"What in the world…?" and other expressions of amazement came to everyone's lips.

"I believe it's that drunken sailor," someone remarked.

"Let me get at him," the landlord said grimly, and pushed his way through the small crowd in the direction of the stairs.

"It can't be him," the night watchman asserted. "I let him out myself by the back door two hours ago and bolted the door after him."

But the little man with the tricolour scarf had snatched his hand out of Josette's grasp. For a moment it seemed as if he was about to join the landlord in his quest after the sailor, but apparently he thought better of it; probably he felt that it would be beneath the dignity of a Government official to chase a mudlark up and down the stairs of a tavern; besides which he well knew in his heart of hearts that no sailor or mudlark would be found inside the house. The laughter had come from outside – there must be an open window somewhere – and its ringing tone was only too familiar to this same Government official with the pale sad face and the badge of office round his waist: it came from a personage that had always proved elusive, whenever the utmost resources of his enemy's intelligence were set to work to run him to earth.

The only thing to do now in this present crisis – for crisis it certainly would prove to be – was to think things over very carefully, to lay plans so secretly and so carefully that no power on earth could counter them. The girl, Josette Gravier, was a magnificent pawn in the game that was to follow the events of this night, just the sort of pawn that would appeal to the so-called chivalry of those damnable English spies: a decoy – what?

So the little man, whose pale face reflected something of the inward rage that tortured him at this moment, turned fiercely on the small crowd of quidnuncs who still stood about quizzing and whispering, and with a peremptory wave of the arm ordered everyone off to bed. They immediately scattered like sheep. The landlord's wife took hold of Josette's hand.

"Come along, little girl," she said; "there is a nice couch in Annette's room: you'll sleep well on that."

"And remember, both of you," the little man said in the end when Josette meekly allowed herself to be led away, "that you are responsible with your lives – your lives," he iterated emphatically, "for the safety of Citizeness Gravier."

The man and woman both shuddered: their ruddy faces became sallow with terror. They understood the threat well enough, even though the amazing turn which the events of this night had taken was past their comprehension.

Silent and obedient the little crowd had dispersed. They all slunk back to bed, there to exchange surmises, conjectures, gossip with their respective room mates. Josette lay down on the couch in Annette's room. She could not sleep, for her brain was working all the time and her heart still beating with the many emotions to which she had succumbed this night. There were moments when, lying here in the darkness, she doubted and feared. That was because of the tricolour sash and the authority which her friend seemed to wield. Before his appearance in this new guise of authority she had almost persuaded herself that he was intimately connected with the hero of her dreams, but there was no reconciling the badge of officialdom of the Terrorist Government with the personality of the Scarlet Pimpernel. Nevertheless, it was this same little man who had saved her from the ill-will of all those horrid people who said such awful things about her and threatened her with the police. It was he who had given her a solemn promise that the precious letters would be restored to her; so what was an ignorant, unsophisticated girl like Josette Gravier to make of all these mysteries? What she did do was to turn her thoughts to Maurice. Surely *le bon Dieu* would not be so cruel as to snatch from her the means by which she could demand his life and liberty. Surely not at this hour when she was so near her goal.

And in a private room on the floor above, Citizen Chauvelin was pacing up and down the floor, with hands clasped tightly behind his back, his pale face set, his thin lips murmuring over and over again:

"Now then, *à nous deux* once more, by gallant Scarlet Pimpernel."

After a time there came a knock at the door. In response to a peremptory "Entrez!" a rough-looking fellow in jersey and breeches undone at the knee came into the room. He had a sealed packet in his large, grimy hands, and this he handed at Chauvelin.

Neither of the men spoke for some time. The man had remained standing in the middle of the room waiting for the other to speak, while Chauvelin sat at the table, his thin delicate hands toying with the packet, his pale eyes hiding their expression of triumph behind their blue-veined lids.

The silence threatened to become oppressive. The newcomer was the first to break it. He pointed a grimy finger at the sealed packet in Chauvelin's hand.

"That is what you wanted," he asked, "was it not, Citizen?"

"Yes," the other replied curtly.

"It was difficult to get. If I had known..."

"Well!" Chauvelin broke in impatiently; "the wind and rain helped you, didn't they?"

"But if I had been caught..."

"You weren't. So why talk about it?"

"And I injured my knee climbing down again from that cursed window," Picard muttered with a surly glance at his employer.

"Your knee will mend," Chauvelin rejoined curtly; "and you have earned good money."

He gave a quiet chuckle at recollection of the night's events. He and Picard. The open door. The open window. The draught. Josette in her shift and kirtle struggling with the door while Picard stole in at the window, and he, Chauvelin, tiptoed noiselessly back down the stairs. Yes! the whole thing had worked wonderfully well, better even than he had hoped. It had been a perfect example of concerted action.

Picard was waiting for his money. Chauvelin gave him the promised two hundred livres – a large sum in these days. The man tried to grumble, but it was no use, and after a few moments he slouched, still grumbling, out of the room.

For close on half an hour after that did Chauvelin remain sitting at the table, toying with the stolen packet. There was a lighted candle on the table, its feeble light flickered in the draught. Chauvelin's pale, expressive eyes were fixed upon the seals. He did not break them, for it was part of the tortuous scheme which he had evolved that these seals should remain intact. He looked at them closely, wondering whose hand had fixed them there: Bastien de Croissy's probably, who had been murdered for his pains, or else the wife's before she entrusted the packet to Josette. The seals told him nothing, and he did not mean to break them: he laid the precious packet down on the table. Then he opened the table drawer. Out of it he took a small lump of soft wax. With the utmost care he took an impression of one of the seals: he examined his work when it was done and was satisfied that it was well done. He then returned the wax impression into the table drawer and locked it.

The stolen packet he slipped into the breast pocket of his coat, and he laid the coat under the mattress in the adjoining room. After which he went to bed.

25

The imaginative brain that invented the torment meted out to Damocles could not in very truth have invented torture more unendurable. Poor old Damocles! All he wanted was to taste for a time the splendour and joys of kingship, and Dionysius, the tyrant King of Sicily, thought to gratify his whim and his own sense of humour by giving the ambitious courtier charge of the kingdom for a while.

So good old Damocles ascended the throne which he had coveted and licked his chops in anticipation of all the luxury that was going to be his, until suddenly he perceived that a sword was hanging over his head by nothing but a hair from a horse's tail. Now we must take it, though legend doesn't say so, that this sword followed the poor man about wherever he went, else all he need have done was to wander through his kingdom and avoid sitting immediately under that blessed sword. As to how the business of the horse's hair was accomplished, say in an open field, is perhaps a little difficult to imagine.

Be that as it may, three worthy Representatives of the People in this autumn of 1793 did in very truth go about their avocations with, figuratively speaking, a sword of doom hanging over their heads.

Three weeks had gone by since Chabot's memorable interview with Josette Gravier, and there was no news of her, no news of Armand Chauvelin, no news, alas! of those compromising letters which were enough to send the whole batch of them to the guillotine.

The Club of the Cordeliers had of late lost a great deal of its prestige, and consequently was not frequented by the most influential members of the Government: it was, therefore, an admirable meeting-place for those who desired to talk things over in the peace and quiet of the club's deserted rooms. Many a time in the past weeks did those three reprobates, quaking in their shoes, hold conclave among themselves, trying to infuse assurance and even hope into one another. Sometimes the great Danton would join them, knowing well that if his three satellites fell, he, too, would be involved in the general *débâcle* that would ensue. Late into the night they would sit and talk, wondering what had become of the little she-devil who had dared to threaten them, hoping against hope that one of the many accidents attendant on a voyage across France had put an end to her.

Then one day there came a letter from Citizen Chauvelin. It was sent to François Chabot, the unfrocked monk turned traitor, renegade and Terrorist, as being the most deeply involved in the affair of the compromising letters. With trembling fingers Chabot broke the seals of this welcome message, for he had already recognised the thin Italian calligraphy of the writer: he was alone in his luxuriously furnished study. At first he could hardly see what he was doing: the words of the letter danced before his eyes, the blood rushed up to his temples, and the paper rustled in his trembling hands. Then slowly he was able to decipher the writing. The first sentence that he read caused him to utter a gurgle of joy: "I have the girl here…"

That was good news indeed. Chabot closed his eyes so as to savour all the more thoroughly the intense joy produced in him by this message. With the girl in his power Chauvelin could have no possible difficulty in getting hold of the letters as well. Now Chabot came to think of it, it was strange that his colleague chose this enigmatic way of commencing his letter. The girl! Yes! the girl was well enough! But what about the letters? He suddenly felt uncomfortable...vaguely frightened of he knew not what. He blinked his eyes once or twice because they had become blurred, and beads of perspiration stood out at the roots of his hair and trickled down his nose. Then at last he settled down to read, and this is what Citizen Armand Chauvelin had written to him from Rouen:

"CITIZEN AND DEAR COLLEAGUE,
I have the girl here under my eye, and by this you will gather that my mission has been successfully accomplished. I am now in Rouen at the hostelry of the *Cheval Blanc*, under the same roof as the little blackmailer. So far I have done nothing about the letters. I can get hold of them any moment, but there are other very grave matters that command my attention. Owing to the inclement weather the diligence cannot ply for some days, and this enforced delay suits my purpose admirably, for I do not wish to leave Rouen just now. The wench cannot in any case escape me and, if you will believe me, I have such high quarry close to my hand that I cannot leave this city until I have secured it. This is not a personal matter but one that affects the very safety of the Republic: how, then, could I risk that by deserting my post? You must try and read between the lines, and then explain the matter to all those who are involved in the affair of the Croissy letters. As I have already told you, I can, of course, get hold of the letters at any time, and I suggest that you give me leave in that case to destroy them before any further mischief is wrought. If you agree to this wise course, send me a courier immediately to the hostelry of the *Cheval Blanc* here in Rouen. But I beg of you not to delay. There are

inimical powers at work here of which you can have no conception, and if, as I believe, the safety of the Republic is as dear to you as it is to me, you will be ready to fall in with my views."

François Chabot read and re-read this letter, which did certainly in some of its phrases appear ambiguous. What, for instance, did Chauvelin mean by the closing sentence? To Chabot it seemed to contain a veiled threat, and there were other points, too…

That evening the four men sat in a corner of the club-room in a very different mood to that of the past few weeks. There they were – François Chabot (Loire et Cher), Fabre d'Eglantine (Paris) and Claud Bazire (Côte d'Or), as unprincipled a lot of rascals as ever defamed the country of their birth. The great Danton had joined them at their earnest request – not so much a scoundrel he as an infuriated wild animal, smarting under many wrongs, lashing out savagely against guilty and innocent alike, and with old ideals long since laid in the dust.

"I would not trust that old fox farther than I could see him," Danton had said as soon as the matter of Chauvelin's letter had been put before him.

"But he can get hold of the letters at any time – there's no doubt about that," one of the others remarked.

"He has probably got them inside his coat pocket by now," the great man retorted, "ready to sell them or use them for his own ends."

"Then what had one better do?"

"Let us send a courier over to Rouen," Fabre d'Eglantine suggested, "with orders to Citizen Chauvelin to come to Paris immediately."

"Suppose he refuses?" Danton said with a shrug.

"He wouldn't dare…"

"And would you dare threaten him if he really has the letters and holds them over you?"

They were silent after that because they knew quite well – in fact had just realised it for the first time – that it was Armand Chauvelin now instead of Bastien de Croissy or Josette Gravier who held the sword of Damocles over their heads.

After a time Chabot murmured, looking to the great Danton for guidance now that the emergency appeared more fateful than before: "What shall we do, then?"

"If you take my advice," Danton said, and strove to appear as if the whole matter did not greatly concern him, "if you take my advice, one of you will go straight to Rouen, see Citizen Chauvelin and get the packet of letters straight from the girl. After that the sooner the wretched things are destroyed the better."

That seemed sound advice, and after discussion it was decided to act upon it, François Chabot declaring his willingness, in spite of the weather, to journey to Rouen by special coach on the morrow.

26

From Meulon, where he spent the night, Chabot sent a courier with a letter over to Rouen to prepare Chauvelin for his arrival.

> "Devoured with impatience" (he wrote), "I am coming in person to receive the precious letters from your hands and discuss with you the terms of your reward, which my friends and I are determined shall be as great as your service to our party."

An ironic smile twisted Chauvelin's thin lips when he read this short epistle. The events had not turned out any differently to what he had expected. Those cowardly fools over there were, in fact, playing into his hands.

He had been interrupted by the courier in an important work which had demanded a great deal of time and skill. Five days had gone by since poor little Josette had been robbed of her precious letters, and today Chauvelin was sitting at the table in the private room which he still occupied in the hostelry of the *Cheval Blanc*. Though it was daylight there was a lighted candle on the table, and when the courier arrived, Chauvelin's deft fingers had been busy making up a small parcel which looked like a packet of letters and which he had been engaged in sealing down with red wax and a brand-new seal.

When the courier was announced he blew out the candle and threw the packet into the table-drawer.

Now that he was alone again he took the packet out of the drawer, and then drew another out of the breast-pocket of his coat. The two packets now lay side by side on the table. Chauvelin applied himself sedulously to a final examination of them. To all intents and purposes they were exactly alike. None but a specially trained eye could detect the slightest difference in them. In shape, in size, in the soiled and crumpled appearance of the outside covering, in the disposition of the five seals they were absolutely interchangeable. It was only to Chauvelin's lynx-like eyes that the difference in the seals was apparent. A very minute difference indeed in the sharpness and clearness of the impress.

He gave a deep sigh of satisfaction. All was well. The work of die-sinking had been admirably done from the wax impression of the original, by a skilled workman of Rouen. Chauvelin could indeed be satisfied: his deep-laid scheme was working admirably: he could await the arrival of Chabot with absolute calm and the certainty that his own delicate hands held all the threads of as neat an intrigue as he had ever devised for the ultimate undoing of his own most bitter enemy.

He slipped the two packets inside his coat pockets; the original one stolen from under the pillow of Josette Gravier he thrust against his breast, the other he put into a side pocket. After which he settled his sharp features into an expression of kindliness and went in search of Josette.

He knew just where to find her, sitting on the bench under the chestnut trees – that beautiful avenue which had once formed part of the old convent garden of the Ursulines, driven away by the relentless edicts of the revolutionary government. The mediaeval building, still splendid in its desolation, showed already signs of decay. The garden was untended, the paths overgrown with weeds, the grass rank and covered with a carpet of fallen leaves, the statuary broken, but nothing could mar the beauty of the age-old trees, of the chestnuts already half-denuded of leaves. And the vista over the river was beautiful, with the two islands and the sleepy backwater, and the sight of the ships gliding with such stately majesty down-stream towards the sea. The place was not lonely, for the riverside was a favourite walk of the townsfolk, and on the quay boatmen plied their trade of letting pleasure boats out on hire. The convent itself had been turned into a communal school for the children of Rouennais soldiers who were fighting for their country, and, after school hours or during recreation time, crowds of children trooped out of the building and ran playing up and down the avenue. Indeed, Josette did not come here for solitude: she liked to watch the children and the passers-by and, anyway, it was nicer than sitting in that stuffy public room of the hostelry where prying eyes scanned her none too kindly.

Her pale-faced little friend had insisted that she should continue to share a room with the landlord's daughter: this room had no egress save through the larger one occupied by the landlord himself and his wife, and Josette was quite aware that her friend had made these people responsible for her safety as well as for her comfort. This, of course, had greatly reassured her, and his promise that he would get the letters back for her had cheered her up – especially for the first twenty-four hours. She had such implicit faith not only in his friendship, but also, since that fateful night, in his power; but for that tricolour sash she would have felt happier still, but somehow she didn't like to think of that kind, sad, gentle creature as a member of a government of assassins.

This was the fifth day that Josette had spent in Rouen, waiting and hoping almost against hope. Once or twice she had caught sight of her friend either in the garden or while he wandered along the riverside, with head bent, hands clasped behind his back, evidently wrapped in thought. When he passed by in front of Josette he always looked up and gave her an encouraging smile. And then, again, she saw him in the public room at meal-times, and always he gave her a smile and a nod.

Then yesterday, here in the old garden, he came and sat down beside her under the chestnut tree, and he was so gentle and so kind that she was tempted to confide in him. She told him about the contents of the stolen packet – about the letters, the possession of which had cost brave Bastien de Croissy his life, and about her own journey to England in order to get the letters from Louise. And as he listened with so much attention and sympathy she went so far as to tell him about Maurice, and how it had been the object of her journey – nay! the object of her life – to use the letters as Bastien had intended to use them: as a leverage to obtain what she desired more than anything in the world – the life and liberty of Maurice Reversac.

"I am not afraid of what I mean to do," she concluded. "I have already bearded Citizen Chabot once, and I know that I can get from him everything I want…" She paused and added with a sigh of longing, "if only I have those letters…!"

Her friend had been more than kind after that, and so confident and reassuring that she slept that night more soundly and peacefully than she had done since she arrived in Rouen.

"Have no doubt whatever, little one," he had said in the end. "You shall have your precious letters back very soon."

And then today, even while she sat at her accustomed place under the chestnut tree, and with dreamy glance watched the people coming and going up and down the riverside all intent on affairs of their own, heedless of this poor little waif with the gnawing anxiety in her heart, she suddenly caught sight of the little man coming towards her with a light, springy step. Somehow, directly she saw his face, she knew that he was the bearer of good news. And so it turned out to be. Even before he came close to her he thrust his hand into the side pocket of his coat and she guessed that he had the letters. She could not repress a cry of joy which caused the passers-by to cast astonished glances at the pretty wench, but she paid no heed to them. She was so excited that she jumped up and ran to her friend. He had indeed drawn the sealed packet from the pocket of his coat, and now he actually put it into her hands. It was so wonderful – almost unbelievable. Josette pressed the packet against her cheek and her young palpitating bosom – the precious, precious packet! She was so happy, so marvellously, so completely happy! She didn't care who watched her; just like a child she spread out her arms and would have hugged that kind peerless friend to her breast only that he put up a warning hand, for, in truth, she was attracting too much attention from the quidnuncs on the quay. At once she asked his pardon for her vehemence.

"I am so happy," she murmured 'twixt laughter and tears, "so happy! I was forgetting…"

"I told you I would get the letters for you, didn't I?" he said, and with kindly indulgence patted her trembling little hands.

"And I shall pray God every day of my life," she responded, sinking her voice to a whisper, "to give you due reward."

"So long as you are happy, my child…"

"I could fall at your feet now," she murmured earnestly, "and thank you on my knees."

None but a hardened, stony heart as that which beat in the Terrorist's breast could have resisted the charm, the exquisite sentiment of this beautiful woman's gratitude. To his enduring shame, be it said that Chauvelin felt neither remorse nor pity as he looked on the lovely young face with the glowing eyes and tender mouth quivering with emotion. His tortuous schemes would presently land her on the hideous platform of the guillotine; that beautiful head with the soft chestnut curls would presently fall into the ghoulish basket which already had received so many lovely heads. What cared he? All these people – men, women, young and old – were so many pawns in the game which he had devised; and he, Chauvelin, was still engaged in moving the pieces: he still had his hold on the pawns. Away with them if they proved to be in the way or merely useless. It was more often than not a scramble as to which party would push the other up the steps of the guillotine.

Chauvelin sat himself down quite coolly on the bench and, with a sneer round his lips which he took care the girl should not see, he watched her as she tucked the precious packet away underneath her fichu.

"I have further good news for you, Citizeness," he said as soon as she had sat down beside him.

"More good news!" she exclaimed; then pulled herself together and turned big inquiring eyes on her friend: "I won't hear it," she said resolutely, "until I know your name."

He gave a light shrug and a laugh: "Suppose you call me Armand," he replied, "Citizen Armand."

"Is that your name?"

"Why, yes?"

Josette murmured the name once or twice to herself.

"It will be easier like this for me," she said with naïve seriousness, "when I pray to *le bon Dieu* for you. And now," she went on gaily, "Citizen Armand, I am ready for your news."

"It is just this: you won't need to go to Paris."

"What do you mean?"

"Just what I say. A courier has just come from Meulon with news that François Chabot, representative of the people, will be in Rouen this evening."

"This – evening?"

"So you see…"

"Yes… I see," she murmured, awed at the prospect of this unexpected event.

"It all becomes so much safer," he hastened to reassure her. "I succeeded in getting that packet back for you this time, but I could not journey all the way to Paris with you, and you might have been robbed again."

"Oh, I see – I do see!" Josette sighed. "Isn't it wonderful?" She felt rather bewildered. It was all so unexpected and not a little startling. Instinctively her hand sought the packet in the bosom of her gown. She drew it out. The outside wrapper was very soiled and crumpled – it had been through so many hands – but the seals were intact.

"I wouldn't break the seals if I were you, little girl," Chauvelin said. "It will be better for you, I think, also for your friend – what's his name? – Reversac, isn't that it? – if the Citizen Representative is allowed to think that you have not actually read those compromising letters. It will make him less ill-disposed towards you personally. Do you see what I mean?"

"I think I do, but even if I didn't," Josette added naïvely, "I should do as you tell me."

No compunction, no pity for this guileless child who trusted him! Chauvelin patted her on the shoulder:

"That's brave!" was all he said. He appeared ready to go, but Josette put a timid hand on his arm.

"Citizen Armand…"

"Yes? What is it now?"

"Shall I see you before…"

"Before the arrival of François Chabot?"

"Yes."

"I will certainly let you know, and see you if I can… By the way," he added as if in after-thought, "would it not be wiser for you to leave the packet with me until this evening?… No?" he went on with a smile as Josette quickly crossed her little hands over her bosom as if some powerful instinct had suddenly prompted her not to part again from her precious possession. "No…? Well, just as you like, my child; but take care of them: those spies and thieves are still about, you know."

"Spies?"

"Of course. Surely you guessed that your letters were not stolen by ordinary thieves?"

"No, I did not. I just thought…"

"What?"

"That being a sealed packet a thief would think that it contained money."

"Enough to warrant such an elaborate plot," Chauvelin remarked dryly, "and you so obviously not a wealthy traveller?"

"I hadn't thought of that. But, then, of course, Citizen Armand, you must know who stole the packet since…"

"Since I got it back for you? I do know, of course."

"Who was it?" Josette asked and gazed on Chauvelin with wide-open frightened eyes.

"If I were to tell you, you wouldn't understand."

"I think I would," she murmured. "Try me!"

"Well," he replied, sinking his voice to a whisper, "did you happen to notice on the first evening you arrived here a big man dressed as a sailor, who made himself conspicuous in the public room of the *Cheval Blanc*?"

"Yes, I did – a horrid man, I thought. But surely he…?"

"That man, who I admit wore a clever disguise, is the head of an English organisation whose aim is the destruction of France."

"You don't mean…?" she gasped.

Chauvelin nodded. "I see," he said, "that you have heard of those people. They call themselves the League of the Scarlet Pimpernel and, under pretence of chivalry and benevolence, are nothing but a pestilential pack of English spies who take money from both sides – their own Governments or ours whichever suits their pocket."

"I'll not believe it!" Josette protested hotly.

"Did you not notice that night as soon as I entered the room that the fat sailor beat a hasty retreat?"

"I noticed," she admitted, "that he did leave the public room soon after you sat down to supper."

"I sent the police after him then, but he had a marvellous faculty for disappearing when he is afraid for his own skin."

"I'll not believe it!" Josette protested again, thinking of Louise's letter and of the hero of her dreams. "Had it not been for the Scarlet Pimpernel…"

"Your friend Louise de Croissy," Chauvelin broke in with a sneer, "would never have reached England – I know that. Did I not tell you just now that pretence of chivalry is one of that man's stock-in-trade? No doubt he wanted to get Citizeness Croissy away, thinking that she would leave the letters with you: when he realised that you hadn't them and that you were journeying to England obviously in order to get them, he followed you. I know he did, and I did my best to circumvent him. I befriended you as far as I could, for he dared not approach you while I was on the watch."

"Oh, I know," Josette sighed, "you have been more than kind."

She felt as if she were floundering in a morass of doubt and misery, tortured by suspicion, wounded in her most cherished ideals. Ignorant, unsophisticated as she was, how could she escape out of this sea of trouble? How could she know whom to trust or in whom to believe? This friend had been so kind, so kind! The precious letters had been stolen from her and he had got them back. Without him where would she be at this hour? Without him she would have nothing wherewith to obtain life and liberty for Maurice. Tears welled up to her eyes; never, perhaps, had she felt quite so unhappy, because never before had she been brought up in such close contact with all that was most hideous in life – treachery and deceit. She turned her head away because she was half-ashamed of her tears. After all, what was the destruction of an illusion in these days when one saw all one's beliefs shattered, all one's ideals crumbled to dust? Josette had almost deified the Scarlet Pimpernel in her mind, and Louise's letter had confirmed her belief in his wonderful personality with the fascinating mystery that surrounded it and the almost legendary acts of bravery and chivalry which characterised it. If any other man had spoken about her hero in the way this pale-faced little friend of hers had done she would have dubbed him a liar and done battle for her ideal; but she owed so much to Citizen Armand, he had been such a wonderful friend, such a help in all her difficulties, and now, but for him, she would have been in the depths of despair.

He was wrong – Josette was certain that he was wrong – in his estimate of the Scarlet Pimpernel, but never for a moment did she doubt his sincerity. She owed him too much to think of doubting him. Whatever he said – and his words had been like cruel darts thrust into her heart – he had said because he was convinced of its truth, and he had spoken only because of his friendship for her. Even now he seemed to divine her thoughts and the reason of her tears.

"It is always sad," he said gently, "to see an illusion shattered; but think of it like this, my child: you have lost a – shall I say *friend*, though I do not like to misuse the word? – who in very truth had no existence save in your imagination; against that you have found one who, if I may venture to say so, has already proved his worth by restoring to you the magic key which will open the prison doors for the man you love. Am I not right in supposing that Maurice Reversac is that lucky man?"

Josette nodded and smiled up at the hypocrite through her tears.

"I hadn't meant to tell you so much," he said, rising ready to go, "only that I felt compelled to warn you. The man who stole your letters once will try to do so again, and I might not be able to recover them a second time."

It was getting late afternoon now, the shadows were deep under the trees, but on the river twilight lingered still. The girl sat with her head bent, her fingers interlocked and hot tears fell upon her hands. The kind friend who had done so much for her was still standing there about to go, and she could not find it in her heart to look up into his face and to speak the words of gratitude which his marvellous solicitude for her should have brought so readily to her lips. Her thoughts were far away with Louise in her pretty room in England, telling her story of the astounding prowess of the Scarlet Pimpernel, his resourcefulness, his devotion, the glamour that surrounded his mysterious personality in his own country; how could all that be true if this kind and devoted friend over here did not deceive himself and her? And if he did not, then were all the tales she had heard tell of the mystic hero nothing but legends or lies?

A confused hum of sounds was in her ears; the boatmen gossiping on the quay, the shuffling footsteps of passers-by the shrieks and laughter of children up and down the avenue and, suddenly through it all, a stentorian voice chanting the first strains of the Marseillaise completely out of tune. Josette felt rather than saw Citizen Armand give a distinct start: she looked up just in time to see him cross over rapidly to the quay. The ear-splitting song had come from that direction. The boatmen were all laughing and pointing to a boat just putting off the shore, in which a fat sailor in tattered coat and shiny black hat thrust at the back of his head was plying the oars. He it was who was singing so intolerably out of tune; his voice resounded right across the intervening space: even when he reached midstream and headed toward the islands, some of the stentorian notes echoed down the avenue. Josette couldn't help smiling. Was that the man who had stolen the letters from under her pillow – the dangerous spy whom it took all her friend's ingenuity to track? Could, in fact, that ugly uncouth creature, with the lank hair, the tattered clothes and the toothless mouth, be the mysterious and redoubtable Scarlet Pimpernel?

Josette could not help laughing to herself at the very thought. Citizen Armand must indeed be moonstruck to think of connecting that buffoon with the most gallant figure of all times. She glanced anxiously about her to find her friend Armand, for she wanted to speak with him again, to convince him how wrong he was, how utterly mistaken he had been. All at once her big sea of troubles ebbed away. She felt happy and light-hearted once more. Her illusions were not shattered: she could still worship her ideal and yet retain her affection for the sad-faced and kindly man who had befriended her. She was happy – oh, so happy! – and her lips were ready now to speak the words of gratitude.

But look where she might, there was no longer any sign of Citizen Armand.

27

It was now eight o'clock in the evening. An hour ago a post-chaise had driven into the courtyard of the *Cheval Blanc* and from it descended Citizen François Chabot, Representative of the People for the department of Loire et Cher. He had been received by the landlord of the tavern with all the honours due to his exalted station and to his influence, and had supped in the public room in the company of that pale-faced little man who had already created so much attention in the hostelry and who went by the name of Citizen Armand.

Josette sitting at another table in a dark angle of the room watched the two men with mixed feelings in her heart. She couldn't eat any supper, for inwardly she was terribly excited. The hour had come when all her efforts on behalf of Maurice would come to fruit. Her friend had sent her word that he would summon her when the Citizen Representative was ready to receive her, so she waited as patiently as she could. Watching Chabot she recalled every moment of her first interview with him; she had been perfectly calm and self-possessed then, and she would be calm now when she found herself once more face to face with him. Though ignorant and unsophisticated, Josette was no fool. She knew well what risk she ran by consenting to meet Chabot here in Rouen with the letters actually upon her person. Events had turned out differently from what she had planned. She had meant to meet Chabot in Paris on neutral ground, with the letters out of his reach until she had the safe conducts for herself and Maurice safely put away. Here it was different.

Danger? There always was danger in coming in conflict with these men who ruled France by terror and the ever-present threat of the guillotine, but there was also that other danger, the risk of the precious letters being stolen again during the final stage of the journey, and no chance of getting them back a second time. Even so, Josette would perhaps have refused to meet Chabot till she could do so in Paris had it not been for Citizen Armand; but it never entered her mind that this faithful and powerful friend would not be there to protect her and to see fair play.

As on that other occasion in the luxurious room of the Rue d'Anjou she was not the least afraid: it was only the waiting that was so trying to her nerves. While she made pretence to eat her supper she tried to catch her friend's eye, but he was deeply absorbed in conversation with Chabot. Once or twice the latter glanced in her direction, then turned back to Armand with a sneer and a shrug.

After supper the two men went out of the room together, and Josette waited quietly for the summons from her friend. At last it came. Looking up, she saw him standing in the doorway: he beckoned to her and she followed him out of the room. She was absolutely calm now, as calm as she had been during the first interview when the precious letters were not yet in her possession. Now she felt the paper crackling against her bosom – the golden key her friend had called the packet, which would open the prison gates for Maurice.

Armand conducted her to a small room at the back of the house, one which had been put at the disposal of the Citizen Representative by the landlord, who probably used it in a general way as a place where he could receive his friends with the privacy which the public room could not offer. It was sparsely furnished with a deal table covered by a faded cloth, on which past libations had left a number of sticky stains: on the table a bottle of ink, a mangy quill pen, a jar of sand and a couple of pewter sconces in which flickered and guttered the tallow candles. There were a few chairs ranged about the place and a wooden bench, all somewhat rickety, covered in grime and innocent of polish. From a small iron stove in an angle of the room a wood fire shed a welcome glow. The only nice bit of furniture in the place was an old Normandy grandfather clock, standing against the wall and ticking away with solemn majesty. There was only one window, and that was shuttered and bolted. The walls had once been whitewashed: they were bare of ornament save for a cap of liberty roughly drawn in red just above the clock and below it the device of the Terrorist Government: "*Liberté, Egalité, Fraternité*." Recently a zealous hand had chalked up below this the additional words: "*Ou la mort*."

When Chauvelin ushered Josette into this room Chabot was sitting at the table. The girl came forward and without waiting to be asked she sat down opposite Chabot and waited for him to speak. She looked him fearlessly in the face, and he returned her glance with an unmistakable sneer. Chauvelin, who had followed Josette into the room, now put the question:

"Shall I go, or would you like me to stay?"

Josette, looking up at him, did not know to whom he had addressed the question, but in case it was to her she hastened to say: "Do please stay, Citizen Armand."

Chauvelin then sat down on the bench against the wall behind Josette, but facing his colleague. For a minute or two no one spoke, and the only sound that broke the fateful silence was the solemn ticking of the old clock. Then Chabot said abruptly:

"Well, little baggage, so you've been to England, I understand."

"Yes, Citizen, I have," Josette replied coolly.

Chabot, his ugly head on one side, was eyeing her quizzically, his thick lips were curled in a sneer. He picked up the pen from the table and toyed with it: stroked his unshaven chin with the quill.

"Let me see," he went on slowly, "what exactly was the object of your journey?"

"To get certain letters, Citizen," she rejoined, unmoved by his attitude of contempt, "which you were anxious to possess."

"H'm!" was Chabot's curt comment. Then he added dryly, "Ah! I was anxious to possess those letters, was I?"

"You certainly were, Citizen."

"And it was in order to relieve my anxiety that you travelled all the way to England, what?"

"We'll put it that way if you like, Citizen Representative."

The girl's coolness seemed to exasperate Chabot as it had done in their first interview. Even now at this hour when she was so entirely in his power, when his scheme of vengeance against this impudent baggage had matured to such perfection, he could not control that feeling of irritation against his victim, and he envied his colleague over there who sat looking perfectly placid and entirely at his ease. Suddenly he said:

"Where are those letters, Citizeness?"

"I have them here," she answered with disconcerting coldness.

"Let's see them," he commanded.

But she was not to be moved into easy submission.

"You remember, Citizen," she said, "under what conditions I agreed to hand you over the letters?"

"Conditions?" he retorted with a harsh laugh. "Conditions? Say, I have forgotten those conditions. Will you be so gracious as to let me hear them again?"

"I told you, Citizen Representative," Josette proceeded wearily, for she was getting tired of this word play, "I told you at the time; I want a safe-conduct in the name of Maurice Reversac and one in mine to enable us both to quit this country and travel whither we please."

"Is that all?" he sneered.

"Enough for my purpose. Shall we conclude, Citizen Representative? You must be as tired as I am of all this quibble."

"You are right there, you impudent trollop!" Chabot snapped at her with a short laugh. "Give me those letters!"

Then as she made no answer, only glanced at him with contempt and shrugged, he iterated hoarsely:

"Did you hear me? Give me those letters!"

"Not till I have the safe-conducts written out and signed by your hand."

"So that's it, is it?" Chabot snarled, and leaned right across the table, peering into her face. He looked hideous in the dim, unsteady light of the candles, with his thick lips quivering, a slight scum gathering at the corners of his mouth and his thin face bilious and sallow with rage. Thus he remained for the space of a minute, gloating over his triumph. The wench was in his power – nothing could save her now; the vengeance for which he had thirsted was his at last; but there was exquisite pleasure in the anticipation of it, in looking at that slender neck so soon to be severed by the knife of the guillotine, on that dainty head with its wealth of golden curls soon to fall into the gruesome basket while those luminous eyes were closed in death-agony.

"Ah!" he murmured hoarsely, "you thought you had François Chabot in your power, you little fool, you little idiot! You thought that you could frighten him, torture him with doubts and fears? You triple, triple fool!"

His voice rose to a shriek: he jumped to his feet and, thumping the table with the palm of his hand, he shouted:

"Here! Guard! *A moi!*"

The door flew open: two men of the Republican Guard appeared under the lintel, and there were others standing in the passage. Josette saw it all. While Chabot was raving and spitting venom at her like an angry serpent she had kept hold on herself. She was not frightened because she knew that Armand, her friend, was close by and that Chabot, even though, or perhaps because he was a Representative of the People would not dare to commit a flagrant act of treachery before his colleague: would not dare to provoke her, Josette Gravier, into revealing the existence of letters compromising to himself here and now. But when the door flew open and she caught sight of the soldiers, she jumped to her feet and turned to the friend to whom she looked so confidently for protection. Chabot now was laughing loudly; with head thrown back he laughed as if his sides would split.

"You little fool!" he continued to snarl. "You egregious little idiot!" He paused, and then commanded: "Search her!" The two soldiers advanced. Josette stood quite still and did not utter a single cry. Her great eyes were fixed on her friend – the friend who was playing her false, who had already betrayed her. At first her glance had pleaded to him: "Save me!" Her dark blue eyes, dark as a midsummer's night, had seemed to say: "Are you not my friend?" But gradually entreaty gave place to horror and then to a stony stare; for Citizen Armand, the friend and protector who had wormed himself into her secrets, gained her trust and stolen her gratitude, sat there silent and unmoved, stroking his chin with his talon-like fingers, an enigmatic smile round his thin lips. Slowly Josette averted her gaze: she turned from the treacherous friend to the gloating enemy. The soldiers now stood one on each side of her – she could actually feel their breath upon her neck; the hand of one of them fell upon her shoulder. With a smothered cry of revolt she shook it off and deliberately took the packet of letters from inside her bodice and laid it on the table.

A hoarse sigh of satisfaction broke from Chabot's throat. His thick, coarse hand closed over the fateful packet; the soldiers stood by like wooden dummies, one on each side of Josette.

"Can I go now?" the girl asked.

Chabot threw her a mocking glance.

"Go?" he mimicked with a sneer. Then the sarcasm died on his lips, and his ugly face, which he thrust forward within an inch of hers, became distorted with a look of almost bestial rage. "Go? No, you evil-minded young jade – you are not going. Like a born idiot you have placed yourself in my power. For the past month you have been laughing at me and my friends in your sleeve, relishing like a debauched little glutton the torment which you were inflicting upon us. Well, it is our turn to laugh at you now, and laugh we will while you rot in gaol, you and your lover; aye! rot, until the day on which your heads fall under the guillotine will be welcomed by you as the happiest one of your lives."

Except that she recoiled with a feeling of physical disgust when the man's venom-laden breath fanned her cheeks, Josette had not departed for one moment from her attitude of absolute calm. The moment that earthly protection failed her and the friend whom she trusted proved to be a traitor, she knew that she and Maurice were lost. Nothing on earth could save either of them now from whatever fate these assassins chose to mete out to them. She prayed to *le bon Dieu* to give her courage to bear it all and, above all, she prayed for strength not to let this monster see what she suffered. The name of Maurice thrown at her with such cruelty had made her wince. It was indeed for Maurice's sake that she suffered most acutely. She had built such high hopes – such fond and foolish hopes apparently – on what she could do for him that the disappointment did for the moment seem greater than she could bear.

She no longer looked at the betrayer of her trust: in her innocent mind she thought that he must be overwhelmed with shame at his own cowardice. *Le bon Dieu* alone would know how to punish him.

At a sign from Chabot the soldiers each placed a hand once more upon the girl's shoulder. They waited for another sign to lead her away. Their officer was standing in the doorway: Chabot spoke to him.

"What accommodation have they got in this city," he asked with a leer at Josette and a refinement of cruelty worthy of the murderer of Bastien de Crossy, "for hardened criminals?"

"There is the town jail, Citizen," the man replied.

"Safe, I suppose?"

"Very well guarded, anyway. It is built underneath the town hall."

"Who is in charge?"

"I am, Citizen, with a score of men."

"And in the town hall?"

"There is a detachment of the National Guard under the command of Captain Favret."

"Quartered there?"

"Yes, Citizen."

Chabot gave another harsh laugh and a shrug.

"That should be enough to guard a wench," he said, "but one never knows – you men are such fools…"

While he spoke Chabot had been idly fingering the packet, breaking the seals one by one. Now the outside wrapper fell apart and disclosed a small bundle of letters – letters…? Letters? Chabot's hand shook as he took up each scrap of paper and unfolded it, and while he did so every drop of blood seemed to be drained from his ugly face and his bilious skin took on a grey ashen hue; for the packet contained only scraps of paper folded to look like letters with not a word on any of them. Chabot's eyes as he looked down on those empty scraps seemed to start out of his head: his face had been distorted before, now it seemed like a mask of death – grey, parchment-like, rigid. He raised his eyes and fixed them on Josette, while one by one the scraps of paper fluttered out of his hand.

But Josette herself was no longer the calm, self-possessed woman of a moment ago. When Chabot fingered the fateful packet and broke the seals one by one, when the outside wrapper fell apart and disclosed what should have been the famous letters, a cruel stab went through her heart at the thought of how different it would all have been if only the man she had trusted had not proved to be a Judas. Then suddenly she saw that here were no letters, only empty scraps of paper: her amazement was as great as that of her tormentor himself. She had received that packet from Louise: she had never parted from it since Louise placed it in her hands – never. But, of course...the last five days...the theft...the miraculous recovery... Oh, *mon Dieu! mon Dieu!* what did it all mean? Her brain was in a whirl. She could only stare and stare on those scraps of paper which fell out of Chabot's bony hands one by one.

No one spoke: the soldiers stood at attention, waiting for further orders. At the end of the room the old grandfather clock ticked away the minutes with slow and majestic monotony. At last a husky groan came from Chabot's quivering lips. He pointed a finger at Josette and then at the papers on the table.

"So," he murmured in a hoarse whisper, "you thought to fool me again?"

"No, no!" she protested involuntarily.

"You thought," he insisted in the same throaty voice, "to extract a safe-conduct from me and to fool me with these worthless scraps..."

He paused and then his voice rose to a shriek.

"Where are the letters?" he shouted stridently.

"I don't know," Josette protested. "I swear I do not know."

"Bring me those letters now," he iterated, "or by Satan..."

Once more he paused, for the words had died on his lips; indeed, how could he threaten his victim further when already he had promised her all the torments, mental and physical, that it was in his power to inflict. "Or by Satan..." What further threat could he utter? Jail? Death for her and her lover? What else was there?

"Bring me those letters!" he snarled, like a wild cat robbed of its prey, "or I'll have you branded, publicly whipped. I'll have you – I – I thank my stars that we've not given up in France all means of punishing hellhounds like you."

"I cannot give you what I haven't got, Citizen," Josette declared calmly, "and I swear to you that I believed that the letters were in the packet which I have given you."

"You lie! You…"

Chabot turned to the officer-in-charge. "Take the strumpet away and remember…" He checked himself and for the next few moments swore and blasphemed; then suddenly changing his tone he said to Josette:

"Listen, little Citizeness; I was only trying to frighten you," and the tiger's snarl became a tabby's purr. "I can see that you are a clever wench. You thought you would fool poor old Chabot, did you not? Thought you would have a bit of a game with him, what?"

He tiptoed round the table till he stood close to Josette; he thrust his grimy finger under her chin, forced her to raise her head: "Pretty dear!" he ejaculated, and pursed his thick lips as if to frame a kiss. But it must be supposed that something in the girl's expression of face caused him to spare her this final outrage: or did he really wish to cajole her? Certain it is that he contented himself with leering at her and ogling the sweet pale face which would have stirred compassion in any heart but that of a fiend.

"So now you've had your fun," he resumed with an artful chuckle, "and we are where we were before, eh? You are going to give me the letters which you went all the way to England to fetch, and I will give you a perfectly bee-ee-autiful safe-conduct for yourself and that handsome young lover of yours – lucky dog! – so that you can go and cuddle and kiss each other wherever you like. Now, I suppose you have hidden those naughty letters somewhere in your pretty little bed and we'll just go there together to fetch them, what?"

Josette made no reply and no movement. What could she do or say? She had only listened with half an ear to that abominable hypocrite's cajoleries. She had no more idea than he had what had become of the letters, or how it was that a packet in appearance exactly like the one which Louise had given her came to be substituted for the original one. She guessed – but only in a vague way – that Citizen Armand had something to do with the substitution, but she could not imagine what his object could possibly have been. While she stood mute and in an absolute whirl of conjecture and of doubt, Chabot waxed impatient.

"Now then, you little baggage," he said, and already he had dropped his insinuating tone, "don't stand there like a wooden image. Do not force me to send you marching along between two soldiers. Lead the way to your room. My friend and I will follow."

"I have already told you, Citizen," Josette maintained firmly, "I know nothing about any packet except the one which I have given you."

"It's a lie!"

"The truth, so help me God! And," she added solemnly, "I do still believe in God."

"Tshah!"

It was just an ejaculation of baffled rage and disappointment. For the next few seconds Chabot, with his hands behind his back, paced up and down the narrow room like a caged panther. He came to a halt presently in front of his colleague.

"What would you do, friend Chauvelin," he asked him, "if you were in my shoes?"

Chauvelin, during all this time, had remained absolutely quiescent, sitting on the bench immediately behind Josette. It was difficult indeed to conjecture if he had taken in all the phases of the scene which had been enacted in this room in the last quarter of an hour: Chabot's violence, Josette's withering contempt had alike left him unmoved. At one time it almost looked as if he slept: his head was down on his breast, his arms were crossed, his eyes closed. But now when directly interpellated by his colleague he seemed to rouse himself and glanced up at the angry face before him.

"Eh?" he queried vaguely. "What did you say, Citizen Representative?"

"Don't go to sleep, man!" the other retorted furiously. "Your neck and mine are in jeopardy while that baggage is allowed to defy me. What shall I do with her?"

"Keep her under guard and perquisition in her room: 'tis simple enough." And Chauvelin's lips curled in a sarcastic smile.

"Perquisition? Why, yes, of course! The simplest thing, is it not?" And Chabot turned to the officer once more. "Sergeant," he commanded, "some of you go find the landlord of this hostelry. Order him to conduct you to the room occupied by the girl Gravier. You will search that room and never leave it until you have found a sealed packet exactly like the one which she laid on the table just now. You understand?"

"Yes, Citizen."

"Then go; and remember," he added significantly, "that packet must be found or there'll be trouble for you for lack of zeal."

"There will be no trouble," the soldier retorted drily.

He turned on his heel and was about to march off with his men when Chauvelin said in a whisper to his friend:

"I would go with them if I were you. You'll want to see that the packet is given to you with the seals unbroken, what?"

"You are right, my friend," the other assented. He signalled to the sergeant, who stood at attention and waited for the distinguished Representative to go out of the room in front of him. In the doorway Chabot turned once more to Chauvelin:

"Look after the hussy while I'm gone," he said, and nodded in the direction of Josette. "I'm leaving some men outside to guard her."

"Have no fear," Chauvelin responded drily; "she'll not run away."

Chabot strode out of the room; the sergeant followed him, and some of the men fell into step and marched in their wake up the passage.

"You can wait outside, Citizen Soldiers!" Chauvelin said to the two men who were standing beside Josette. He had his tricolour scarf on, so there was no questioning his command: the soldiers fell back, turned and marched out of the room, closing the door behind them. And between those four white-washed walls Josette was now alone with Chauvelin.

25

"Was I not right, little one, to carry out that small deception?"

If at the moment when Mother Eve was driven out from the Garden of Eden she had suddenly heard the serpent's voice whispering: "Was I not right to suggest your eating that bit of apple?" she would not have been more astonished than was Josette when that gentle, insinuating voice reached her ears.

She woke as from a dream – from a kind of coma into which she had been plunged by despair. She turned and encountered the kindly familiar glance of Citizen Armand, sitting cross-legged, unmoved on the bench, his head propped against the wall. In the feeble light of the guttering candles he appeared if anything paler than usual, and very tired. Josette gazed on him tongue-tied and puzzled, indeed more puzzled than she had ever felt before during these last few days so full of unexplainable events. As she did not attempt to speak he continued after a moment's pause:

"But for the substitution which I thought it best to effect, your precious letters would now be in the hands of that rogue, and nothing in the world could have saved you and your friend Reversac from death." And again he continued: "The situation would be the same as now but we shouldn't have the letters."

He thrust his long thin hand into the inner pocket of his coat and half drew out a packet, wrapped and sealed just as was the other which had contained the pretended letters. Josette gave a gasp, and with her habitual, pathetic gesture pressed her hands against her heart. It had begun to beat furiously. She would have moved only that Armand put a finger quickly to his lips.

"Sh-sh!" he admonished, and slipped the packet back inside his coat.

There was a murmur of voices outside; one of the soldiers cleared his throat, others shuffled their feet. There were sounds of whisperings, of movements and heavy footsteps the other side of the closed door – reminders that watch was being kept there by order of the Citizen Representative. Josette sank her voice to a whisper:

"And you did that…? For me…? Whilst I…"

"Whilst you called me a traitor and a Judas in your heart," he concluded with a wan smile. "Let's say no more about it."

"You may forgive me… I cannot…"

"Don't let's talk of that," he resumed with a show of impatience. "I only wished you to know that the reason why I didn't interfere between Chabot and yourself was because in the existing state of our friend's temper my interference would have been not only useless but harmful to you and your friend. All I could do was to manoeuvre him into ordering the perquisition in your room and get him to superintend it so as to have the chance of saying these few words to you in private."

"You are right, as you always have been, Citizen Armand," Josette rejoined fervently. "I cannot imagine how I ever came to doubt you."

As if in response to her unspoken request he rose and came across the room to her, gave her the kindest and most gentle of smiles and patted her shoulder.

"Poor little girl!" he murmured softly.

She took hold of his hand and managed to imprint a kiss upon it before he snatched it away.

"You have been such a wonderful friend to me," she sighed. "I shall never doubt you again."

"Even though I were to put your trust to a more severe test than before?" he asked.

"Try me," she rejoined simply.

"Suppose I were to order your arrest…now?… It would only be for a few days," he hastened to assure her.

"I would not doubt you," she declared firmly.

"Only until I can order young Reversac to be brought here."

"Maurice?"

"Yes! For your ultimate release I must have you both here together. You understand?"

"I think I do."

"While one of you is here and the other in Paris, complications can so easily set in, and those fiends might still contrive to play us a trick. But with both of you here, and the letters in my hands, I can negotiate with Chabot for your release and for the necessary safe-conducts. After which you can take the diligence together to Tréport and be in England within three days."

"Yes! yes! I do understand," Josette reiterated, tears of happiness and gratitude welling to her eyes. "And I don't mind prison one little bit, dear Citizen Armand," she added naïvely. "Indeed I don't mind anything that you order me to do. I do trust you absolutely. Absolutely."

"I'll try and make it as easy for you as I can, and with luck I hope to have our friend Reversac here within the week."

Excited and happy, not the least bit frightened, and without the slightest suspicion, Josette saw Chauvelin go to the door, open it and call to the soldiers who were on guard in the passage. She heard him call:

"Which of you is in command here?" She saw one of the men step briskly forward; heard his smart reply:

"I am, Citizen!" and finally her friend's curt command:

"Corporal, you will take this woman, Josephine Gravier, to the Commissariat of Police. You will give her in charge of the Chief Commissary with orders that she be kept under strict surveillance until further orders." He then came across to the table, took up the quill pen that was lying there and a printed paper out of his pocket, scribbled a few words, signed his name and strewed the writing with sand. The tallow candles had now guttered so low, and emitted such a column of black smoke, that he could hardly see: he tried to re-read what he had written and was apparently satisfied, for he handed the paper to the soldier, saying curtly:

"This will explain to the Chief Commissary that the order for this arrest is issued by a member of the Third Sectional Committee of Public Safety – Armand Chauvelin – and that I hereby denounce Josephine Gravier as suspect of treason against the Republic."

The corporal – a middle-aged man in somewhat shabby uniform – took the paper and stood at attention, while Chauvelin, with a peremptory gesture, beckoned to Josette to fall in with the men. Loyal and trusting until the end, the girl even forbore to throw a glance on the treacherous friend who was playing her this cruel trick: she even went to the length of appearing overcome with terror, indeed she played to perfection the role of an unfortunate aristo confronted with treason and preparing for death.

"Now then, young woman," the corporal commanded curtly. Three men were waiting in the passage. With faltering steps and her face buried in her hands, Josette allowed herself to be led out of the room. The corporal was the last to go; the door fell to behind him with a bang. Chauvelin stood for a moment in the centre of the room, listening. He heard the brief word of command, the tramp of heavy feet along the passage in the direction of the front door, the shooting of bolts and rattle of chains. He rubbed his pale, talon-like hands together, and a curious smile played round his thin lips.

"You'll have your work cut out, my gallant Pimpernel," he murmured to himself, "to get the wench away. And even if you do, her lover is still in Paris, and what will you do about him? I think this time..." he added complacently.

Then he paused and once more lent an attentive ear to the sounds that came to him from the other side of the house; to the banging and the stamping, the thuds and thunderings, the loud and strident shoutings and medley of angry voices, all gradually merging into a terrific uproar.

And as he listened the enigmatic smile on his lips turned to a contemptuous sneer.

29

It was late in the evening by now and most of the clients of the hostelry had already retired for the night. Awakened by the terrible hubbub some of them had ventured outside their doors, only to find that the corridors and stairs were patrolled by soldiers, who promptly ordered them back into their rooms. On the downstairs floor the landlord and his wife, in the room adjoining the one which their daughter had shared with Josette Gravier, had been rudely ordered to give up all keys and on peril of their lives not to interfere with the soldiers in the discharge of their duty. The Representative of the People, who had arrived at the hostelry that very evening, appeared to be in a towering rage: he it was who ordered a rigorous search of both the rooms, the landlord vaguely protesting against this outrage put upon his house.

He and his family were, however, soon reduced to silence, as were the guests on the floors above, and the stamping and the banging, the thuds and thunderings, the shouts and imprecations were confined to the two rooms in the house where a squad of soldiers, under the command of their sergeant and egged on by Chabot, carried on a perquisition with ruthless violence.

Within a quarter of an hour there was not a single article of furniture left whole in the place. The men had broken up the flooring, pulled open every drawer, smashed every lock: they had ripped up the mattresses and pillows and pulled the curtains down from their rods. Chabot, stalking about from one room to the other with great strides and arms akimbo, cursed the soldiers loudly for their lack of zeal.

"Did I not say," he bellowed like a raging bull, "that those letters must be found?"

The sergeant was at his wits' ends. The two rooms did, indeed, look in the feeble light of the hanging lamp above as if a Prussian cannon had exploded in their midst. The landlord with his wife and daughter cowered terror-stricken in a corner.

"Never," they protested with sobs, "never has such an indignity been put upon this house."

"You should not have taken in such baggage," Chabot retorted roughly.

"Citizen Chauvelin gave orders..."

"Never mind about Citizen Chauvelin. I am giving you orders, here and now."

He strode across the room and came to a halt in front of the three unfortunates. They struggled to their feet and clung to one another in terror before the fearsome Representative of the People. Indeed, Chabot at this moment, with face twisted into a mask of fury, with hair hanging in fantastic curls over his brow, with eyes bloodshot and curses spluttering out of his quivering lips, looked almost inhuman in his overwhelming rage.

"The hussy who slept in here...?" he demanded.

"Yes, Citizen?"

"She had a sealed packet – a small packet about the size of my hand...?"

"Yes, Citizen."

"What did she do with it?"

"It was stolen from her, Citizen Representative, the first night she slept in this house," the landlord explained, his voice quaking with fear.

"So she averred," the woman put in trembling.

"Did any of you see it?"

They all three shook their heads.

"The girl didn't sleep in this room that night, Citizen," the woman explained. "She shared a room with two female travellers who left the next day on the diligence. Citizen Chauvelin then gave orders for her to sleep in my daughter's room and made us responsible for her safety."

Chabot glanced over his shoulder at the sergeant.

"Find out in the morning," he commanded, "at the Commissariat all about the female travellers and whither they went, and report to me." He then turned back to the landlord. "And do you mean to tell me that none of you saw anything of that sealed packet supposed to have been stolen? Think again," he ordered roughly.

"I never set eyes on it, Citizen," the man declared. "Nor I, I swear it!" both the two women averred. Chabot kept the wretched family in suspense for a few minutes after that, gloating over their misery and their fear of him, while his bloodshot eyes glared into their faces. Behind him the sergeant now stood at attention, waiting for further orders. There was nothing more to be done, since every nook and cranny had been ransacked, and short of pulling down the walls no further search was possible. But Chabot's lust of destruction was not satisfied. He had the feeling at this moment that he wanted to set fire to the house and see it burned to the ground, together with that elusive packet of letters which meant more than life to him.

"Sergeant!" he cried, and was on the point of giving the monstrous order when a quiet, dry voice suddenly broke in: "There are other ways than fire and brimstone, my friend, of recovering what you desire to possess."

Chabot swung round with an angry snarl and saw Armand Chauvelin standing in the doorway, a placid, slender figure in sober black with inscrutable face and smooth unruffled hair.

"The hussy?" Chabot yelled, his voice husky with choler.

"She is safer than she was when you left her half an hour ago, for I've had her arrested and sent to the Commissary of the district under a denunciation from me. She is safe there for the present, but she certainly won't be for long if you spend your time raving and swearing and pulling the house down about our ears."

"What the devil do you mean – she won't be safe for long? Why not?"

"Because," Chauvelin replied with earnest significance, "there are influences at work about here which will be exerted to their utmost power to get the wench out of your clutches."

"I care nothing about the wench," Chabot muttered under his breath. "It's those accursed letters..."

"Exactly," Chauvelin broke in quietly, "the letters." Chabot was silent for a moment or two, swallowing the blasphemies that forced themselves to his lips. He glared with mixed feelings of wrath and vague terror into those pale, deep-set eyes that regarded him with unconcealed contempt. Something in their glance seemed to hypnotise him and to weaken his will. After a time his own glance fell; he cleared his throat, tugged at his waistcoat and passed his grimy, moist palm over his curly hair. And in order to gain further control over his nerves he buried his hands in his breeches pockets and started once more to pace up and down the room. The soldiers had lined up in the passage outside: their sergeant had stepped back against the doorway and was doing his best not to smile at the Citizen Representative's discomfiture.

"You are right," Chabot said at last to Chauvelin with a semblance of calm. "We must talk the matter of the letters over before we decide what we do with the baggage."

Then he turned to the sergeant.

"Which are the men who took the wench to the Commissariat?" he asked.

"I don't think they are back, Citizen," the sergeant replied.

"Don't think!" Chabot snarled. "Go and find out."

The man moved away and Chabot called after him:

"Report to me in the public room – you'll find me there."

He gave a sign to Chauvelin. "Let's go!" he said curtly. "The sight of this room makes me see red."

He did not throw another glance on the unfortunate landlord and his family, the victims of his unreasoning rage. They stood in the midst of their devastated room looking utterly forlorn, not knowing yet if they had anything more to fear. The house appeared singularly still after the uproar of a while ago, only the measured tread of soldiers patrolling the corridors echoed weirdly through the gloom.

Chabot stalked on ahead of his colleague and made his way to the public room. There he threw himself into a convenient chair and sprawled across the nearest table, ordering the man in charge to bring him a bottle of wine. Then he called loudly to his colleague to come and join him.

But Chauvelin did not respond to the call. He turned into the small private room where the fateful interview had just taken place. He closed the door, locked and bolted it. He then went across to the window and examined its shutter. It was barred as before. There was no fear that he would be interrupted in the task which now lay before him. The candles had burned down almost to their sockets: Chauvelin picked up the snuffers and trimmed the wicks. Then he sat down at the table and drew the original sealed packet out of his breast pocket.

The time had come to break the seals. There was no longer any reason to keep the packet intact. The first act in the drama which he had devised for his own advancement and the destruction of his powerful enemy had been a brilliant success. The wench Josette Gravier and her lover were both in prison – one in Rouen, the other in Paris. Such a situation would of a certainty arouse the sympathy of the Scarlet Pimpernel and induce him to exert that marvellous ingenuity of his for the rescue of the two young people. But this time Chauvelin was more accurately forewarned than he had ever been before. All he need do was keep a close eye on the wench; the English spy, however elusive he might be, must of necessity attempt to get in touch with the girl, and unless he had the power of rendering himself invisible, his capture was bound to follow. It may safely be said that no fear of failure assailed Chauvelin at this hour. He considered his enemy as good as captured already. It would be a triumph for his perseverance, his inventive genius and his patriotism! Once more he would become a power in the land, the master of these men – these venal cowardly fools – who would again fawn at his feet after this and suffer at his hands for all the humiliation they had heaped upon him these past two years.

The compromising letters would be an additional weapon wherewith to chastise these arrogant upstarts – not excluding the powerful Danton himself, perhaps not even Robespierre. Armand Chauvelin saw himself on the very pinnacle of popularity, the veritable ruler of France. To what height of supreme power could not he aspire, who had brought such an inveterate enemy of revolutionary France to death?

And all the while that these pleasant thoughts, these happy anticipations ran through Armand Chauvelin's mind, his delicate hands toyed with the packet of letters – the keystone that held together the edifice of his future. He fingered it lovingly as he had done many a time before. Here it was just as it had been when Picard placed it in his hands: he had never broken the seals, never seen its contents, never set eyes on the letters which caused men like Chabot, Bazire and Fabre d'Eglantine and even the popular Danton to tremble for their lives. But now that the first act of the little comedy which he had devised had been successfully enacted in this very room, he felt that he could indulge his natural curiosity to probe into the secrets of these men. He felt eager and excited. These letters might reveal secrets that would be a still more powerful leverage than he had hoped for the fulfilment of his ambition.

His fingers shook slightly as they broke the seals. The wrapper fell apart just as that other had done in Chabot's hands, and the contents were revealed to Chauvelin's horror-filled gaze. For here were no letters either; like the wrapper and like the seals the contents were the same as those which had turned Citizen Chabot from a human being into a raging beast: scraps of paper made to appear like letters – nothing more!

Chauvelin stared at them and stared; his pale, deep-set eyes were aflame, his temples throbbed, his whole body shook as with ague. What did the whole thing mean?

Where did this monstrous deception begin? What was the initial thread which bound this amazing conspiracy together? Did it have its origin in Bastien de Croissy's tortured brain – in that of his despairing widow? Or did that seemingly guileless girl after all…? But no! this, of course, was nonsense. Chauvelin passed his trembling hand over his burning forehead. He felt as if he had been stunned by a heavy blow on the head. Idly he allowed the scraps of paper to glide in and out between his fingers. There was not a word written on any of them. Mere empty scraps of paper!… All save one!… Mechanically Chauvelin picked that one up…it was soiled and creased, more so than the others. He passed his hand over it to smooth it out. The candles were guttering and smoking again…he could hardly see…his eyes, too, were dim – not with tears, of course; just with a kind of film which threw a crimson blur over everything. He was compelled to blink once or twice before he could decipher the words on that one scrap of paper. He did succeed in the end, but only read the first few words:

"We seek him here…"

That maddening doggerel, the sight of which had so often been to him the precursor of some awful disaster! For the first time in his career Chauvelin felt a sense of discouragement. He had been so full of hope only a few minutes ago – so full of certainty. This awful disappointment came like a terrific, physical crash upon his aching head. With arms stretched out upon the table, that one scrap of paper crushed in his hand, he thought of the many failures which had gradually brought him down from his exalted rank to one of humiliation. Calais, Boulogne, Paris, Nantes and many more – and now this! He had felt it coming when his enemy had so impudently faced him in the public room of this hostelry. The big fat sailor – that unmistakable laugh – the pepper-pot to remind him of his greatest discomfiture over at the *Chat Gris* in Calais: these and more all seemed to flit past Chauvelin's fevered brain in this moment of bitter disappointment. He had even ceased to think of Josette, communing only with the past. The minutes sped by; the old Normandy clock ticked away, majestic and indifferent.

A few minutes later Chabot's clamorous voice broke in on the lonely man's meditations. He roused himself from his apathy, threw a quick glance around. Then as the familiar voice drew nearer and nearer he gathered the scraps of paper hastily together and thrust them in his pocket out of sight. He went to the door and opened it just in time to meet his colleague, whose walk was not as steady as it had been when rage alone had governed his movements. Since then a bottle of red wine and one of heady Normandy cider had gone to his head; his lips sagged and his eyes were bleary. Lurching forward he nearly fell into Chauvelin's arms.

"I have been waiting for you for half an hour," the latter said with a show of reproach. "What in the world have you been doing?"

"I was in a high fever," Chabot muttered thickly. "A raging thirst I had – must have a drink…"

"Sit down there," Chauvelin commanded, for the man could hardly stand. "We must have more light."

"Yes…more light… I hate this gloom…"

Chabot fell into a chair; he stretched his arms over the table and buried his head in the crook of his elbow, and was soon breathing audibly. Chauvelin looked down on him with bitter contempt. What a partner in this great undertaking which he already had in mind! However, there was nothing for it now…this drunken lout was the only man who could lend him a hand at this juncture. He clapped his hands, and after a moment or two the maid in charge appeared. Chauvelin ordered her to bring more candles and a jug of cold water.

Chabot was snoring. With scant ceremony Chauvelin dashed the water over his head. The maid retired, grinning.

"What in hell…?" Chabot cried out, thus rudely awakened from his slumbers.

The cold water had partially sobered him. He blinked for a time into the fluttering candle-light, the water dripping down the tousled strands of his hair and the furrows of his cheeks.

"We've got to review the situation," Chauvelin began drily.

He sat down opposite Chabot, leaning his elbows on the table, his thin veined hands tightly clasped together.

"The situation?" Chabot iterated dully. "Yes, by Satan!…that hussy…what?"

"Never mind about the hussy now! You are still anxious, I imagine, that certain letters which gravely compromise you and your party do not fall into the hands, say, of the *Moniteur* or the *Père Duchesne* for publication."

Chauvelin spoke slowing and deliberately so as to allow every word to sink into the consciousness of that sot. In this he succeeded, for at mention of those fateful letters the last cloud of drunkenness seemed to vanish from the man's sodden brain. Rage and fear had once more sole possession of him.

"You swore," he countered roughly, "that you would get those letters…"

"And so I will," Chauvelin returned calmly, "but you must do your best to help."

"You have allowed yourself to be hoodwinked by a young baggage – you..."

"If you take up that tone with me, my friend," Chauvelin suddenly said in a sharp, peremptory tone, fixing his colleague with a stern eye, "I will throw up the sponge at once and let the man who now has the letters do his damnedest with them."

The threat had the same effect on Chabot as the douche of cold water. He swallowed his choler and said almost humbly:

"What is it you want me to do?"

"I'll tell you. First, about the packet of letters..."

"Yes!...the packet of letters – the real packet... Who has it – where is it?... I want to know..." And with each phrase he uttered Chabot beat on the table with the palm of his hand, while Chauvelin's quick brain was at work on the last phases of his tortuous scheme.

"I'll tell you," he replied quietly, "who stole the packet of letters from the girl Gravier. It was the English spy who is known under the name of 'the Scarlet Pimpernel.' "

"How do you know?"

"Never mind how I know: I do know. Let that be sufficient! But as true as that you and I are alive at this moment the Scarlet Pimpernel has those letters in his possession..."

"And he can send the lot of us to the guillotine?" Chabot interposed in a raucous whisper.

"He certainly will," Chauvelin retorted drily, "unless..."

"Unless what? Speak, man, unless you wish to see me fall dead at your feet!"

"...unless we can capture him, of course."

"But they say he is as elusive as a ghost. Why, you yourself..."

"I know that. He is not as elusive as you think. I have tried – and failed – that is true. But never before have I had the help of an influential man like you."

Chabot bridled at the implied flattery.

"I'll help you," he said, "of course."

"Then listen, Citizen. Although we have not got the letters, we hold what we might call the trump card in this game…"

"The trump card?"

"Yes, the girl Gravier. I told you I had ordered her arrest…"

"True, but…"

"She is at the present moment at the Commissariat, under strict surveillance…"

Chabot jumped to his feet, glared into his colleague's pale face and brought his heavy fist crashing down upon the table.

"You lie!" he shrieked at the top of his voice. "She is not at the Commissariat."

Chauvelin shrugged.

"Where, then?" he asked coolly.

"The devil knows – I don't!"

It was Chauvelin's turn to stare into his colleague's eyes. Was the man still drunk, or had he gone mad?

"You'd oblige me, Citizen," he said coolly, "by not talking in riddles."

"Riddles?" the other mocked. "Tscha! I tell you that that bit of baggage whom you ordered to be taken to the Commissariat never got there at all."

"Never got there?" Chauvelin queried with a frown. "You are joking, Citizen."

"Joking, am I? Let me tell you this: the sergeant and the soldiers whom I sent to inquire after the wench came back half an hour ago and this is what they reported: neither the soldiers nor the hussy were seen at the Commissiariat…"

"But where…?"

"Where the wench is no one knows. The Commissary at once sent out a patrol. They found the four soldiers in the public garden behind St Ouen, their legs tied together by their belts, their caps doing duty as gags in their mouths; but not a sign of the girl."

"Well – and?"

"The soldiers were interrogated. They are all under arrest now, the cowardly traitors! They declared that while they crossed the garden on their way to the Commissariat they were suddenly attacked from behind without any warning. They had seen no one and hadn't heard a sound: the place was pitch dark and entirely deserted. It seems that the lights have been abolished in this God-forsaken city ever since oil and tallow got so dear, and the townsfolk avoid going through the garden, as it is the haunt of every evil-doer in Rouen. The men swore that they did their best to defend themselves, but that they were outnumbered and outclassed. Anyway, the miscreants, whoever they were, brought them down, bound and gagged them and then made off in the darkness, taking the wench with them."

"But didn't the men see anything? Were they footpads who attacked them, or – or...?"

"The devil only knows! Two of the soldiers declared that they were attacked by men in the same uniform that they wore themselves, and one thought that he recognised a sailor whom he had seen about on the quay the last day or two – a huge, powerful fellow, whose fist would fell an ox."

"Ah?"

"Anyway, the hell-hounds made off in the direction of the river."

"Ah?" Chauvelin remarked again.

"Why do you say 'Ah?' like that?" Chabot queried roughly. "Do you know anything of this affair?"

"No, but it does confirm what I said just now."

"What's that?"

"That those infernal English spies are at work here."

"Why do you say that?"

"Everything points to it: the mode of attack, the disappearance of the girl, the big sailor. Footpads would not have attacked soldiers with empty pockets, nor would they have carried off a girl who has neither friends nor relations to pay ransom for her."

"That's true."

"When did the sergeant tell you all this?"

"Not so long ago – might be a quarter of an hour…"

"Why didn't you let me know at once?"

"It was none of your business. I am here to give orders, not you."

"And what orders did you give? You didn't seem to be in a fit condition to give any orders at all."

"Rage at being baffled again went to my head. If you had not taken it upon yourself to order that girl's arrest…"

"You were about to tell me," Chauvelin broke in harshly, "what orders you gave to the sergeant."

"I ordered him to bring the four delinquents here, as I wish to interrogate them."

"Well – and are they here?"

"Wait, Citizen – all in good time! The sergeant had to go to the Commissariat – then he would have to…"

"I know all that," the other interrupted impatiently. He went to the door and opened it, clapped his hands and waited until the night-watchman came shuffling along the corridor.

"As soon as the sergeant returns," he said to the man, "bring him in here."

Chabot opened his mouth in order to protest; he was jealous of his prerogatives as a Representative of the People, a position of far greater authority than a mere member of the Committee of Public Safety. But there was something in Chauvelin's quiet assumption of command that overawed him and he felt shrunken and insignificant under the other's contemptuous glance. His ugly mouth closed with a snap, and he saw the watchman depart with a glowering look in his eyes. He sat down again by the table and stared stupidly into vacancy; his clumsy fingers toyed with the objects on the table; his thin legs were stretched straight out before him. Now and then he glanced towards the open door and listened to the several sounds which still resounded through the house.

Although the guests had been peremptorily ordered to keep to their rooms they could not be prevented from moving about and whispering among themselves, since sleep had become impossible. The uproar of a while ago, when furniture was being smashed and floors and walls were battered, had awakened them all from their first sleep. Since then vague terror and the ceaseless tramping of soldiers who patrolled the house had kept everyone on the alert. The unfortunate landlord and his family had taken refuge in a vacant room, but for them, more so than for any of their clients, sleep was impossible.

Thus, a constant, if subdued, hubbub reigned throughout the house. Chabot seemed to find a measure of comfort in listening to it all. Like so many persons who profess atheism, he was very superstitious, and all the talk about the mysterious spy, who worked in the dark and was as elusive as a ghost, had exacerbated his nerves. Chauvelin, on the other hand, paced up and down the room; his thin hands were tightly clasped behind his back, his head was down on his chest. His busy mind was ceaselessly at work. Obviously he had lost the first round in this new game which he had engaged in against the Scarlet Pimpernel. And not only that: he had lost what he had so aptly termed the *trump card* in the game. Josette Gravier was just the type of female in distress who would appeal to the adventurous spirit of Sir Percy Blakeney: while she was a prisoner in Rouen the Scarlet Pimpernel would not vacate the field, and there would have been a good chance of laying him by the heels. There was none now that the girl was in safety, for Chauvelin knew from experience that there was no getting prisoners like her out of the clutches of the Scarlet Pimpernel, once that prince of adventurers had them under his guard.

Indeed, the Terrorist would have felt completely baffled but for one fact – yet another trump card which he still held and which if judiciously played…

At this point his reflections were interrupted by the arrival of the sergeant, followed by the four delinquent soldiers. This time Chauvelin made no attempt to interfere. Let Chabot question the men if he wished. He, Chauvelin, knew everything they could possibly say. He listened with half an ear to the interrogatory, only catching a word or a phrase here and there: "We saw nothing…we heard nothing… They were on us like a lightning flash… Yes, we had our bayonets…impossible to use them… It was dark as pitch… They wore the uniform of the National Guard…the same as ours, at least as far as one could see in the dark…all except one, and he looked like a boatman…a huge fellow with a powerful fist… I had seen him on the quay before…and here in the public room… How could we use our bayonets?… They were dressed the same as we were… They hit about with their fists…the big sailor felled me down…and me too… I saw stars… So did I… When I recovered my legs were tied together and my woollen cap was stuffed into my mouth…" and more in the same strain.

The city gates being closed after dark no one could possibly pass them before dawn on the morrow, but there was always the river and no end to the ingenuity and daring of the Scarlet Pimpernel. But there was that last trump card – the ace, Chauvelin fondly hoped.

When Chabot finally dismissed the soldiers the two men once more put their heads together.

"There is not much we can do about the girl Gravier," Chauvelin remarked drily. "Luckily, we hold the man Reversac. It is with him we can deal now."

"The girl's lover?" the other asked.

"Of course."

"I see what you mean."

"Lucky that you do," Chauvelin mocked. "You know where he is, I presume."

"In the Abbaye. I had him taken there myself. A stroke of genius, methinks," he added complacently, "to have the fellow arrested."

"Well, you have had a pretty free hand these last few weeks while that cursed English spy turned his attention to our friend Carrier at Nantes."

"I suppose the death of all those priests and women appealed to him… As for me…"

"So did Josette Gravier as your victim appeal to him, and so will Maurice Reversac."

"Thank our friend Satan, we've got him safe enough!"

"Yes, he is our trump card," Chauvelin concluded, "and we must play him for all he is worth."

He renewed his pacing up and down the room, while Chabot, quite sober now but with not two ideas in his muddled brain, stared stupidly in front of him.

"Paris will not do," Chauvelin resumed after a little while, mumbling to himself rather than speaking to his colleague. "That damned Pimpernel has too many spies and friends there and hidden lairs we know nothing about."

"Eh? What did you say?" Chabot queried tartly.

"I said that we must get Reversac away from Paris."

"Why? We've got him safe enough."

"You have not," Chauvelin asserted forcefully. He came to a halt the other side of the table, and fixing his pale eyes on Chabot asked him: "Have you ever asked Fouquier-Tinville how many prisoners have escaped from Paris alone through the agency of the Scarlet Pimpernel?"

"No, but…"

"Considerably over two hundred since the beginning of this year."

"I don't believe it!"

"It's true, I tell you; and the same number from Nantes. Carrier is at his wits' end."

"Carrier is a fool."

"Perhaps. But you understand now why I want to get Reversac away from Paris. By dint of bribery if nothing else, the Scarlet Pimpernel will drag him out of your clutches."

Chabot reflected for a moment, and Chauvelin, guessing the workings of his mind, added with earnest significance:

"If we lose Reversac we shall have nothing to offer in exchange for the letters."

"The letters…" Chabot murmured vaguely. "Yes," Chauvelin remarked drily: "you haven't found them, have you?"

By way of a reply Chabot uttered a savage oath. "Where the girl is, there are the letters," the other went on, "get that into your head, and the letters are in the possession of the English spies. Now remember one thing, my friend: while we hold the girl's lover we can still get the letters, by offering a safe-conduct in exchange for them. And incidentally – don't forget that – we have the chance of laying our hands on the Scarlet Pimpernel, for whose capture there is a reward of ten thousand livres."

As Chabot had exhausted his vocabulary of curses he relieved his feelings this time by blaspheming.

"Ten thousand," he ejaculated.

"Not to mention the glory."

"Damn the glory! But I hate to let the baggage and her lover go."

"You need not."

"How do you mean – I need not? You've just mentioned safe-conducts…"

"So I did. But I can endorse those with a secret sign. It is known to every chief Commissary in France and nullifies every safe-conduct."

"Splendid!" Chabot exclaimed and beat the table with the palm of his hand. "Splendid!" he exclaimed and jumped to his feet. "Now I begin to understand."

The two men exchanged roles for the moment. It was Chabot now who paced up and down the room, mumbling to himself, while Chauvelin sat down at the table and with idle hands toyed with the quill pen, the snuffers, or anything that was handy. Presently Chabot came to a standstill in front of him.

"You want to get Reversac away from Paris?" he asked.

"Yes."

"And bring him here?"

"Yes."

"The journey down will be dangerous if, as you say, the English spies are on the war-path."

"We must minimise the danger as far as we can."

"How?"

"A strong escort. And there will be the additional chance of capturing the Scarlet Pimpernel."

"You think he will be sure to try and get at Reversac?"

"Absolutely certain."

"And forewarned is forearmed, what?"

"Exactly."

"Splendid!" Chabot reiterated gleefully.

"And if we succeed in capturing one or more of those confounded spies, just think how marvellous our position will be with regard to the letters. We shall have something to bargain with, eh?"

"The Scarlet Pimpernel himself?"

"The whole damned crowd of them, as well as the girl and her lover!"

"You can have the lot," Chabot ejaculated, "so long as I have the accursed letters!"

"If you follow my instructions, point by point," Chauvelin concluded, "I can safely promise you those."

They sat together for another hour after that, elaborating Chauvelin's plan, lingering over every detail, leaving nothing to chance, gloating over the victory which they felt was assured.

It was midnight before they finally went to bed. And at break of day Chabot was already posting for Paris armed with instructions from Chauvelin to the secret agents of the Committee of Public Safety.

30

Snow lay thick on the ground; it was heavy going up the hills and slippery coming down. In an ordinary way the diligence between Meulon and Rouen would have ceased to ply in weather as severe as this. Already at Meulon, when an early start was made, the clouds had looked threatening. "We'll have more snow, for sure," everyone had declared, the driver included, who muttered something about its being madness to attempt the journey with those leaden-coloured clouds hanging overhead.

But in spite of these protests and warnings a start was made in the early dawn. Such were the orders of Citizen Representative Chabot (Loire et Cher), who was travelling in the diligence, and his word, of course, was law. Outside the hostelry of the *Mouton Blanc* a small crowd had gathered despite the early hour, to watch the departure of the diligence. All along people, who stood about at a respectful distance because of the soldiers, declared that this was no ordinary diligence. Though it was one of the small ones with just the coupé and the rotonde, it was drawn by four horses with postilion and all the banquette behind the driver was unoccupied, although the awning was up, and this was odd, declared the gaffers, because the banquette places being the cheapest, three or four passengers usually crowded there, under the lee, too, of the luggage piled upon the top.

In the coupé sat the Citizen Representative himself, and he had that compartment entirely to himself. In the rotonde there was a young man sitting between two soldiers in uniform, and three other men were on the seats opposite. Moreover, and this was the most amazing circumstance of all, what looked at first sight like the usual pile of luggage on the top was no luggage at all, but three men lying huddled up under the tarpaulin, wrapped in greatcoats, for it was bitterly cold up there.

No! It decidedly was no ordinary diligence. And it was under strong escort, too: six mounted men under the command of an officer – a captain, what? So not only was the traveller in the coupé a great personage, but the prisoner must also be one of consequence, for no sooner was he installed with the soldiers in the rotonde than the blinds were at once drawn down, nor was anyone allowed to come nigh the vehicle after that. Naturally all this secrecy and the unusual proceedings created further amazement still, but those quidnuncs who came as near as they dared were quickly and peremptorily ordered back by the soldiers: and later in the day, at Vernon outside the *Boule d'Or*, two boys, who had after the manner of such youngsters succeeded in crawling underneath the coach, were caught when on the point of stepping on the foot-board. The captain in command of the guards seized them both by the ears and ordered them to be soundly flogged then and there, which was done by a couple of soldiers with a will and the buckle end of their belts. The howls that ensued and the sudden report of a pistol-shot, discharged no one could ever tell whence, startled the horses into a panic. The leaders reared, the ostler unable to hold them fell, and fortunately rolled over unhurt in the snow. A more serious catastrophe was just averted through the presence of mind of a passer-by, a poor old vagabond shivering with cold, who did not look as if he had any vitality in him, let alone the pluck to seize the near leader by the bridle as he did and bring the frightened team to a standstill.

The driver and the postilion were having a drink of mulled cider at the moment that all this commotion was going on. They came rushing out of the hostelry just in time to witness the prowess of that miserable old man. The driver was gracious enough to murmur approbation, and even the captain of the guard had something pleasant to say.

It had been so very neatly done.

"I was a stud-groom once," the old man explained with a self-deprecating shrug, "in the house of aristos. 'Tis not much I don't know about horses."

The captain tendered him a few sous.

"This is for your pains, Citizen," he said, and nodded in the direction of the hostelry close by: "you'd better go in there and get a hot drink."

"Thank you kindly, Citizen Captain," the man rejoined as his thin hands, blue with cold, closed over the money. He seemed loth to go away from the horses. They were fine, strong beasts, relays just taken up here and vety fresh. The poor man had evidently spoken the truth: there was not much he did not know about horses. One could see that from the way he looked at them and handled them, adjusting a buckle here and there, fondling the beasts' manes, their ears and velvety noses, inspecting their fetlocks and their shoes.

"Good smith's work here," he said approvingly, tapping one shoe after another.

"That's all right, my man," the Captain broke in impatiently. "We must be off now. You go and get your drink."

The vagabond demurred and looked down with a rueful glance on his ragged clothes.

"I can't go in there," he said with a woebegone shake of the head, "not in these rags. The landlord doesn't like it," he went on, "because of other customers…"

The Captain gave a shrug. He didn't really care what happened to that wretched caitiff. Indeed, he was anxious to get away as he had been ordered by the Citizen Representative to make Gaillon before dark. Citizen Chabot was not a man to be lightly disobeyed, and as he had suffered much from cold and discomfort his temper throughout this journey had been of the vilest. So losing no more time the Captain now turned on his heel and went to give orders to his men. The young postilion, more charitably disposed, perhaps, towards the poor wretch, or in less of a hurry to make a start, said:

"I'll bring you out a drink, old gaffer," and he ran back into the hostelry, leaving the driver and the whilom stud-groom to exchange reminiscences of past aristo stablings. He returned after a couple of minutes with a mug of steaming cider in his hand.

"Here you are, Citizen," he said.

The vagabond took the mug but seemed in no hurry to drink. He had a fit of coughing and swayed backwards and forwards on his long legs as if already he had had a drop too much. The driver, in the meanwhile, took the opportunity of administering correction to the ostler for failing to hold the horses properly when they shied, and for rolling about in the snow when he should have held on tightly to the bridles.

"Call yourself a stableman," he said contemptuously while the postilion stood by, grinning: "why, look at this poor man here..."

But the "poor man here" seemed in a sorry plight just now. The coughing fit shook him so that the steaming cider squirted out of the mug.

"Let me hold the mug for you, old man," the postilion suggested.

"You drink it, Citizen," the man said between gasps. "I can't. It makes me sick."

Nothing loth, the postilion had a drink, was indeed on the point of draining the mug when the driver with a "Here! I say!" took the mug from him and drank the remainder of the cider down.

Chabot put his head out of the window: "Now then, over there!" he called out with a loud curse. And "*En avant!*" came in peremptory command from the captain of the guard. The driver made ready to climb up on the box when the old vagabond touched him on the shoulder: "You wouldn't give me a lift," he suggested timidly, "would you, Citizen?"

"Not I," the other retorted gruffly. "I daren't...not without orders." And he nodded in the direction of the captain.

"He wouldn't know," the poor man whispered. "When you move off I'll climb on the step. I'll keep close behind you and hide in the banquette under cover of the luggage. They couldn't see from the back... My home is in Gaillon and it's three leagues to walk in this damnable weather!"

He looked so sick and so miserable that the driver hesitated. He was possessed of bowels of compassion, even though he was a paid servant of the most cruel, most ruthless government in the world. But despite his feelings of pity for a fellow-creature he would probably have refused point-blank to take up an extra passenger without permission but for the fact that he was not feeling very well just then. That last mugful of steaming cider, coupled with the action of the cold frosty air, had sent the blood to up his head. His temples began to throb furiously and he felt giddy; indeed he had some difficulty in climbing up to his box and never noticed that the vagabond was so close on his heels. Fortunately the Captain at the rear of the coach noticed nothing: he and the soldiers were busy getting to horse. As for Chabot, he had once more curled himself up in the corner of the coupé and was already fast asleep.

Once installed on the box with the reins in his hands the driver felt better, but even so he was comforted by the knowledge that the ex-stud-groom had installed himself behind him. The man was so handy with horses – far more handy than that young postilion – and if that giddy feeling were to return...

It did, about half a league beyond Vernon. That awful sense of giddiness and unconquerable drowsiness! And it was not a moment ago that he had noticed the postilion's strange antics on his horse, his swaying till he nearly fell, and the rolling of his head.

"What the devil can it be?" he muttered to himself when that nasty sick feeling seemed completely to master him. What a comfort it was to feel a pair of strong hands take the reins out of his. Whose those hands were he was too sleepy to guess, and it was so pleasant, so restful, to close one's eyes and to sleep. Daylight was fast drawing in, and with twilight down came the snow: not large, heavy, smooth flakes but nasty thin sleet, which a head wind drove straight into one's face, and which fretted and teased the horses already over-excited by certain judicious touches of the whip. As for the postilion, it was as much as he could do to keep his seat. It was only the instinct of self-preservation that kept him on the horse's back at all.

It was a bad time, too, for the soldiers. They had to keep their heads down against the wind and the driven snow, and to put spur to their horses at the same time, for the diligence, which had lumbered along slowly enough up to now, had taken on sudden speed, and the team galloped up every hill it came to in magnificent style.

Chabot once more thrust his head out of the window and shouted: "Holà!" He had been asleep ever since that halt at Vernon, but this abrupt lurching of the coach had not only wakened but also frightened him.

"Why the hell are you driving like a fury?" he cried. But the head wind drowned his shouts and his reiterated cries of "Holà!"

The horses did not relax speed. Someone was holding the reins who knew how and when to urge them on, and the sensitive creatures responded with a will to the expert touch. It was as much as the mounted men could do to keep up with the coach.

It was not until the Captain chanced to look that way and caught sight of the Citizen Representative's head out of the coupé window, and of his arms gesticulating wildly, that he called out "Halte-là!" whereupon the diligence came immediately to a standstill. Instinct caused driver and postilion to pull themselves together, for the Citizen Representative's voice, husky with rage and fear, was raised above the howling of the wind.

"Tell that fool," he yelled, "not to drive like a fury! He will have us in the ditch directly."

"It is getting dark," the driver made effort to retort, "and this infernal snow is fretting the horses. We must make Gaillon soon."

"At least you know your way, Citizen?" the captain asked.

"Know my way?" the other mumbled. "Haven't I been on this road for over fifteen years?"

"*En evant,* then!" the captain ordered once more.

The horses tossed their heads in the keen, cold air, and forward lurched the clumsy diligence. The driver clicked his tongue and made a feeble attempt at cracking his whip. It was not so much giddy that he felt now but more intolerably sleepy than before.

"Give me back the reins, Citizen," a soothing voice whispered in his ear. The driver thought it might be the devil who had spoken, for who else could it be in this infernal weather and this blinding snow? Who but a devil would want to drive this cursed diligence? But he really didn't care…devil or no he was too infernally sleepy to resist, and the reins were taken out of his hands as before and firmly held above his head. He ventured on a peep round under the awning of the banquette, but all he could see was a pair of legs, set wide apart, with the strong knees that looked as if chiselled in stone, and the powerful hands holding the reins. He remembered the vagabond who climbed up to the banquette behind him and had apparently escaped the officer's notice.

"That old vagabond," he muttered to himself, and then added grudgingly: "He does know how to handle horses."

Another three leagues at galloping speed. But twilight was now sinking into the arms of night. Whoever was holding the reins had the eyes of a cat, for the postilion was no use. But surely Gaillon could not be far. From Vernon it was only a matter of three leagues altogether, and why was the river on the left and not on the right of the road? And why was it so narrow, more like the Eure than the Seine? Its slender winding ribbon gleamed through the bare branches of the willow trees, its icy surface defying the gloom.

"Where the hell…!" the driver mumbled to himself from time to time as his bleary eyes roamed over the landscape. Some little way ahead a few cottages and a church with square tower loomed out of the snow, the tiny windows blinking like sleepy eyes through the sparse intervening trees. But this was certainly not Gaillon. The driver rubbed his eyes. He was suddenly very wide awake. He snatched at the reins, held them tight and the team came to a halt, the steam rising like a cloud from their quivering cruppers. The captain swore and called loudly: "*En avant!*" and then: "Is this Gaillon?" He rode up abreast of the driver. "Is this Gaillon?" he iterated, pointing to the distant village.

"No, it's not," the driver replied. "At least…"

"Then where the devil are we?"

And the driver scratched his head and vowed he was damned if he knew!

"Must have taken the wrong turning," he said ruefully.

"You said you had been on this road for over fifteen years."

"But not," the driver growled, "in such confounded weather." He went on muttering about the usual way of diligences…they did not ply in the winter, save in settled weather…sometimes one was caught in a snowstorm, but not often…and it was not fit for horses with all that snow on the ground…it had been madness to start from Mantes this morning and expect to make Gaillon by nightfall. And more to this effect, while the officer with eyes trying to pierce the gloom was evidently debating within himself whether he should beard the irate Representative of the People and rouse him from sleep.

"Where did you miss your road?" he asked roughly. And: "Can't we go back?"

"The only turning I know," the driver muttered, "is close to Vernon. We should have to go back three leagues..."

This time the captain blasphemed. Curses were no longer adequate.

"What's the name of that village?" he queried when he had exhausted most of his vocabulary. "Do you know?"

The driver did not.

"Is there a hostelry where we can commandeer shelter for the night?"

"Sure to be," the other rejoined.

"*En evant*, then!"

The driver did a good deal more muttering and grumbling and hard swearing when he heard the captain say finally: "The Citizen Representative will have something unpleasant to say to you about this delay."

Something unpleasant! Something unpleasant! He, too, would have something unpleasant to say to that old vagabond who did know all about horses and nothing about the way to Gaillon. Where they were now, the devil knew! He himself had been on the main road for fifteen years. Paris, Mantes, Vernon, Rouen, he knew all about them; and his home was in Paris; how, then, could he be supposed to know anything of these country roads and God-forsaken villages? Le Roger it was, probably, in which case he, the driver, had vaguely heard of a dirty hole there where bed and supper might be found. As for stabling for all these horses... If he dared he would denounce that old vagabond for getting them into this trouble, but he was afraid of the punishment which, of course, he deserved for having taken the man on board without permission.

But the time would come, and very soon too, when the shoulders of the old villain would smart under the whip, so thought the driver as he clutched that whip with special gusto, and then cracked it and clicked his tongue. And the team made another fresh start – in darkness this time and with the wind howling as the lumbering vehicle sped in the teeth of the gale.

The snow swirled round the heads of men and beasts and stung their faces as with myriads of tiny whip-lashes. Another ten minutes of this intolerable going through the ever-increasing gloom, with heads bent against the storm and stiffened hands clutching at the sodden reins. Then at last the driver's eyes were gladdened by the sight of a scaffold pole on which dangled with dismal creakings an iron lantern: its feeble light revealed the sign beneath: *Le Bout du Monde*.

The End of the World! An appropriate as well as a welcome sign. A desolate conglomeration of isolated cottages, two or three barns grouped at some distance round the tumble-down *auberge* seemed all there was of the village, with the ice-bound river winding around it and a background of snow-covered fields.

The driver pulled up and looked about him with misgivings and choler. It didn't seem as if a good supper and comfortable beds could be got in this God-forsaken hole. There was only one thing to look forward to with glee, and that was the castigation to be administered to that infernal vagabond. There was any amount of noise and confusion going on to drown the howls of the victim – what with the soldiers dismounting, the horses fretting and stamping, chains rattling, hinges creaking, doors banging, the Representative of the People yelling and cursing and calling for the landlord, a rushing and a running and a swearing as the landlord came racing out of the *auberge*.

The driver called over his shoulder: "Now then, down you get!"

But there came no sign or movement from the banquette. The driver peered through the darkness and under the awning, but of a certainty the miserable vagabond was not there. Down clambered the driver in double quick time; he paid no heed to the orders shouted at him, to the curses from the irate Representative of the People; he pushed his way through the crowd of soldiers, he jostled the prisoner and the passengers: he even fell up against the sacrosanct person of Citizen

Representative Chabot. Like a lunatic he ran hither and thither, peering in every angle, every barn, behind every tree, but there was no sign of that old rogue who had sprung out of the snow at Vernon only to disappear in the darkness around the *Bout du Monde*.

The End of the World! In very truth, had not such an action been forbidden by decree of the National Convention, the driver, when he finally realised that the man had really and truly vanished, would of a certainty have crossed himself.

The devil couldn't do more, what?

31

There was, of a truth, a great deal of confusion and any amount of cursing and swearing before men and beasts, not to mention the coach and saddlery, were housed under shelter for the night. Accommodation was more than scant in this poverty-stricken village and wholly inadequate at the hostelry itself. There were close on a score of men all requiring bed and supper and eleven horses to stable and to feed. The resources of the *Bout du Monde* were nowhere near equal to such a strain.

The landlord, indeed, was profuse in apologies. Never, never before had his poor house been honoured by such distinguished company. Le Roger was right off the main Paris–Rouen road; seldom did a coach come through the village at all, let alone with so numerous an escort: as for a diligence with a team and postilion, such a thing hadn't been seen here within memory of the oldest inhabitant. Sometimes travellers on horse-back bound for Elboeuf chose this route rather than the longer one by Gaillon, but...

At this point Chabot, fuming with impatience, broke in on the landlord's topographical dissertation and curtly ordered him to prepare the best food the house could muster for himself and the captain of the guard, together with a large jug of mulled cider. As for the rest of the party, they would have to make shift with whatever there was.

The captain and the landlord then worked with a will. There was a large thatched barn at some distance from the *Bout du*

Monde where all the horses were presently jostled in, and such hay and fodder as could be mustered in the village was all commandeered by the soldiers for the poor tired beasts. A couple of men were told off to watch over them. Under the roof of another small barn close by and open to the four winds the coach and saddlery was then stowed. So far, so good. As for the men, they swarmed all over the small hostelry, snatching at what food they could get, raiding the outhouse for wood wherewith to pile up a good fire in the public room, where presently, after their scanty meal of lean pork, hard bread and dry beans, they would finally curl themselves up on the floor in their military cloaks, hoping to get to sleep.

The wretched prisoner was among them. No one had troubled to give him any food or drink. As presumably he was being taken to Rouen in order to be guillotined there was not much object in feeding him. But orders were very strict as to keeping watch over him; and the soldiers of the guard were commanded to take it in turns, two by two, all through the night to keep an eye on him. At the slightest disturbance all the men were to be aroused, the prisoner's safety being a matter of life and death for them all. Having given these orders and uttered these threats, Representative Chabot, in company of the captain, followed the landlord up a flight of rickety stairs to the floor above, where they were served with supper in a private room under the sloping roof. In this room, which was not much more than a loft, there was a truckle bed, hastily made up for the Citizen Representative, and in the corner a mattress and pillow for the Citizen Captain. This was the best the landlord could muster for the distinguished personages who were honouring his poor house, and anyway, a good fire was roaring in the iron stove, and the place was away from the noise and confusion of the overcrowded public room.

Chabot's temper was at its worst. Having eaten and drunk his fill, he lay down on the truckle bed and tried to get some sleep; but ne'er a wink did he get. All night he tossed about, furious with everything and everybody. From time to time he tumbled out of bed to throw a log on the fire, for it was very cold: he made as much noise as he could then and tramped heavily once or twice up and down the room so as to wake the captain, who was snoring lustily. During moments of fitful slumber he was haunted by a ghostlike procession of all those who had contributed to his present discomfort: he dreamed of the time, not far distant he hoped, when he would belabour them with tongue and whip-lash to his heart's content. There was the hussy Josette Gravier, who had dared to threaten and then to hoodwink him; there was her lover, Reversac, the wretched prisoner downstairs, who, luckily, could not possibly escape the guillotine; there was, too, that fool of a driver who had landed him, François Chabot, Representative of the People, in this God-forsaken hole, and the captain of the guard, whose persistent snoring chased away even the semblance of sleep. Even his colleague, Chauvelin, were he here, should not escape the trouncing.

The hours of the night went by leaden-footed. At the slightest noise Chabot would rouse himself from his hard pillow and sit up in bed, listening. The prisoner – that valuable hostage for the return of the letters – was well guarded, but the very importance of his safety further exacerbated Chabot's nerves. But nothing happened, and after a while the silence of the night fell on the *Bout du Monde*.

At last in the distance and through the silence a church clock struck six. It was still quite dark; only the fire in the iron stove shed a modicum of light with its glow into the room. The getting away of the coach with its mounted escort would certainly take some time and, anyway, as he, Chabot, could not sleep there was no reason why anyone else should. He jumped out of bed and roused the captain.

"Why, what's the time?" the latter queried, his eyes still heavy with sleep.

"Damn the time!" Chabot retorted roughly. " 'Tis, anyway, late enough for you to stop snoring and begin to see to things."

Very ill-humoured, but not daring to murmur, the captain rose and pulled on his boots. One slept in one's clothes these days, especially on a journey like this; and there was, of course, no question of washing at the *Bout du Monde* save, perhaps, at the pump outside, and it was much too cold for that. The captain's toilet on this occasion meant slipping on his coat, fastening his belt and smoothing his hair; and it all had to be done in the dark. He peeped out of the window.

"The wind has dropped," he remarked, "but there's a lot more snow to come down."

"Anyway," Chabot rejoined, "we start whatever the weather."

He, too, had pulled on his boots, but was still in his shirtsleeves, and his coarse curly hair stood out from his head in tufts like an ill-combed poodle dog. He took to marching up and down the room, striding about in the darkness and swearing hard when he barked his shins against a chair. As the captain went out of the room he called to him:

"Tell the landlord to bring candles and a large jug of hot cider with plenty of spice in it."

He resumed his walk up and down the room, varying his oaths with blasphemies, and spat on the floor in the intervals of picking his teeth. He went to the door once or twice and listened to the confused sounds which came from below. A score of men roused from sleep, the inevitable swearing and shouting and tramping up and down the passage. The dormer window in this room gave on the back of the house where it was comparatively quiet; but after a time Chabot heard the men's voices down there, the jingle of their spurs and their heavy footsteps as they went off evidently to see to the horses. The barn where the horses were stabled was at some little distance in the village, and Chabot congratulated himself that he had roused that lazy lout of an officer in good time. He was hungry and cold in spite of the fire in the room, and swore copiously at the landlord when the latter brought him the jug of steaming cider and a couple of lighted candles. The remnants of last night's supper were still on the table; he pushed the dirty plates and dishes impatiently on one side, then poured himself out a mugful of hot drink while the landlord excused himself on the plea that he had such a lot to do with so big a crowd in his small house. Should his daughter come up and attend to the distinguished Representative's commands?

But Chabot was, above all, impatient to get away.

"We must make Rouen before dark," he said tartly, "and the days are so short. I want no attention. You go and speed up the men and give a hand with the horses so that we can make a start within the hour."

He drank the cider and felt a little better, but he could not sit still. After marching up and down the room again once or twice he went to the window and tried to peer out, but the small panes were thick with grime and framed in with snow and it was pitch-dark outside. His nerves were terribly on edge and he cursed Chauvelin for having expected him to undertake this uncomfortable journey alone. Then there was the responsibility about the prisoner and this perpetual talk of English spies. "Bah!" he muttered to himself as if to instil courage into himself: "a score of these louts I've got here can easily grapple with them."

Then why this agonising nervousness, this unconquerable feeling of impending danger? Suddenly he felt hot: the blood had rushed up to his head, beads of perspiration gathered on his forehead. He went to the window and unlatched it, but the cold rush of air made him shiver. He feared that he was sickening for a fever. He tried to close the window again, but the latch was stiff with rust and his fingers soon became numb with the cold.

"Curse the blasted thing!" he swore between his teeth as he fumbled with the latch.

"Let me do it for you, Citizen," a pleasant voice said close to his ear.

Chabot swung round on his heel, smothering a cry of terror. A man – tall, broad-shouldered, dressed in sober black that fitted his magnificent figure to perfection – was in the act of closing the window. With firm dexterous fingers he got the latch into position.

"There! that's better now, is it not, my dear Monsieur? I forget your name," he said with a light laugh. Then added: "So now we can talk."

He brushed one slender hand against the other and with a lace-edged handkerchief flicked the dust off from his coat.

"Dirty place, this End of the World, what?" he remarked. Chabot, tongue-tied and terror-stricken, had collapsed upon the truckle bed. He gazed on this tall figure which he could only vaguely distinguish in the gloom. Like the driver of the diligence a while ago, he would have crossed himself if he dared, for this, of a surety, must be Lucifer: tall, slender, in black clothes that melted and merged into the surrounding darkness, allowing the flickering candlelight to play upon a touch of white at throat and wrist and on the highly polished leather of the boot.

"Who are you?" he gasped after a time, for the stranger had not moved, and Chabot felt that all the while a pair of eyes, cold and mocking, were fixed upon him from out of the gloom. "Who are you?" he reiterated under his breath.

"The devil you think I am," the other responded lightly, "but won't you come and sit down?"

He motioned towards a chair by the table.

"I haven't much time, I'm afraid; and," he went on lightly, "you'll be more comfortable than on that hard bed."

Then as Chabot made no effort to move, but sat there, one hand resting on the bed, the glow of the firelight upon him, the stranger remarked:

"Why, look at your hand, my dear Monsieur What's-your-name; it looks as if you had dipped it in a sanguinary mess."

Mechanically Chabot looked down on his hand to which the stranger was now pointing. In that crimson glow it certainly looked as if… Hastily he withdrew it and rubbed it against his coat. Then, as if impelled by some unknown force, he rose and made a movement towards the table, but stopped halfway and suddenly made a dash for the door. But the stranger forestalled him, had him by the wrist before he could seize the latch, and with a grip that was irresistible drew him back to the table and forced him down upon a chair. He sat down opposite to him on the other side of the table and reiterated quietly:

"Now we can talk."

Chabot up to this moment was absolutely convinced that this was the devil made manifest. His education, conducted within the narrow limits of a seminary, had in a way prepared him for such a possibility, and during the brief years which he spent as a Capuchin friar he had had every belief implanted into him of demons and evil spirits, of material hell and bottomless pit. Cold, terror, discomfort of every sort all helped to unnerve him. Fascinated, he watched that tall dark figure, pouring with white slender hand the mulled cider into a mug and handing it over to him.

"Drink this, man," came the mellow voice out of the darkness, "and pull yourself together. We have no time to lose."

Chabot took the mug, but set it down on the table untasted.

"Well," the stranger said lightly, "as you like; but try and listen to me. I am not a manifestation of your familiar as you suppose, only a plain English gentleman. I happen to have in my possession certain letters which in a moment of carelessness you were rash enough to write to a certain Bastien de Croissy…"

At mention of "letters" Chabot uttered a hoarse cry: his fingers went up to his necktie, for he suddenly felt as if he would choke. "You!" he murmured, "you…?"

"Yes! I, at your service; I know all about those letters, for that is what you were about to say, was it not?"

He held Chabot with his eyes, and Chabot was fascinated by that glance. The eyes held him and he tried to defy them, made a supreme effort to pull himself together. Slowly it dawned upon him that here was no devil made manifest, but rather an emeny who was trying to hit at him, to hoodwink him about those letters as that young baggage had tried to do. Another of her lovers probably – yes! that was it: an English lover picked up in England recently: one of those spies, perhaps, of whom his friend Armand Chauvelin was often wont to talk, but certainly another lover, and if he, Chabot, was fool enough to bargain he would be made a fool of once more. This thought had the effect of soothing his nerves: he suddenly felt quite calm. That choking sensation was gone; he took up the mug of cider and drank it down. His hand was perfectly steady; and he was in no hurry. The captain would be back directly and together they would laugh over the discomfiture of this fool when he found himself securely bound with cords in the company of the other prisoner, Maurice Reversac, the hussy's latest lover.

It was all very easy and very amusing. No! there was no hurry. In fact, this hour would have been very dull and very long but for this diversion. The candles were guttering and Chabot took the snuffers and used them very efficiently and deliberately. He pretended not to notice the stranger's nonchalant attitude, sitting there opposite to him, with his arms resting on the table and his very clean white hands interlocked.

"That wick would be all the better for another snick," he remarked; and Chabot tried to imitate his careless manner by saying: "You think so, Citizen?" and carefully trimmed the offending wick.

He really was enjoying every moment of this unexpected interview. How stupid he had been to be so scared! The devil, indeed! Just an English jackanapes who had put his head in the lion's jaw previous to laying it under the knife of the guillotine; moreover, a spy could be shot without trial within the hour, in fact, and the captain could see to it that this one didn't talk. He, the captain, would be back directly, and, anyway, there were at least a dozen men in the public room down below, so what was there to fear when all was well and quite amusing?

The stranger had made no movement. Chabot leaned over the table, resting his head in his hand.

"You know, Mr the Englishman," he said with well-assumed unconcern, "that you have vastly interested me."

"I am glad," rejoined the other.

"About those letters, I mean."

"Indeed?"

"Now I should be very curious to know just how you came to be in possession of them."

"I will gratify your curiosity with all the pleasure in life," the stranger replied. "I took them out of the pocket of Madame de Croissy while she was asleep."

"Nonsense!" Chabot retorted with an assumption of indifference, although the name de Croissy had grated unpleasantly on his ear. "What in the world had the Widow Croissy got to do with any supposed letters of mine?"

"You forget, my dear sir," the Englishman retorted blandly, "that the letters were written by yourself to that lady's husband; that in order to obtain possession of them you murdered that unfortunate man in a peculiarly cruel and cowardly manner; the lady thereupon was persuaded for obvious reasons to leave for England, taking the letters with her."

"Bah! I've heard that story before."

"Have you now?" the stranger remarked with an engaging smile. "Isn't that funny?"

"Not nearly so funny as your lie that you took those letters – whatever they were – out of the woman's pocket, and that she never noticed the loss."

"How very clever of you to say that, my dear Citizen What's-your-name: a masterpiece, I call it, of skilful cross-examination. You would have made a wonderful advocate at any bar." He gave a short laugh, and Chabot spat like a cat that's being teased. "As a matter of fact," the stranger resumed, quite unperturbed, "the lady certainly might have noticed her loss. You were right there. But, you see, I took the precaution of substituting a sealed packet exactly similar to the one I had stolen and placed it in the lady's pocket."

Then as Chabot made no reply, was obviously thinking over what his next move should be in this singular encounter, the Englishman continued:

"In fact, you will observe, Sir, that my process was identical to the one employed by our mutual friend Chambertin when he stole what he thought was the precious packet of letters from little Josette Gravier and substituted for it another contrived by himself to look exactly similar. I am very fond really of Monsieur Chambertin; for a clever man he is sometimes such a silly fool, what?"

"Chambertin?" Chabot queried, frowning.

"Beg pardon – I should say Chauvelin."

"Do you mean to pretend that it was he?"

"Why, of course. Who else?"

"And that he had those damned letters?"

"No, no, my dear Monsieur What-d'you-call-yourself," the stranger retorted with a light laugh. "I have those blessed – not damned – letters here, as I had the honour of explaining to you just now."

And with his elegant, slender hand he tapped the left breast of his coat. Chabot watched him for a moment or two under beetling brows. The man's coolness, his impudence had irritated him, and while he had thought that he was playing a cat's game with a mouse, somehow the roles of cat and mouse had come to be reversed. But it had lasted too long already. It was time to put an end to it, and the moment was entirely opportune, for just then Chabot's ears were pleasantly tickled by the sound of the captain's voice down below ordering the landlord to bring him some hot cider. He had evidently returned from the barn, leaving the men to feed and saddle the horses.

Chabot chuckled at thought of the stranger's discomfiture when presently the captain would come tramping up the stairs, and, in anticipation of coming triumph, he fixed his antagonist with what he felt was a searching as well as an ironic glance.

"Suppose," he began slowly, "that before going any further you show me those supposed letters."

"With all the pleasure in life," the Englishman responded blandly. And to Chabot's intense amazement he drew out of his breast-pocket a small sealed packet exactly similarly in appearance to the one which poor little Josette Gravier had so trustingly kept in the bosom of her gown. Chabot chortled at sight of it.

"Will you break the seals, Monsieur the Englishman?" he queried with withering sarcasm, "or shall I?"

But already the stranger's finely shaped hands were busy with the seals. Chabot, his ugly face still wearing a sarcastic expression, drew the candles closer. Soon the seals were broken, the wrapper fell apart and displayed, not scraps of paper this time, but just a few letters, written by divers hands. Chabot felt as if his eyes would drop out of his head as he gazed. The flickering candles illumined the topmost letter with its unmistakable signature – his own – François Chabot. And there were others: he remembered every one of them, gazed on the tell-tale signatures – his – Bazire's – Fabre's.

"Name of a dog!" he cried, and made a quick grab for the letters. But the stranger's hands, delicate and slender though they were, were extraordinarily firm and quick. In a moment he had the letters all together, the wrapper round them, a piece of twine, picked out the devil knew whence, holding the packet once more securely together. Chabot could not take his eyes off him. He watched him as if hypnotised, mute, blind to all else save that calm, high-bred face with the firm lips and the humorous twinkle in the eyes. But when he saw the stranger on the point of putting the packet back inside his coat, he cried, hoarse with passion: "Give me those letters!"

"All in good time, my dear sir. First, as I have already had the honour to remark, we must have a good talk."

Chabot rose slowly to his feet. The captain's voice rising from the public room below, the tramp of the soldiers' feet, his whole surroundings recalled him to himself. Fool that he was to fear anything from this insolent nincompoop!

"I give you one last chance," he said very quietly, even though he could not disguise the tremor of his voice. "Either you give me those letters now – at once – in which case you can go from here a free man and to the devil if you choose; or…"

At this same moment the sound of several voices was wafted upwards. Some of the soldiers had apparently assembled somewhere underneath the window and were talking over some momentous happening. Chabot and the stranger could hear snatches of what they said:

"Luckily the horses were not…"

"The wind unfortunately…"

"The saddles are…"

"So is the coach…"

"What in the world are we going…"

"Better see what the Citizen Captain…"

And so on, until after a time they moved away to the front entrance of the house, which was right the other side. The stranger was smiling while he lent an attentive ear. But Chabot only thought of the fact that now the guard would soon be assembled inside the house. Twenty trained men to cope with this insolent spy. His pale yellow eyes gleamed in the dim light like those of a cat. He was gloating over his coming triumph, licking his chops like a greedy cur in sight of food.

"Or," he concluded between clenched teeth, "I'll call the captain of the guard and have you shot as a spy within the hour."

By way of reply the stranger rose slowly from the table. To Chabot's excited fancy he appeared immensely tall: terrifying in his air of power and physical strength, and instinctively this scrubby worm, this cowardly assassin, this unfrocked friar cowered before the tall, commanding figure of the stranger in abject terror of his own miserable life. He edged round the table, while the Englishman deliberately walked to the window; then he made a dart for the door, expecting every second to feel that steel-like grip once more upon his arm. With his hand already on the latch he looked over his shoulder at his enemy, who was at the moment engaged in opening the window. The gust of wind that ensued was so strong that Chabot could not pull the door open; moreover, his hands were shaking and his knees felt as if they were about to give way under him: only later did he become aware that the door was locked. He heard the stranger give a curious call, like that of sea-mews who are wont to circle about the Pont-Neuf in Paris when the winter is very severe. The call was responded to in the same way from below, whereupon the stranger flung the packet out of the window. Three words were wafted upwards, words with a foreign sound which Chabot could not understand. Subsequently he averred that one of those words sounded something like "Raitt!" and the other like "Fouk's," but of course that was nonsense.

The stranger then went back to the table and sat down. Once more he reiterated the irritating phrase which so exasperated the Terrorist: "Now we can talk."

Chabot fumbled with the door-knob. He had just heard the men trooping back into the house.

"No use, my friend," the stranger remarked drily. "I locked that door when I came in. And here's the key," he added, and put the rusty old key down on the table.

"Come and sit down," he resumed after a second or two as Chabot had not moved, had in fact seemed glued to that locked door; "or shall I have to come and fetch you?"

"You devil! You hound! You abominable…" Chabot muttered inarticulately. "Get me back those letters or…"

"Come and sit down," the other reiterated coolly. "You have exactly five minutes in which to save your skin. My friend is still outside, just under this window; if within the next five minutes he hears no signal from me he will speed to Paris with those letters, and three days after that they will be published in every newspaper in the city and shouted from every house-top in France."

"It's not true," Chabot muttered huskily. "He cannot do it. He couldn't pass the gates of Paris."

"Would you care to take your chance of that?" the stranger retorted blandly. "If so, here's the key…call your guard…do what you damn well like…"

He laughed, a pleasant infectious laugh, full of the joy of living through this perilous, exciting adventure, full of self-assurance, of arrogance, as you will, a laugh to gladden the hearts of the brave and to strike terror in those of the craven.

"One minute nearly gone," he renewed, and from his breeches pocket drew a jewelled watch attached to a fob, and this he held out for the other man to see.

Birds and rabbits, 'tis averred, are so attracted by the python which is about to gulp them down that they do not attempt to flee from him but become hypnotised, and of themselves draw nearer and nearer to the devouring jaws. In very truth there was nothing snake-like about the tall Englishman with the merry, lazy eyes and the firm mouth so often curled in a pleasant smile, but Chabot was just like a hypnotised rabbit. He crossed the room slowly, very slowly, and presently sat down opposite his tormentor.

"Nearly two minutes gone out of the five," the latter said, "and I verily believe I can hear your friend the captain's footfall in the hall below."

It was then that Chabot had an inspiration. In this moment of crushing humiliation and of real peril he remembered his friend Chauvelin, saw him as in a vision sitting with him in the small private room of the *Cheval Blanc* at Rouen. What did he say when there was talk of the prisoner Reversac and his sweetheart Josette? Something about safe-conducts for them to be offered in exchange for the letters. Safe-conducts? And in his quiet, incisive voice Chauvelin had added, "I can endorse those with a secret sign. It is known to every Chief Commissary in France and nullifies every safe-conduct."

Yes, that was it: "Nullifies every safe-conduct." And Chauvelin knew the secret sign as did every Chief Commissary in France. So now to play one's cards carefully, and above all not to show fear; on no account to show that one was afraid.

And Chabot, sitting at the table, stroked his scrubby chin and said:

"I suppose what you want is a safe-conduct for some traitor or other, what?"

But the inspiration proved only to be a mirage and the sense of triumph very short-lived. The very next moment Chabot's fond hopes were rudely dashed to the ground, for the stranger replied, still smiling:

"No, my friend, I want no safe-conduct endorsed by you or your colleague with a secret sign to render them valueless."

And Chabot fell back in his chair; he was sweating at every pore. He marvelled if after all his first impression had not been the true one; since this man appeared to be a reader of thought was he not truly the devil incarnate?

"What is it you do want?" he uttered, choking and gasping.

"That you unlock that door – here's the key – and call to the gallant captain of the guard."

He held the key out to Chabot, who, fascinated, hypnotised, took it from him.

"Go and unlock that door, Monsieur What's-your-name, and call your friend the captain."

Slowly, as if moved by some unseen and compelling power, Chabot tottered towards the door. The stranger spoke to him over his shoulder: "When he comes you will tell him that you desire someone to go over to the village to the house of Citizen Pailleron with a message from you. Pailleron has a nice covered wagonette which he uses for the purpose of his trade as carrier between here and Elboeuf. Your messenger will explain to him that Citizen Representative François Chabot requires the wagonette immediately for his personal use. A sum in compensation will be given to him before a start is made."

Chabot made a final effort to turn on his tormentor: "This is madness!" he cried. "I'll not do it. If I call the captain it will be to have you shot..."

"Another minute gone," quoth the stranger blandly, "and I am sure the captain is coming up the stairs."

"You hellish fiend!"

"My friend down below will be wondering if he should speed for Paris or..."

The key grated in the lock. Chabot's trembling hands were fumbling with the latch.

"Come! that is wise," the Englishman said, "but for your own sake I entreat you to command your nerves. The captain is coming up. You will explain to him about the wagonette, also that you will be leaving here within the hour in the company of two friends, one of them being the young man, Maurice Reversac, at present detained through an unfortunate misunderstanding, and the other your humble servant."

Chabot was like a whipped cur with its tail between its legs. He slunk away from the door and came back across the room, and, like a whipped cur, he made a final effort to bite the hand that smote him.

"You must think me a fool…" he began, trying to swagger.

"I do," the other broke in blandly. "But that is not the point. The point is that I am looking to you to effect the ultimate rescue of two innocent young people out of your murderous clutches. Josette Gravier is in comparative safety for the moment, and Maurice Reversac is close at hand. I propose to convey them to Havre and see them safely on board an English ship *en route* for our shores, which you must admit are more hospitable than yours. For this expedition your help, my dear Monsieur What's-your-name, will be invaluable, so you are coming with us, my friend, in Citizen Pailleron's wagonette, and I myself will have the honour to drive you. And when we are challenged at the gates of any city, or commune, or at a bridge-head, you will show the guard your pretty face and reveal your identity as Representative of the People in the National Convention and stand upon your rights as such to free passage and no molestation for yourself, your driver and your son – we'll call Maurice Reversac your son for convenience's sake – and at Elboeuf, as well as at Dieppe, on the quay or at any barrier your pleasant countenance and your gentle, authoritative voice will command the obsequiousness they deserve. So I pray you," he concluded with perfect suavity, "call the captain of the guard and explain to him all that is necessary. We ought soon to be getting on the way."

He leaned back in his chair, gave a slight yawn, then rose, and from his magnificent height looked down on the cringing figure of the unfrocked friar. Chabot tried vainly to collect his thoughts, to make some plan, to think, to think, my God! to think of something, and above all to gather courage from the fact that this man, this abominable spy, this arrogant devil, was still in his power: now, at this moment, he could still hand him over to be shot at sight…or else at Rouen; with Chauvelin waiting for him, he could…he could…

But the other, as if divining his thoughts, broke in on them by saying: "You could do nothing at Rouen, my friend, for let me assure you that within twenty-four hours my friend who now has your letters in his possession will be on his way to Paris, there to deliver them at the offices of the *Moniteur* and of *Père Duchnese*, unless I myself desire him to hand them over to you."

"And if I yield to your cowardly threats," Chabot hissed between his teeth, "if I lend myself to this dastardly comedy, how shall I know that your associate, as vile a craven as yourself, will give me the letters in the end?"

"You can't know that, my friend," the other retorted simply, "for I cannot expect such as you to know the meaning of a word of honour spoken by an English gentleman."

"How shall I know if I do get the letters that none have been kept back?"

"That's just it: you can't know. But remember, my friend, that there is one thing you do know with absolute certainty, and that is, if my plan to save those two young people fails, if I do not myself request my friend to give up the letters to you, then as sure as we are both alive at this moment those letters will be published in every news-sheet throughout France; your name will become a byword for everything that is most treacherous and most vile, and not even the dirtiest mudrake in the country will care to take you by the hand."

The stranger had spoken with unwonted earnestness, all the more impressive for the flippant way in which he had carried on the conversation before. Chabot, always a bully, was nothing if not a coward. Any danger to himself reduced him to a wriggling worm. That his peril was great he knew well enough, and he had realised at last that there was no threat that he could utter which would shake that cursed English spy from his purpose.

There was a moment of tense silence in the room, whilst the captain's footsteps were heard slowly coming up the stairs. The stranger gave a gay little laugh and sat down once more opposite his writhing victim. He poured out two mugfuls of cider, and the moment that the door was thrown open he was saying with easy familiarity:

"Your good health, my dear François, and to our proposed journey together."

He held the white-livered recreant with his magnetic eyes and made as if to raise the mug to his lips; then he paused and went on lightly:

"By the way, did you happen to see the *Moniteur* the day before yesterday? It has a scathing attack, inspired of certainty by Couthon, against Danton and some of his methods."

Chabot clenched his teeth. At this moment he would have sold his soul to the devil for the power to slay this over-weening rapscallion.

The captain, seeing the Citizen Representative in conversation with a friend, halted respectfully at the door. He stood at attention, until Chabot looked round at him with tired, bleary eyes.

"What is it, Citizen Captain?" he inquired in a thick, tired voice, while the stranger, as if suddenly aware of the officer's presence, rose courteously from the table.

"I have to report, Citizen Representative," the captain replied, "that during the night certain miscreants found their way to the coach and saddlery, to which they did a good deal of mischief."

"Mischief? What mischief?" Chabot muttered inarticulately, while the stranger gave a polite murmur of sympathy.

"They've cut the saddle-girths, the reins and the stirrup-leathers, and the spokes of two of the coach wheels are broken right across. The damage will take more than a day to repair."

"I hope, Citizen Captain," the stranger said affably, "that you have laid hands on the rascals."

"Alas, no! the mischief was done at night. The barn lies some way back from this house; no one heard anything. The ruffians got clean away."

Chabot was speechless; not only had the quantity of spiced cider got into his head, but rage and despair had made him dumb.

"My dear François," the Englishman commented with good-humoured urbanity, "this is indeed unfortunate for all these fine soldiers who will have to spend a day or two in this God-forsaken hole. I know what that means," he went on, turning once more to the captain, "as I have been through such experience before, travelling on my business in these outlying parts."

"Ah! You know Le Roger then, Citizen?" the captain asked.

"I have been here once before. I am a commercial traveller, you know, and go about the country a good deal. I only arrived last night from St Pierre half an hour after you did, and was happy to hear that my old friend François Chabot was putting up for the night. Then luckily I happened to bespeak Citizen Pailleron's covered wagonette to take me on today to Louviers, but it will be a pleasure as well as an honour for me to drive the Citizen Representative to Rouen if he desires."

"It will be heavy going."

"Perhaps, but my friend Pailleron has excellent horses which he will let me have."

"This is indeed lucky," the captain assented.

Still he seemed to hesitate. As Chabot remained tongue-tied, the stranger touched him lightly on the shoulder.

"It is lucky, is it not, my dear François?" he asked.

Chabot looked up at his tormentor. "Go to hell!" he murmured under his breath.

"The Citizen Captain is waiting for orders, my friend."

"You give them, then."

The stranger gave a light laugh. "I am afraid the cider was rather heady," he explained to the officer. "Will you be so good, captain, as to send round to Citizen Pailleron and let him know that the Representative of the People is ready to start. I believe the snow has left off for the moment; we can make Louviers before noon."

There was nothing in this to rouse the captain's suspicions. The Citizen Representative, though suffering perhaps from an excess of hot, spiced drink, nodded his head as if to confirm the order given by his friend. That this tall stranger was his friend there could be no doubt; the two of them were conversing amicably when he, the captain, first entered the room. And it certainly was the most natural conclusion for any man to come to, that so distinguished a personage as a Representative of the People in the National Convention would not wish to remain snowed up in this desolate village for two days at least, but would gladly avail himself of the means of transit offered to him by a friend. And certainly whatever doubt the officer might have had in his mind was finally dissipated when the stranger spoke again to Citizen Chabot.

"My dear François," he said, once more touching the other on the shoulder, "you have forgotten to speak to our friend the captain about the young man, Reversac."

"The prisoner?" the captain asked.

"Even him."

"He is quite safe at this moment in the public room, and we…"

"That's just the point," the stranger rejoined; and, unseen by the captain, he tightened his grip on Chabot's shoulder. "Do, my dear François, explain to the Citizen Captain…"

Chabot winced under the grip, which seemed like a veritable strangle-hold upon his will-power. He had not an ounce of strength left in him, either moral or physical, to resist. It was as much as he could do to mutter a few words and to gaze with bleared vision on his smiling enemy.

"Do explain, my dear François," the latter insisted.

Chabot brought the palm of his hand down with a crash upon the table.

"Damn explanations!" he snapped savagely. "The prisoner Reversac comes with me. That's enough."

And as the captain, momentarily taken off his balance by this unexpected command, still stood by the door, Chabot shouted at him: "Get out!"

It was the stranger who, with perfect courtesy, went to the door and held it open for the officer to pass out.

"That cider was much too heady," he said, dropping his voice to a whisper, "but the Citizen Representative will be all right when he gets into the cold air." After which he added, "He does not wish to lose sight of the prisoner, and I shall be there to look after them both."

"Well! It is not for me to make comment," the soldier remarked drily, "so long as the Citizen Representative is satisfied..."

"Oh! He is quite satisfied, I do assure you. You are satisfied, are you not, you dear old François?"

But even while he asked this final question he quickly closed the door on the departing soldier, for in very truth the blasphemies which Chabot uttered after that would have polluted even the ears of an old Republican campaigner.

32

Less than half an hour later a covered wagonette to which a couple of sturdy Normandy horses were harnessed drew up outside the front door of the *Bout de Monde*. The word had soon enough gone round the village and among the men that the Representative of the People was leaving Le Roger in company of a friend, taking the prisoner with him.

He came out of the hostelry wrapped in his big coat. He looked neither to right nor left, nor did he acknowledge the respectful salutes of the landlord and his family assembled at the door to bid him good-bye. The prisoner, hatless, coatless and shivering with cold, was close behind him. But it was the Representative's friend who created most attention. He was very tall and wore the finest of clothes. It was generally whispered among the quidnuncs that he was a commercial traveller who had made much money by smuggling French brandy into England.

While François Chabot and the prisoner stowed themselves away as best they could under the hood of the wagonette, the stranger climbed up on the box and took the reins. He clicked his tongue, tickled the horses with his whip, and the light vehicle bumped along the snow-covered road and was soon lost to sight.

Grey dawn was breaking just then; the sky was clear and gave promise of a fine sunny day. The men who had formed the escort for the diligence and those who had travelled inside in order to guard the prisoner sat around the fire in the public room in the intervals between scanty meals, and discussed the amazing adventures of the past twenty-four hours. They had begun, so it was universally admitted, with the mysterious report of a pistol outside the hostelry at Vernon and the strange appearance of the whilom stud-groom who looked such a miserable tramp. What happened on the road after that no one could aver with any certainty, for the driver, who knew himself to be heavily at fault, never said a word about having taken the tramp aboard on the banquette, and allowing the reins to slip out of his hands into the more capable ones of the stud-groom.

Indeed, while the others talked the driver seemed entrenched in complete dumbness. He drank copiously, and as he was known to become violent in his cups he was left severely alone. The damage done in the night to the coach and saddlery had further aggravated his ill-humour. He put it all down to spite directed against him by some power of evil made manifest in the person of that cursed vagabond. It was supposed that the villagers had set themselves the task to bring the miscreants to book, but the hours sped by and nothing was discovered that would lead to such a happy result. The snow all round the barn where coach and saddlery had been stowed had been trampled down so heavily that it was impossible to determine in which direction the rapscallions had made good their escape.

33

To François Chabot the journey between Le Roger and the coast was nothing less than a nightmare. He was more virtually the prisoner of that impudent English spy than any aristo had ever been in the hands of Terrorists. And while thoughts and plans and useless desires went hammering through his fevered brain, the wagonette lumbered along on the snow-covered road, and on the driver's seat in front of him sat the man who was the cause of his humiliation and his despair. Oh, for the courage to end it all and plunge a knife into that broad back! But what was the good of wishing, for there was that terrible threat hanging over him of the letters to be published where all who wished could read, and the certainty of disgrace with the inevitable guillotine? Chabot could really thank his stars that he did not happen to have a knife handy. He might surely, in a moment of madness, have killed his tormentor and also the young man who sat squeezed beside him in the interior of the wagonette.

They reached Louviers at noon. At the entrance to the city they were challenged by the sentry at the gate. The Englishman jumped down from the box. At a mere sign from him Chabot showed his papers of identity: –

> "François Chabot, Representative of the People in the National Convention for the department of Loire et Cher…"

He declared the young man sitting next to him to be his son, and the other a friend under his own especial protection. The sentry stood at attention: the officer gave the word:

"Pass on in the name of the Republic!"

A nightmare, what? or else an outpost of hell!

They avoided Rouen, made a circuit of the town and turned into a country lane. Presently the driver pulled up outside a small, somewhat dilapidated house, which lay *perdu* in the midst of a garden all overgrown with weeds, and surrounded by a wall broken down in many places and with a low iron gate dividing it from the road. He jumped down from the box, fastened the reins to a ring in the wall; then, with his usual impudent glance, peeped underneath the hood of the wagonette. He thrust a parcel and a bottle into Chabot's lap and said curtly:

"Eat and drink, my friend. Monsieur Reversac and I have business inside the house."

The whilom prisoner stepped out of the wagonette and together the two men went inside the house. One or two people passed by while Chabot sat shivering in the draughty vehicle. He ate and he drank, for he was hungry and thirsty, but he had entirely ceased to think by now. He no longer felt that he was a real live man, but only an automaton made to move and to speak through the touch of a white slender hand and the glance of a pair of lazy deep-set blue eyes.

Many minutes went by before he heard the rickety door of the old house creak upon its hinges. The two men came down the path towards the wagonette, but they were not alone. There was a girl with them, and Chabot uttered a hoarse cry as he recognised the baggage, Josette Gravier, who had made a fool of him and was now a witness of his humiliation.

This, perhaps, was the most galling experience of all. He, the arrogant bully who had planned the destruction of these innocents, was now the means of their deliverance and their happiness. He closed his eyes so as not to see the triumph which he felt must be gleaming in theirs.

How little he understood human nature! Josette and Maurice had no thought of their enemy, none of the terrible torments which they had endured; their thoughts were of one another, of their happiness in holding each other by the hand; above all, of their love. In the hours of sorrow and peril of death they had realised at last the magnitude of that love, the joy that would be theirs if it pleased God to unite them in the end.

And this happiness they had now attained, and owed it to the brave man who had been the hero of Josette's dreams. When first she discovered his identity, when she knew that she owed her rescue to him, and when today he had suddenly walked into the old house where she had been patiently waiting for him under the care of a kindly farmer and his wife, she would gladly, if he had allowed it, have knelt at his feet and kissed his hands in boundless gratitude.

For these two, also, the journey seemed like a dream, but it was a dream of earthly Paradise; hand in hand they sat and hardly were conscious of the presence of that ugly, ungainly creature huddled up, silent and motionless, in a corner of the wagonette.

For them, too, he was just an automaton, moved at will by the mysterious Scarlet Pimpernel. He only bestirred himself when the wagonette was challenged at a bridge-head or the barriers of a *commune*; then, in answer to a demand from the sentry, he would poke his ugly head forward from under the hood and in a kind of dead, toneless voice recite his name and quality. And Josette and Maurice invariably giggled when they heard themselves described as the son and daughter of that hideous man, and that tall, handsome stranger as his friend.

The sentry then would give the word:

"Pass on in the name of the Republic!"

and the wagonette, driven by the mysterious stranger, would once more lumber along on its way.

The journey was broken at a small hostelry, about half a league beyond Elboeuf. The food was scanty and ill-cooked, the beds were hard, the place squalid, the rooms cold; but the idea of sleeping under the same roof with Maurice made Josette in her narrow truckle-bed feel as if she were in heaven.

When they neared the coast the first tang of the sea coming to Josette's nostrils brought with it recollections of that former journey which she had undertaken all alone for Maurice's sake. And when, presently. they came into Havre, and after the usual formalities at the gates of the city were able to leave the wagonette, these recollections turned to vivid memories. Guided by the tall mysterious stranger, they walked along the quay, whilst the past unrolled itself before Josette's mental vision like an ever-changing kaleidoscope. She remembered Citizen Armand, heard again his suave, lying tongue, met his pale eyes with their treacherous, deceptive glance. And she snuggled up close to Maurice, and he put his arm round her to guide her down the bridge to the packet-boat, which was on the point of starting for England.

To follow them thither were a sorry task. Many French men and women there were these days – Louise de Croissy and little Charles-Léon among them – who, fleeing from the terrors of a Government of assassins, found refuge in hospitable England. Helped by friends, made welcome by thousands of kindly hearts, they eked out their precarious existence by working in fields or factories until such time as the return of law and order in their own beautiful country enabled them to go back to their devastated homes.

Heureux le peuple qui n'a pas d'histoire. Of Maurice and Josette Reversac there is nothing further to record, save the fulfilment of their love-dream and their happiness.

34

"And now we'll go and get those blessed letters."

Sir Percy Blakeney, known to the world as the Scarlet Pimpernel, had stood on the quay watching the packet-boat sailing down the mouth of the river. His arm was linked in that of François Chabot, once a Capuchin friar, now Representative of the People in the National Convention. He held Chabot by the arm, and Chabot stood beside him and also watched the boat gliding out of the range of his vision.

The nightmare was not yet ended, for there was the journey back to Rouen in the wagonette with himself, François Chabot, chained to the chariot wheel of his ruthless conqueror.

A halt was made on the road outside the same old house where they had picked up Josette Gravier. This time Sir Percy bade Chabot follow him into the house. How it all happened Chabot never knew. He never could remember how it came about that presently he found himself fingering those fateful letters: they were all there – three written by himself, two written by his brother-in-law, Bazire, and two by Fabre d'Eglantine – seven letters: mere scraps of paper; but what a price to pay for their possession! An immense wave of despair swept over the recreant. Perhaps at this hour the whole burden of his crimes weighed down his miserable soul and it received its first consciousness of inevitable retribution. The wretch spread his arms out on the table and, laying down his head, he burst into abject tears.

When the paroxysm of weeping was over and he looked about him the tall mysterious stranger was gone.

It was twilight of one of the most dismal days of the year. Looking up at the window, Chabot saw the leaden snow-laden clouds sweeping across the sky. Heavy flakes fell slowly, slowly. All round him absolute silence reigned. The house apparently was quite deserted. He staggered rather than walked to the door. He tramped across the path to the low gate in the wall. Here he stood for a moment looking up and down the narrow road and the heavy snowflakes covered his shoulders and his tufty, ill-kempt hair. There was no sign of the wagonette beyond the ruts made by the wheels in the snow, and for a long time not a soul came by. Presently, however, a couple of men – farm-labourers they were by the look of them – came along and Chabot asked them:

"Where are we?"

The men stopped and in the twilight peered curiously at this hatless man, half-covered with snow.

"What do you mean by 'Where are we?' " one of them asked.

"Just what I am asking," Chabot replied in that same dead tone of voice. "Which is the nearest town or village? I am stranded here and there is no one in this house."

The men seemed surprised.

"No one there?"

"Not a soul."

"Farmer Marron and his wife were still here," one of the men said, "two days ago, and they had a wench with them for a little while."

"They must have gone to Elboeuf where the old grandmother lives," the other suggested. "I know they talked of it."

"Elboeuf?" Chabot queried. "How far is that?"

"A league and a quarter," the man replied, "not more." A league and a quarter, and it was getting dark and snow was falling fast. It was so cold, so cold! And Chabot was very tired.

"Well, good-night, Citizen," the men called out to him. "We are going part of the way to Elboeuf. Would you like to join us?"

A league and a quarter, and Chabot was so tired.

"No, thank you, Citizens," he murmured feebly. "I'll tramp thither tomorrow."

He turned on his heel and went back into the lonely house. The arch-fiend who had brought him hither had seemingly left him some provisions and a bottle of sour wine. There was a fire in the room and upstairs in a room above there was a truckle bed and on it a couple of blankets.

Chabot curled himself up in these and fell into a fitful sleep.

The next day he tramped to Elboeuf and the day after that took coach for Rouen to meet his colleague Armand Chauvelin and give him the trouncing he deserved, for it was because of him, his intrigues and his wild talk of the Scarlet Pimpernel, that he, François Chabot, had been brought to humiliation and despair. The interview between the two men was brief and stormy. They parted deadly enemies.

A week later Chabot was back in his luxurious apartment in the Rue d'Anjou and a month later he perished on the guillotine. He had been denounced as suspect by Armand Chauvelin of the Committee of Public Safety for having on the 15 Frimaire an II de la République connived at the escape of two traitors condemned to death: Josette Gravier and Maurice Reversac, and for having failed to bring to justice the celebrated spy known as the Scarlet Pimpernel.

Baroness Orczy

The Elusive Pimpernel

In this, the sequel to *The Scarlet Pimpernel,* French agent and chief spy-catcher Chauvelin is as crafty as ever, but Sir Percy Blakeney is more than a match for his arch-enemy. Meanwhile the beautiful Marguerite remains wholly devoted to Sir Percy, her husband. Cue more swashbuckling adventures as Sir Percy attempts to smuggle French aristocrats out of the country to safety.

The Laughing Cavalier

The year is 1623, the place Haarlem in the Netherlands. Diogenes – the first Sir Percy Blakeney, the Scarlet Pimpernel's ancestor – and his friends Pythagoras and Socrates defend justice and the royalist cause. The famous artist Frans Hals also makes an appearance in this historical adventure: Orczy maintains that Hal's celebrated portrait *The Laughing Cavalier* is actually a portrayal of the Scarlet Pimpernel's ancestor.

Baroness Orczy

The League of the Scarlet Pimpernel

More adventures amongst the terrors of revolutionary France. No one has uncovered the identity of the famous Scarlet Pimpernel – no one except his wife Marguerite and his arch-enemy, citizen Chauvelin. Sir Percy Blakeney is still at large, however, evading capture…

Leatherface

The Prince saw a 'figure of a man, clad in dark, shapeless woollen clothes wearing a hood of the same dark stuff over his head and a leather mask over his face'. The year is 1572 and the Prince of Orange is at Mons under night attack from the Spaniards. However Leatherface raises the alarm in the nick of time. The mysterious masked man has vowed to reappear – when his Highness' life is in danger. Who is Leatherface? And when will he next be needed?

Baroness Orczy

The Scarlet Pimpernel

A group of titled Englishmen, under the leadership of a mysterious man, valiantly aid condemned aristocrats in their escape from Paris to England during the French Revolution. Their leader is the Scarlet Pimpernel – a man whose audacity and clever disguises foil the villainous agent Chauvelin. Who is he and can he keep one step ahead of the revolutionaries?

The Triumph of the Scarlet Pimpernel

It is Paris, 1794, and Robespierre's revolution is inflicting its reign of terror. The elusive Scarlet Pimpernel is still at large – so far. But the sinister agent Chauvelin has taken prisoner his darling Marguerite. Will she act as a decoy and draw the Scarlet Pimpernel to the enemy? And will our dashing hero evade capture and live to enjoy a day 'when tyranny was crushed and men dared to be men again'?

OTHER TITLES BY BARONESS ORCZY AVAILABLE DIRECT FROM HOUSE OF STRATUS

Quantity	Title	£	$(US)	$(CAN)	€
	By the Gods Beloved	6.99	12.95	19.95	13.50
	The Case of Miss Elliott	6.99	12.95	19.95	13.50
	Eldorado	6.99	12.95	19.95	13.50
	The Elusive Pimpernel	6.99	12.95	19.95	13.50
	The First Sir Percy	6.99	12.95	19.95	13.50
	I Will Repay	6.99	12.95	19.95	13.50
	The Laughing Cavalier	6.99	12.95	19.95	13.50
	The League of the Scarlet Pimpernel	6.99	12.95	19.95	13.50
	Leatherface	6.99	12.95	19.95	13.50
	Lord Tony's Wife	6.99	12.95	19.95	13.50
	The Old Man in the Corner	6.99	12.95	19.95	13.50
	The Scarlet Pimpernel	7.99	12.95	19.95	14.50
	Sir Percy Hits Back	6.99	12.95	19.95	13.50
	The Triumph of the Scarlet Pimpernel	7.99	12.95	19.95	14.50

ALL HOUSE OF STRATUS BOOKS ARE AVAILABLE FROM GOOD BOOKSHOPS OR DIRECT FROM THE PUBLISHER:

Internet: **www.houseofstratus.com** including synopses and features.

Email: **sales@houseofstratus.com**
info@houseofstratus.com
(please quote author, title and credit card details.)

Tel: **Order Line**
0800 169 1780 (UK)
800 724 1100 (USA)
International
+44 (0) 1845 527700 (UK)
+01 845 463 1100 (USA)

Fax: **+44 (0) 1845 527711 (UK)**
+01 845 463 0018 (USA)
(please quote author, title and credit card details.)

Send to:
House of Stratus Sales Department
Thirsk Industrial Park
York Road, Thirsk
North Yorkshire, YO7 3BX
UK

House of Stratus Inc.
2 Neptune Road
Poughkeepsie
NY 12601
USA

PAYMENT

Please tick currency you wish to use:

☐ £ (Sterling) ☐ $ (US) ☐ $ (CAN) ☐ € (Euros)

Allow for shipping costs charged per order plus an amount per book as set out in the tables below:

CURRENCY/DESTINATION

	£(Sterling)	$(US)	$(CAN)	€(Euros)
Cost per order				
UK	1.50	2.25	3.50	2.50
Europe	3.00	4.50	6.75	5.00
North America	3.00	3.50	5.25	5.00
Rest of World	3.00	4.50	6.75	5.00
Additional cost per book				
UK	0.50	0.75	1.15	0.85
Europe	1.00	1.50	2.25	1.70
North America	1.00	1.00	1.50	1.70
Rest of World	1.50	2.25	3.50	3.00

PLEASE SEND CHEQUE OR INTERNATIONAL MONEY ORDER
payable to: HOUSE OF STRATUS LTD or HOUSE OF STRATUS INC. or card payment as indicated

STERLING EXAMPLE

Cost of book(s): .... Example: 3 x books at £6.99 each: £20.97

Cost of order: .... Example: £1.50 (Delivery to UK address)

Additional cost per book: .... Example: 3 x £0.50: £1.50

Order total including shipping: .... Example: £23.97

VISA, MASTERCARD, SWITCH, AMEX:

☐☐☐☐☐☐☐☐☐☐☐☐☐☐☐☐☐☐☐☐

Issue number (Switch only):

☐☐☐

Start Date: ☐☐/☐☐

Expiry Date: ☐☐/☐☐

Signature: ______________________________

NAME: ______________________________

ADDRESS: ______________________________

COUNTRY: ______________________________

ZIP/POSTCODE: ______________________________

Please allow 28 days for delivery. Despatch normally within 48 hours.

Prices subject to change without notice.
Please tick box if you do not wish to receive any additional information. ☐

House of Stratus publishes many other titles in this genre; please check our website (**www.houseofstratus.com**) for more details.